ISBN 978-1-9162544-3-5

Meaningless Mud Publishing

To

The Crown Posada

ISBN 978-1-9162544-3-5

Meaningless Mud Publishing

To

The Crown Posada

"CROWN POSADA"

By

Clifford Jones

A Professor Copley Mystery

Chapter One

The clock chimed one.

It did not strike again.

Instead, there was a sound of yawn aching timber splintering bell dropping thunder.

A cloud of dust; a perfumed cloud of age matured pigeon droppings; cascading out of the bell tower vents.

A clang. A thud. A dull empty sound of bronze on concrete.

"I told you it wasn't up to it. I bloody well told you"

"Thank you, Toby. I take your point. It appears that the rot was worse than I anticipated. I put it down to shoddy workmanship."

"It was erected in 1799 Copley."

"My point exactly. Shoddy workmanship; obviously, not maintained. Jolly poor show I think."

"Copley. I don't think your mastering the significance of the situation. You've just destroyed the bell tower of St Edwards college Oxford. I think there might be a few ramifications "

"Nonsense. The towers still standing. Nothing wrong with it.

"The tower is. I grant you that. I don't think anything inside it is. No. I take it back, definitely, nothing inside is. Just look through that window."

Copley stared through a dust smothered pane to see a pigeon staring back, perched on a bell. Half a bell to be precise.

"I seem to have underestimated the amount of deterioration. My fault entirely. I appear to have fucked up somewhat"

"Somewhat. I should say so. The Dean isn't going to be pleased with you."

"Dry rot. Bound to collapse. Better that it collapsed in such a controlled way. It could have come down on some innocent bystanders or even a student."

Copley paused to consider the prospect of crushing as many students as possible to death. Bus loads in fact. He was rattled back into reality by Toby tugging at his arm.

"Copley. The Dean."

Copley focused on the approaching figure. Calculated the distance and the nearest exit from the quad and with three bounds was well on the way, stopping only to doff his hat at a fellow academic. Even under fire Copley respected protocol; even in a hasty retreat. This was going to be an eight-pint problem.

Duly bar stooled and comfortably refreshed in the Bear & Staff, Copley waited for Toby to bring the news. Whilst he waited his mind wandered. He regretted the whole business. What was he thinking of coming back to Oxford? The scene of many of his greatest disasters of which this was by no means the worst. In fact, there was no doubt in Copley's mind that this minor unfortunate incident with dry rot, was a mere fancy, compared with his past escapades. A new bell. Work for bell founders. Repairs to the fabric; from a college that could well afford it a thousand times over. He'd merely encouraged things along. Copley wondered if he'd given the bats a hard time, but as they were above the bell in the roof rafters, they were well out of the drop zone, unlike the rats, of which there had been an ample sufficiency, as he had scaled the rickety staircase. Despite the unfortunate incident he had been successful, the inscription was there, on its side, but complete, used as nothing more than a useful piece of cut stone. Incorporated into the tower by masons unaware of its relevance; under the noses of the great and good, the academic elite that wouldn't have gone within half a mile of workmen and thus seen the stone and its inscription. Perhaps it had been unwise to pull on the bell rope quite so hard. Toby would calm the waters. It was his patch. Copley was merely visiting. Copley had one "get out of jail free" card, the significance of the inscription; for the time being Copley would keep it to himself. Copley looked at the empty pint glass. It was enough to have the barman start on pouring a fresh pint.

Allowing for the unexpected demolition, Copley was satisfied. A couple of photographs of the inscription was all he had needed. Throughout his career new finds, often as not, led to the asking of awkward questions. This was different, this wasn't a new find. The inscription had been known of for at least five years, the plaster falling off the wall and an historian with an interest in bats. Toby Rutherford. Good old dependable Toby. He'd studiously recorded the inscription; informed the department of archaeology and his fellow ancient historians and precisely diddly squat had happened. Nobody had taken any notice. No. That wasn't true. Nobody wanted to take any notice. Because it was not what anybody wanted to know. Anybody in academia that towed the line; let the facts pass them by to continue to spew out their hackneyed theories as certain indisputable fact. One of those inconvenient pieces of evidence that could be quietly overlooked.

Copley let the beer fill his thoughts. Dowsing the anger towards most of his colleagues. The way they had simply ignored Toby; they knew the truth. Yet nobody would face up to it. Better, by far to let it stay hidden. Unbending history snapped egos clean through. This was truly a sharp gut-wrenching revelation. Painful. One always avoids pain. Five years. Five years for a slow revelation. A hypothesis. A managed acceptance. No. Just forget it. Let it rot. Until Toby. Dependable Toby, picks up the phone and rings me in Newcastle.

Copley considered. Drank deep. Time to go home. Toby could sort the mess out.

Three hours later Copley was on the train.

He drank deep from his glass. First class was quiet; he could observe a couple, of retiring years, holding hands; with gentle deep smiles. The sort of smile defiant and resilient against time passing; love. Copley felt oddly emotional; slightly lost, an urge to hold Evelyn. A wave of need. It passed. He hid his unbidden thoughts in a deep quaff from his glass. The train sped on.

Evelyn met him at the station.

"Copley"

"Greetings my darling."

"Don't darling me. Toby Rutherford has been on the phone; apparently St Edwards are willing to overlook the damage, as long as you don't step foot within the college again. What's this all about Copley?

"Ignorance. It's all about ignorance. The need to keep everyone ignorant."

Evelyn swung the car out of the station and joined the continual log jam of a one-way system.

"I expect it of you, but not Toby. Have you been corrupting decent if slightly boring Rutherford? You vanish to Oxford; arrive back with a trail of devastation. What exactly have you done?"

"I wrecked St Edwards bell tower."

"Copley"

"Only the interior and the bell. Dry rot. Not my fault really. It just collapsed."

"It just collapsed."

"I might have helped it along. Nobody got hurt"

Evelyn swung the car onto the coast road.

"Words fail me Copley. Why Toby?"

"I'm sorry I should have told you."

"Yes. You should. What was so important that you had to just vanish; you know better than that?"

"Toby found an inscription."

"Toby hasn't excavated anywhere in years"

"He's into bats."

"Bats?"

"He was looking for some when he came across an inscription in the tower. On its side, just used as building rubble."

"What's so important that you drop everything?"

For starters, Toby found the inscription five years ago and for the last five years nobody has been in the slightest interested. No. I take that back. Oxfords finest were informed, viewed it and quietly forgot about it. "

"So why the sudden rush if nobody wants to know?"

"It took Toby five years to work up the courage to contact me. From the very start he was told not to let me anywhere near it; I wasn't to know. After being ignored and treated like dirt he decided to send me a photo. I decided to go and check it out for myself. For which I apologize. I know it caused you a great deal of extra work. But it was, I assure you, worth every bit of your effort."

"What will happen to Toby now they know you know?"

"Nothing. All puff, wind and bluff; even the damage; easily sorted. All they want is me to keep quiet about the inscription."

"Will you?"

"No. Have I ever?"

Evelyn swung the car into Percy Park and pulled up in front of the four storey house.

"Home sweet home"

"Copley stop moaning"

"I didn't say a word"

"It's a lovely house."

Copley dragged his bag off the back seat and followed Evelyn up the steps and in through the front door,

"Why here?"

"Because you decided to have a few chaps round."

"How was I to know they would abseil off the roof."

"Pissed as farts and naked. Only they didn't crash through our windows did they. Add that to the catalogue of members of the department regularly found asleep in the shrubbery; I think we needed to move before the neighbours put a contract out on you."

"Sorry Evelyn"

"That's the second sorry in less than two minutes; you must be sickening for something. I'll get the kettle on. Put your stuff in the washing machine."

Copley duly complied and headed into the utility room and bundled his dirty clothes into the washing machine. An envelope dropped on the floor. It was in Toby's handwriting. Copley opened the envelope. A single small folded sheet of paper fell onto the floor; Copley picked it up and unfolded it. Two words in capitals

CROWN POSADA

Copley refolded the paper and put it in his pocket.

"Copley. Don't forget the conditioner."

Copley forgot the conditioner.

The following morning Copley and Evelyn sat on the Metro heading into Newcastle along the ancient ever-changing river. Copley enjoyed the Metro; he could people watch. It passed the time; he could imagine lives in the raw and change it every day. Playing at tin God. Not today. Copley felt the warmth of Evelyn against him, that same warmness as of the bed less than an hour gone. He felt whole in Evelyn's presence, her love.

Monument. The train disgorged most of its passengers; Evelyn took Copley's hand and after passing through the ticket barriers they headed up the brightly lit slope into Fenwick's. Breakfast, overlooking Greys monument; traitorously drinking good Italian coffee.

"Copley. When exactly are you going to tell me what the inscription said? I know perfectly well what a little shit you can be if you think you can have the upper hand and lord it over the rest of the department. It would be useful to know, before, no doubt, I will be digging you out of another hole of your own making. I didn't say anything last night, you were tired."

"I wasn't. I wasn't tired. It was the note."

"What note?"

"Toby slipped a note into my bag; must have done it when I was packing, he popped into my room. I expected him to have been upset. Strangely, now I think of it, he was very pragmatic; I just thought that reality had dawned for him. For all the threats, my unfortunate incident with the bell rope; all of that and not a word, or action would be taken against him"

What did it say?"

"Two words; in capitals. Crown Posada."

"Crown Posada"

"Precisely."

"Why would Toby put a note in your pocket for one of your drinking holes?

"Toby has had five years to consider the inscription. Five years of being ignored and shunned."

"Let's see this inscription."

Copley handed over his phone and Evelyn swiped through the images.

"It's awkward to photograph on its side. Toby did the translation; it's on the next photo. I agree with his work, the state of preservation is excellent; there's not a chance of another interpretation; which is why a lot of academics would prefer to consider it a hoax, or just pretend it didn't exist."

Copley watched Evelyn closely as she read the text. He was thinking back to the night Toby had contacted him and seeing the inscription for the first time. To him it was confirmation of a suspicion. Imagination. Archaeologists needed bucket loads to truly succeed. Copley had oft wondered, mulled, rejected and shelved many ideas; snippets of chances grasping at the improbable. Sometimes. Just occasionally, the hunches, the niggling germ of a faint possibility, paid out. The Crown Posada came to mind. Many of his greatest theories were the result of gloriously fruitful hours in pubs and the Posada was one of those establishments where ideas ricocheted off the walls.

Evelyn studied the image on the phone, Toby's careful hand, spelling out the translated script.

I Gnaeus Julius Agricola Legate Augusti Pro Praetore sealed the canal started by Quintus Petillius Cerialis beneath the rock at the first bridge of the Votandi across the great river

"The first bridge across the river below the rock. Which would be Newcastle?"

"Now you understand why I vanished to see Toby, I needed to see the inscription for myself; long before Pons Aelius, we have a bridge, a canal and obviously a large tribal settlement friendly to the Romans. None, other than, perhaps, the canal, is that much of a surprise. Just because Hadrian orders a bridge constructed doesn't mean it's the first and the first safe bridging point is always going to be important, especially if that coincides with safe anchorage on a dangerous fast flowing river."

"I suppose the obvious question, for which you will have undoubtedly an answer for; is why is an inscription stone from Newcastle built into the bell tower of an Oxford College?"

"John Tradescant the Younger is most likely the culprit. Toby has provided a very interesting lead as to the stones original location."

"Why the Crown Posada?"

"Therein lies a tale."

Copley attracted the waitress and ordered more coffee.

"You know the Crown Posada Evelyn; you've dragged me out of there more than once; I know you know where I am; either The Free Trade or the Crown Posada. Copley can be relied upon; if everything turns to rat shit, off I go. Now I will tell you something you probably don't know. I go to The Free Trade and take in the view and I think things through. I plot, I scheme, I curse to myself; often as not I am pleasantly occupied with chat about beer. The atmosphere is open, light, exposed. Whereas, at the Posada, I listen; I'm warm, comforted in the dark space; I listen, calculate and imagine. The tower and the cave. They both serve me well, they complement each other. Yes, the beer is a joy, the company enlightening and oft as not erudite; the liquid curtain parting me from the woes of life. I make no excuses nor will I ever."

The coffee arrived.

"Why am I telling you this? You know me better than anyone alive. Better than I do at times; I know my ways are those you let me wander along. I couldn't survive without you. So, in this roundabout way I have spent too long in both but in doing so have gained an intricate knowledge and to a degree and understanding of their past. The Free Trade sits on a watchpoint, a lookout, going back as far as human beings wary of each other. Keeping an eye on who paddled their way up and down the river. Oh, there are many stories to tell of the spot, but Toby's note is important. The Crown Posada, well; it's unique. Simply that."

"Yes. But what's it got to do with the inscription in Oxford?"

"Toby like everyone else knows my reputation; the man who walks through time; talks to the past and like everyone else would undoubtedly treat me as a complete headcase, but for the fact you keep me in a position of power and influence and everyone just views me as having mildly eccentric behaviour. I get results and that means money in the coffers. You see to most of that as well. Toby wants me to locate this canal."

"That's a lie Copley. You want to find this canal. But why the Crown Posada?"

"Ok. I do want to find this canal. The Crown Posada is the key, because it's more than it seems, always has been. Always will be. It's our way to the past"

"Our way?"

"Yes. Our way. You are coming with me. I'm not doing this alone. I warn you; this isn't something we do lightly; this is different. I trust you with my life; I want you with me in this; wherever it takes us. Because without you I might not get back. How many times have you rescued me from the Posada?"

"Dragged you out more like. Are you serious?"

"Absolutely. It may be a complete waste of time. I haven't the faintest where or how a canal would fit into the landscape. Before you say anything and certainly, before you say anything about work; this isn't going to take long. Nobody will miss me; everybody will miss you. But for once I want to share rather than drag you into things"

"What's brought this on? What have you done Copley? What aren't you telling me?"

"Nothing. I swear. I can't lie with you. You know that. No. I just sat on the train on the way back from Oxford and thought it was better to come clean about this from the start. I just had a feeling; don't know exactly what; just that it would be nice to do this together. I'm not easy Evelyn; I know I'm not. It's me. I never was. But I do care. I watched an old couple; sitting hand in hand, just happy with each other. Where does it go? Time. It just drips way by the gallon. I love you. I decided there and then that you are part of this, whatever it is, from here on in. No hidden agendas. Bottom line; an inscription suggests a canal built or at least adopted by Cerialis, before Agricola; suggesting formal Roman control at least as far as the Tyne in 74AD. Which screws up Tacitus's account of his son in law's daring do. The chances of finding any trace of a canal is nigh on impossible. I needed to see the original just in case Toby had misinterpreted any of the text, he hadn't. The bridge I suspect is below the later Hadrianic one, but why does none of the establishment of Roman influence appear in Tacitus. Eboracum seems to be the limit of Romanization. What's going on here?"

"Copley my love. I'm touched. But we have to be getting on. Time's passing and I have your department to run."

"You haven't"

"Pardon"

"I emailed the Dean last night. You are on sick leave for twenty-eight days. He owed me a favour. Several actually, mostly courtesy of you. "

Evelyn glared. Copley knew that glare only too well. Laser beams ready to be fired.

"All courtesy of you. Anyway; we are going to investigate, and we are starting at The Crown Posada."

"Copley"

Copley expected a firestorm. The wrath of Evelyn, to fall upon him with a force eleven blasts. Instead; a wide smile. A girlish glint.

"Alright then. But I don't want to work from home. This could be fun. Whatever has got into you I say bring it on."

"Nor do I. We have an appointment at ten thirty, plenty of time."

"Where?"

"Here; with the Kevin Whyte, Sir John Fitzherbert's director."

"Why?"

"I intend to rent the old flat above the pub to use as a base whilst we undertake the research. It's been abandoned since fire regulations meant an additional fire escape was required.

"How can we use it?"

"I've also invited the Fire Service and a scaffolding company; between us we can work out a temporary solution."

"Who is footing the bill for this; you are not seriously putting this down to departmental expenditure. Copley. I mean it"

Evelyn was getting ready to pounce.

"No. Toby is paying. Not Toby personally; St Edwards will be. Part of the reconstruction budget will be heading to Newcastle courtesy of an accounting error. Cost centers are such useful things, one can be quite creative. Scaffolding; fire service and temporary office costs are not going to stick out like sore thumbs. Toby has discovered that the college's accountant has an interesting second career. Madam Whip I believe. Honestly, what is becoming of academia. You would expect better than that?"

"All I have to say to that is; boots, Copley. Boots. No doubt Toby found out and tried the goods. You are all dirty little boys. More fool her for giving way to Toby."

"That wouldn't happen here. "

"Dead right Copley"

"Actually, Toby hasn't done anything yet. He will be discovering at approximately ten thirty tonight when I will be ringing him with the plan. Tomorrow when his backside will have cooled down somewhat. I've known about Madam Whip for some time; he will implement his part of the deal."

"Copley you are a devious bastard."

"Yes, my dear Evelyn. I am. Which is why you adore me."

"If you carry on like this, I will tear them off."

"Seriously Evelyn none of this is heading the department's way. I'm certain we can gain access to the top floors of the pub safely and I believe it's imperative we are physically present in and around the area, plus nobody from the department can get a look in. Priority number one, nobody gets a preview of our work. If Toby suggests the inscription stone came from approximately where the Posada stands then it's important to prove it, one way or another at the start."

"This isn't an excavation. You can hardly tear the place apart"

"No, No it's not an excavation. More an immersion."

"An immersion?"

You'll see, or not as the case maybe. It depends on whether the place responds to you. You know how I work, but we've never shared this sort of exploration; you've experienced the results, the reaction. Never the process. I want you to understand. It's important to me. To us."

"What's brought this on Copley? This sudden desire to be all inclusive."

"Time. I lie in bed and think of how much of my life is down to your effort on my behalf and how I carry on when I should be sharing and caring. Couldn't be who I am without you. Sorry Evelyn. Nothing else I can say. Me diving onto the first train to Oxford like that just tipped things over the edge. I apologize."

"Thank you, Copley, I'm touched you are a pompous arrogant pig-headed savage; but you are my pompous savage."

Evelyn kissed Copley on the cheek and took his hand and held it. Copley physically relaxed, melted to Evelyn's touch. He always did. Bliss.

They sat silent, just smiling and looking into each other, deep beyond their eyes. Remembering; lifting the cloak of the daily common place, looking at their souls swimming in each other.

"If we get the use of the space above the Posada, we will need some basic equipment."

Evelyn, ever practical, brought them both back to earth. Bliss could wait awhile, and Copley's tongue would be busy making good for his extremely devious behaviour. Bad boys would always be put to work.

"We won't need much, I know the power supply is on and the loo works; it's all been locked up for years."

"Why do we actually need it at all? The Posada isn't that old a building"

"It makes things much easier and whilst the present structure isn't ancient its what's beneath and behind that's important. You'll see."

Copley smiled; Evelyn smiled. Instead of heading to the University the routine was broken. Copley had expected Evelyn to remonstrate, she hadn't; he would normally be on his guard; the eyes told him to relax; Evelyn was enjoying an unexpected change.

"As we've got a little time in hand, I think I will just do a little shopping; won't be long Copley"

Copley smiled and accepted the kiss on the cheek with a broad smile.

"Enjoy darling"

Copley watched as Evelyn walked along the glass corridor. He felt elated, he realised he was still smiling, he rather enjoyed it. He sipped his coffee and began to wonder if he had not been too ambitious asking to use the disused part of the Posada; but he instinctively knew that it was a vital component in the whole; how he wasn't sure, it just was.

His gaze dropped to his cup; the froth of the coffee clinging to its nearly empty sides. His mood became reflective. He felt as if he was clinging on. Yes, he was at the top of his game, but only because of Evelyn and yes, he had, to a degree excluded her. He was quite naturally selfish, honestly so; a desire to be in control. Truth was Evelyn had to be there, to curb him, to get him out of the scrapes. He was doing the right thing. He was doing the only thing he could, he was including her from the start. Copley dreaded the fact he knew changing his ways was nigh on impossible and the thought of Evelyn walking away from him would be too hard to manage. Evelyn was his life.

Good old Toby. Copley had listened over a beer to Toby revealing the gory entrails of his failed marriage. It brought Copley up sharp. Toby was no Copley, but the consequences he could readily relate to. Copley was determined to stop the rot; he may have pissed all over the foundations for too long, but he was going to sort it. He had no idea what exactly what he was going to do; the Crown Posada was a good starting point. Toby had not mentioned it and the note in the pocket was odd. Copley mused as to why Toby would do such a thing, academics, especially archaeologists could be somewhat eccentric. Copley had known some in his time that, frankly, were certifiable, but put them in a trench they were incredibly professional focused individuals. Toby was no exception. He probably had decided that Copley had taken a few beers onboard and thus was likely to forget the conversation and thus provided an aide memoir would help him along. Toby had never verbally identified or discussed the possible canal site in detail; this was of no consequence; least that was Copley's memory of events- slightly hazy around the edges. Nothing odd there. Or was there? Copley mused. He enjoyed a good muse. He calculated, considered and did nothing. The scintillas of ideas were not forming into anything cohesive. A pint would normally clear the haze, the mind muddle. Taking over all of the unoccupied part of the Posada was perhaps a tad ambitious especially as he knew fine well the present structure could have nothing to do with anything earlier than the 1880's. The cellar, that was a different scenario. All Copley was doing was setting up camp, as if he was going to dig. Perhaps he would. Impossible. No space, no team. What was he doing? He was doing what Toby had instructed. He was involving Evelyn right from the start, because the voice in his head, that cry of survival that shouted at him from time to time, had screamed at him to have her by his side. He knew that there was something, some reason. Just as Oxford academics had discarded the inscription. There had to be a reason. A reaction. Caused by what? All he knew was Toby had been ignored for five long years, yet very productive ones in respect of research. The Crown Posada stood amidst the thriving commerce of the river; its foundations were undoubtedly Roman, if not earlier. A building inscription, a public statement that eventually become just a convenient piece of pre-cut masonry, nothing unusual in reuse, along comes John Tradescant sometime in the 1650's, sees the stone and persuades a bemused landlord to sell it to him. Tradescant packs it off by boat to London and then has it hauled up to Oxford. Somehow its message, creates a negative reaction and it lingers on, overlooked, only to end up a hundred years later in the fabric of a bell tower. All perfectly feasible.

"A remarkable survivor. Like me"

Copley vocalized. Just as Evelyn walked back to their table.

"Talking to yourself Copley."

"Yes Evelyn."

Copley noticed the Fenwick bags.

"Enjoyed yourself?"

"Yes Copley; just a few essentials and I'm having some other bits delivered next week"

"Bits"

"A new freezer and some curtains for the lounge."

"You've only been gone less than twenty minutes."

"I've been meaning to buy the curtains for weeks. Today was heaven sent. I don't usually have the time."

"I'm glad my proposal has been of some benefit."

"Cheer up Copley; I bought you some new shirts."

Copley looked at the bags. He approved; he knew the drill, he had to approve to keep the peace. But he could not hide his doubt over the Crown Posada. Copley knew this was unusual for him. Doubt. Why was he feeling unsure?

"Sorry Evelyn. I've arranged all this, now I feel as if I've over undone it. Somethings wrong. I just feel. Sorry Evelyn, I shouldn't have bothered. This was a mistake"

"Too late, Copley here comes the Fire Brigade"

"Bugger"

"Copley, pull yourself together. We are doing this."

Before Copley knew it the Fire Service and estate manager from Sir John Fitzherberts were sat affably agreeing a plan. By good fortune the adjacent hotel was having a new lift installed, this meant extensive scaffolding, which allowed for a temporary additional fire escape, from the back of the Crown Posada and thus Copley could have unrestricted use of the upper floors.

Copley had taken a back seat; Evelyn had cast her spell over the company, and all was well. Copley felt a mixture of relief mixed with fear. He had absolutely no idea why he had decided to base himself actually in the pub, other than Toby's note. Being away from the University was to be recommended at all times, but this was different. Something about the inscription being found after all this time; the fact Copley had let Evelyn lead, not only at the meeting, but the move to the coast. Why had he not fought that one off? Copley began to wonder if he was slipping into his dotage. His pompous egotistical self-assured self was melting away, was time washing him clean and empty. Copley pulled himself out of his thoughts.

"Thank you all for agreeing to this rather unusual request; I assure you I deem it critically important to be immersed in the environment. Somewhere under Side is a remarkable forgotten wonder of the ancient world."

Copley was awakening. He felt a lecture coming on.

Copley engaged in the introductory pleasantries, but Evelyn had led, giving the outline, gaining the foothold; Copley was content to let her lead. Indeed, he was letting the whole business swim past him. Something was troubling him. Was it the fact that he felt the passing of time, the necessity of allowing others to lead because he couldn't? Was he admitting the obvious that he had always leant on others? Perhaps he had, perhaps the reality was his complete reliance on Evelyn. It was right she should lead. At least as far as Copley was willing. At the moment Copley hadn't the faintest how, or where he was going.

Copley snapped back into reality. Everyone was looking at him. Professional as ever Copley went into lecture mode.

"Quintus Petillius Cerealis first served in Britannia during the Boudican rebellion of 60 to 6I; where he got a very bloody nose at the battle of Colchester, resulting in him not getting his promotion. By 69 he was back in Britannia with and note this, a new marine legion the Legio II Adutrix; combining the talents of his old legion the IX Hispana he went in pursuit of the rebel prince Venutius; resulting in complete control of the territory Carlisle to Tynemouth. He had learned his lessons from the Boudican catastrophe well. Now his second in command was Julius Agricola, who was to go on and reoccupy the same territory and venture even further North. Much of which was based on the tactics of Cerealis, not that Tacitus his biographer would have you know."

Copley noted his audience had not completely glazed over so continued.

"Cerealis never underestimated the local population after Boudica; not just as a result of their fighting capability, but also the need to deal fairly with the tribes. It saved an awful amount of time and effort. Evidence of this approach is apparent by the fact Cerealis manages to cross from York to Carlisle without sign of serious entanglement, straight across a civil war within the Brigante. Cerealis seems to have had good intelligence of the Carvetti in the West, the Cumbrian side; the Votandi in the East, above the Tyne. The Brigante themselves divided between the queen and the prince. Through this Cerealis moves a legion to occupy Carlisle and strategically place troops across the region. A part of this strategy of containment is the improvement of the West to East trading routes which follow natural boundaries. Namely the Solway and Irthing to the West and the South Tyne and Tyne to the East. Ancient trackways that with minor works can be improved to allow for easier movement of cavalry. But also, for general trade. Now the marine factor becomes important. The campaign to Carlisle has been supported by marine elements working their way up the Cumbrian coast, a coast known to the Romans for centuries because of trading in iron, lead and copper. Tacitus states that Agricola ventured up every river he could but places this activity in the period of his re-invasion of the territory nine years later. Certainly, Agricola merely had to retrace Cerealis steps and that of his own, making the whole trip one of a gentle stroll down memory lane, least as far as Carlisle and Tynemouth. There is no reason to disbelieve that the marine forces also penetrated deep up the Tyne, or at least tried and that is where local knowledge counted for so much. The River Tyne was dangerous, extremely so; prone to extremes and with numerous moving hazards as the course changed through the year. Reaching the site of the later fort at Newcastle would have been feasible, beyond that spur of rock the elements were increasingly untenable. We must also take into account Cerealis is campaigning, long term stablished structure is not required, but establishment of infrastructure that encourages compliance trade and tax is all for the better and the improvement of Dere Street to Roman standards is one such project and it is heading straight past a tribal crossing point which we now call Corbridge. A solution to bulk transport to this point was a necessity to allow for provisioning troops working up and down the Northern length of the road. The river is tempting, but local knowledge and the experience of crossing on barge ferries identifies it is a river not to be taken lightly. Corbridge is the modern name for the Roman Corstopitum, which actually takes its name from a Votandi Gaelic one "Coire" a round hollow in a mountain and the Roman word Strepitum, meaning resounding noise. A hole that makes a noise, a chasm perhaps.

Having a spot called "Noisy Hole" would suggest a well-known location and no doubt one where any self-respecting Roman wold enquire as to where and what it was. There is sound archaeological evidence of a Bronze and later Iron age enclosure around what later became the town forum, suggesting an established busy spot when Cerealis popped in with a few thousand troops.

Corbridge may have been just a bridging ferry point of the river, but there was undoubtedly something else. A hole that makes a noise is contact with the Gods or in more practical terms a hole where air or gases escape. There is nothing obvious about the present site of the Roman or later town, other than they sit on the alluvial bank of a great river; there is no great chasm or echo chamber obvious in the landscape, nor record of one. Whatever it was has vanished and I believe deliberately so. Just as the inscription suggests a closing up; firmly blocking the use for some unknown reason a canal in Newcastle. I believe the two sites are physically connected. That Cerealis exploited an existing natural feature that the locals used to transport bulk goods to and from Newcastle, without navigating the treacherous river. Eighteen odd miles of subterranean works. If it seems fanciful then I would suggest such a distance is nothing compared to the tunnels beneath Rome and many other Roman cities. I personally don't doubt Cerealis would have exploited whatever was available whist he was in campaign mode, if it worked, he would use it. My interest is in why Agricola blocked it." The audience was still. Copley knew he had played them along, a little history and then the fantastical part, followed by the big question. Enough to interest this audience; he was testing out the water here, all he was seeking was permission to use a few rooms in a pub, admittedly right where he wanted to be, but the reaction, that is what he was after. The look on the faces. It had worked. A fire chief and a pub chain manager; they just sat; taking it in.

"Of course, the late Bronze Age coracle burial nowhere near the river helped me no end."

That seemed to do it. Always offer up a smidgen of collaborative evidence as a taster, never did any harm. Nothing like a short lecture to brighten Copley's mood. He felt revitalized. His clouds of worry were lifting.

Copley became aware of a silence, greater than just the immediate company; the entire café had listened in, without choice. Copley having given forth in lecture hall mode. Copley never had any time for lecture hall 'gubbins' he knew how to use the equipment; he could use it to excellent effect if it was promoting himself; otherwise it was of no interest and microphones tended to restrict his performance. Thus, the diners of Fenwick's were given a brief resume of Cerealis campaign in the North for gratis.

Evelyn look skyward, the stunned silence eased, and life returned to the business of ordering poached egg on toast.

"Eighteen miles"

The fire officer was thinking aloud.

"Not impossible."

Sir John Fitzherberts manager nodded, affirming the fire chiefs' thoughts."

"Ashington to Woodhorn and beyond, you could travel a canny few miles out of the sunshine. Eighteen miles is a bit of a stretch; it would be dug through alluvial clays, that would be easy enough, problem would be any grits; further away from the present river the better."

Copley smiled, if there was one thing about the people of the North East, he could absolutely rely upon was their knowledge of the ground beneath their feet; an understanding of the wealth they had hewed for generations.

"Agreed. It would have to be well up the slope. Where was this burial Professor?" Sir Johns representative was readily engaged.

"Under the large storehouse near the forum in Corbridge"

"That's pretty close to the river Professor"

"It is now, but it wasn't then."

"I think you would need to be well North of the town. A coracle isn't a big craft. I wouldn't want to go eighteen miles through a dark tunnel in one. But I think it's a fantastic theory. Just hope you can prove it,"

The fire officer and Sir Johns representative made their farewells and departed.

"He has a point. It is too close to the river."

Copley looked out of the window across to the Monument and gazed far beyond, clutching for something credible.

"We have the Crown at this end, a base. We can set up camp. It's a start. Cheer up Copley. You may be an infuriating old fart most of the time, but you are very rarely wrong. This is without doubt one of your stranger one's, but you've had worse and they have proved to be right. Just as long, as nobody gets hurt. Anyway, you have me along."

"I'm truly glad of that"

Copley looked at Evelyn with a deep desire and just a little dread. The chaps were right. The coracle burial was too close to the river; he was jumping to conclusions. He had to find the tunnel mouth. Perhaps it would be easier to start at Newcastle and work back?

"Evelyn. Would you like to select a small team of your choice; you know all the personnel we will need; I want you to lead the

Newcastle approach and with your permission I'm going to field walk the Corbridge end, at least to start with. Is that fine with you?"

"Perfectly. Thank you, Copley. I don't think you've got it wrong; you need some fresh air. Get out there and delve. It's what you do best."

Copley couldn't disagree entirely, getting his own way is what he really did best, but a tad of field walking and eyeing the landscape came close. Especially as there were some excellent ales to be tried in the vicinity.

"Right Evelyn; I leave you to the Newcastle end and I will station myself in Corbridge"

"Alone Copley. This one you do by yourself. It will do you good. Just you and a notebook."

Copley frowned but didn't argue. Evelyn was in command. She always was really, Copley merely liked to think he was. He knew it. Evelyn had saved him more times than he like to think. His mind wandered to comfy Corbridge pubs and was suddenly brought back to earth by the waitress with the bill.

Copley settled himself as best he could into the seat of an aged train heading wearily towards Carlisle; not all trains stopped at Corbridge, he sat on the slow stopping service rattling its steel way along the Tyne valley. The river had an evil look on it; a grey heavy look; no glinting babbling brook, naught compared to the days before its upper reaches were managed; tamed it was not; tempered at best. The Romans had fought a constant battle with the river and at best had compromised; even building timber sacrificial parts and removable sections of bridges to deal with the worst of the deluge. Arriving at Corbridge Copley was only too aware that the river valley was wide and flat, the railway lying on the southern lower banks and a causeway of a road reaching out across the river plain to the North and the bridge into the town beyond, paralleling the same approach that the Romans took to the immediate West. The Roman town a green shadow, spent and wasted, slowly slipping towards a watery end.

Copley walked along the road towards the bridge, the fields were glistening damp, the river high; his mind wandering to Evelyn; knowing that she would be enjoying all the necessary setting up at the Crown Posada. He was glad to be out of it. He was still ill at ease over the move to Tynemouth, he resented it, he felt as if he was being put out to grass, the first step towards retirement. He would never retire. Copley walked by the pub, over the bridge and into Corbridge. Evelyn had booked a B&B and as Copley approached the smart Victorian villa he decided, from deep within, that he would go sober for the entire trip. Something told Copley he needed all his senses in good form; just as he had felt odd on the trip back to Newcastle and his panic attack in the café, something was niggling away at him.

After all the usual niceties and necessities of sorting himself into his very well-appointed room, Copley wasted no time in changing into walking kit and heading out towards the Roman town. As ever Copley had been formulating a theory; it clarified itself from a murk into a practical plan as he strode past the new houses on Corchester

Lane, and was honed by the time he marched by the entrance to Roman Corbridge and down the dip where the pavement ran out at the entrance to the lane for Corbridge Mill. He crossed the road and with some difficulty made his way through the hedge and clambered over the fence. Copley climbing anything was a comical sight, normally involving him falling off or over. Annoyingly for Copley he managed perfectly, no audience to witness his dexterity.

The fields folded towards the beck, modern farming had planed off, shaped and obscured the past, much like a thick icing on a rock bun; yet, allowing for the road engineering and farming the beck still had that certain feel to it, not completely natural features and not modern works Such thoughts and diversions passed quickly enough as Copley reached the culvert beneath the A69. It was time to get wet and make his way through the cattle stop, which fortunately was lying at a crazy angle, the result of a fallen sapling from the embankment above. Copley sat down, undid his backpack and took a pair of flip flops out. Something under his soles in the water. He put his boots over his shoulder, rolled his trousers to the knee and place his socks in his pocket. The cool water on his shins, the fine grits beneath his feet reminded him of his childhood, building dams on the stream, simple pleasures. His mind was jolted back to reality with the sound of a lorry horn high above on the road, masked from sight but ever present. Copley could stand quite normally in the concrete tunnel; the sound of traffic muffled by the earth above. Copley waded through the near knee-deep channel his mind on the barbed wire ahead. He reached into his breast pocket, one small but very sharp wire cutters. Copley never went walking without his snippers. He hated barbed wire; it inflicted pain, ripped flesh and clothes and generally got in the way of archaeologists. It certainly didn't stop determined livestock. The wire yielded with a satisfying click. Copley waded through, stopping to carefully coil the ends to the posts for his return. The sound of traffic above contrasted with the green field and gentle flowing waters. There was a very defined southern edge to the beck. Potential evidence of canal works thought Copley as he waded up to the bank, removed his flip flops, dried himself with his little towel and placed his socks and boots back on. He could see his next obstacle the new and old bridges over the`A68. Copley intended to go over the top, the A68 b3ing a single carriageway and he wanted to look at the old bridge in some detail. The trees, planted to hide the junction shrouded the intrusion of the main road. A great scythe of engineering across the landscape, cloaked in a green scab, thought Copley, a divide not unlike the Wall; was it just him, but did things seem somehow disconnected from the southern side? An imposition on nature reflected in every step, every feature. The beck wandered in a leisurely snake along a wide corridor; the edges of which seemed too well defined for nature or the earnest efforts of a farmer, least to Copley's eyes. A broad area of water, immediately by the bridge carrying Dere Street North and South. Copley was fermenting a scenario.

He struggled up the embankment over the fence and down and across the A68. Not a single car in sight; down onto the old road and Corburn bridge, marooned by progress, but worthy of preservation. Copley studied the stone, making his way down to the arch, looking at the foundation stones; he smiled to himself. Re-used Roman stone, it was not mere observation, others had recorded the sight. Research was all. There certainly was nothing unusual in the sight of Roman stonemasons work still in use in and around the Wall. What occurred to Copley, was the positioning of the bridge; it launched itself from the South bank at an angle to the North; whilst the present structure was modern in the realm of things the skewed nature of the crossing, considering it was approximate to the Roman road was initially a puzzle to Copley. The present gap crossed by the bridge was about a fifth of the width it would have been in Roman times; it seemed to be positioned at the end of the broad section of water, at the transition; the beck ran in a narrower path to the East, the northern bank immediate east of the present bridge were noticeably higher; the present old ramp skirted a mire of water beneath, "Issues" as the ordnance so helpfully describes, water draining out of the slope of the earth above it. Such signs of the Gods, along with springs were of such religious significance that a bridge would run alongside rather than disturb the feature. One that would supply a water cart or top up a canal pound. Copley was pleased with his physical and theoretical progress so far. Leaving the bridge behind he walked above the beck on the Northern bank on his way to Leazes Lane. The weather was blessedly sunny, the way was hard underfoot and Copley eyed the field edge and the little path with a critical gaze. Towpath. He mused.

In Newcastle, the Crown was preparing for its visitors. The great door to the upper floors was being cleaned, the threshold swept; locks oiled and checked; contracts cleaners were tidying the first-floor back offices. All was a hive of activity and all before nine of the morning. Evelyn stepped out of the organised chaos, stood with her back to the line of vans disgorging men and equipment into the upper heights; she was gazing at the Crown Posadas stained glass windows.

"They look better from the inside."

The voice was attached to a smile and a wave of red hair.

"Arthur Nicholson" manager of the finest and oldest purpose-built public house in Newcastle."

Evelyn shook the hand and followed Arthur through the iron gates and door into the Crown Posada. Evelyn knew it well enough; she had dragged Copley out of it on many occasions she would prefer to forget, but she gazed at it with different eyes. The exterior was always odd; when the rest of Side was reinventing itself with the Baltic trade in the nineteenth century many of the buildings were rebuilt or refaced to reflect the countries traded with. The Crown Posada, or to be precise Crown Buildings had gone from an eight storey multi occupancy, multi layered wooden structure to a cramped but refined three storeys. From plain wooden planking at street level to a statement in fine polished grey granite, sandstone ashlar and stained glass. Designed by Will Newcombe in 1880 the Crown Posada was the counter blast to the Northern climes; its high mansard roof and dormers echoing the French second empire architecture; coupled with the pre-Raphaelite windows; this was no ale house. Built with solid refinement and bedecked with a ceiling of chasm deep recessed panelling, adorned with fussy ornamentation; this was something very different indeed. This was a statement, a theatrical allusion to Southern climes, grapes appear along with juniper berries in the stained glass, wine barrels and at last hop vines, one gentle nod to beer. Wine in a land of beer. More strikingly, the size and shape of the Posada, a small snug immediately inside the inner door; a bar no more than fourteen customers long and a seating area not much longer, narrowing to a passageway to the toilets. Along the right-hand wall tall mirrors offered a pretension of size; filling the tall space higher than wide. Dark wallpaper, brass fittings, heavy chandeliers and a Dansette record player for entertainment. "Coffee?"

"Thank you, white, no sugar"

Arthur sank into the floor on a near vertical staircase which seemed to have fallen off a passing tramp steamer. Neck breakingly steep; designed for minimum space over safety. Evelyn sat on a bar stool thinking how different it was; she was used to seeing it full to bursting. Shoulder to shoulder, a cacophony of noise; at least when Copley was in.

Evelyn could sense the place; the past was very much alive, not just the night before, there was a foundation, broad, deep, complex. A binding. Evelyn could accept Copley's attraction to the intimacy; he could watch a listen in the space not much larger than their lounge. What he heard, what he saw. It explained a lot. Sitting looking around, it was plain that the walls were doing the same, watching, listening; sucking in the tittle tattle, laughter, plots, schemes; profits and losses. The World in a shoulder's width.

"One coffee, no sugar. Welcome to the Crown Posada."

"Thank you. I can see what Copley sees in the place; I've never had the chance before; I'm usually too busy dragging him out of here."

"Copley has been talking about writing a history of the place for years; from time to time he gives us all a snippet"

"Lecture"

"Yes. He does go on a bit"

"A bit"

"We all tolerate it, because it's interesting and its fascinating to think what this place was like before it was rebuilt."

"Which is why we are upstairs"

"I don't understand; I can see the point of recording the present building, but there's nothing of the old one left, least not inside, Copley says there are remains out the back, but everything save for the cellar was flattened in the rebuild."

"That's right; but with your help we may well be able to assess the cellar and conduct some works out the back."

"Why do you need the offices, not that I mind; it's good to see something done with upstairs; I wish the building works next door would include an additional fire escape so they could be brought back into permanent use. Surely you could have just walked back to your department."

"Copley decided that I should lead the project and treat it as if it was a field project as if it were anywhere. His motto has always been"

"Set up your HQ in the nearest pub"

"You've heard it then"

"Just a few times. He has a point. Local information is everything and a pub is the place for it. Where is Copley if you don't mind me asking?"

"He's staying at Corbridge for the next couple of weeks."

"Corbridge.

"The other research area. We have two sites to investigate."

"Copley is stuck in Corbridge and you are upstairs here. I bet that went down well."

"He was fine about it. You know what he's like when he puts his mind to something"

"Like a terrier with its teeth in your ankles. He doesn't let go. "

"No. He doesn't and that's Copley. I promise you there won't be any interference with your routines or customers; any work or physical research will be conducted at night or early morning. The cellar won't be disturbed. We aren't digging it up. We will want to conduct some laser measurement and some scanning, but it won't interfere with your beer."

"I had a memo from head office; you have all the team's assistance. Just tell us what you need, and we will help out. Are you actually going to stay upstairs.?"

"Yes. Only because we will be working at night after you close; your head office has very kindly supplied security cover. "

"It can get a little noisy along Side and the Quay until two thirty in the morning; we close at midnight; and we are normally away by half past, but it can be interesting outside; normally it's just a lot of happy pissed people, most are no trouble at all, but there's always the odd one and you can never really tell. Just be careful if you are outside; I don't think I would want to be up there by myself.", but with security you've no issues."

"Don't worry, there will be a team. No lone working and it won't be every night."

"What would you like me to tell the locals, or do you want to?"

"I'm happy with you telling them Arthur. I will be in with the team so everyone gets to know us and of course I will keep you fully informed as to progress. We won't just be studying the Crown Posada; we will need to record quite a few structures related to it in the area."

"I'm sure it's going to be fine; I'm just pleased that the history of this place is going to be recorded and we can put a new board up in the snug with some facts in it."

"Copley has mentioned it just once or twice"

"I bet he did"

They both smile, sip their coffee and let the building soak up another few seconds of time; for a small space it consumed emotions and stored them in every nook and cranny. The mirror glass shone all the better for the hopes and dreams that polished it with every phrase, every passing fancy, ever slur and laugh.

The iron gate could be heard opening and the first beer delivery of the day arrived. Arthur was called away, leaving Evelyn to muse on what was so special about this cake slice of a building. Copley had muttered loud and long, normally half pissed, that there was something about it. How one Oxford academic and an inscription had found her running her own research project. On what grounds did anyone consider a tunnel underneath the Crown Posada and one that ran all the way to Corbridge? How long had she known Copley? Longer than she wanted to remember. His smile had caught her; his imagination; his desire; his loyalty and his drive. For all his pomposity Copley was hers; he would hold her tight, wail against the world. But he was hers; they worked. It was hard work, but it worked, Through thick and thin and there had been a lot of thin, until Copley, courtesy of Evelyn, got in front of a TV camera and then he was away, like a rocket and she had made sure his trajectory was tweaked to keep him in her orbit.

The iron gate swung again and this time it was a delivery of furniture for upstairs.   Evelyn called down to Arthur to say goodbye and was then away out of the bar door and headed towards the big blue door that led to the upper storeys.

Copley had made his way along the Cor, noting that whilst it had all the appearance of a natural burn there were signs of man's influence and sections that with little imagination could be considered navigation works. Least Copley was of a mind to consider the possibility. Aydon Castle glared down at Copley, strategically placed at the junction between the Cor to the right and a tributary to the left, he was in a tight worn down natural little glen, near ravine. Suddenly his theory was looking as if was about to run out of possibilities. Up to this point the terrain had not concerned him. Nigh on two thousand years of flood and humankind playing with the landscape could change anything; perhaps he was just worn out and the need for beer was urgent. He decided to backtrack a little and make his way up onto the footpath that would take him to Gallow Hill then alongside the A69 and back along Deadridge Lane, a pint within twenty-five minutes and plenty of time to consider options. As he did so he noted the amount of material that had collapsed into the burns course quite recently, a process that would have been a constant for millennia. Finding a tunnel wasn't going to be easy; proving that the Cor was canalled and navigable was a tall enough order. Nothing was impossible. It all had possibilities, but to Copley they were looking a tad thin.

Within the hour Copley was back in his room, showering and thinking about his foray. Overall it had gone very well, his photos and his dictated notes made sense. It was a proper start. He was also aware that he was, as ever, being too hard on himself. It was far too early to come to any conclusions. Copley told himself to take it slow, Suddenly. The day seemed to be turning to night. Copley looked at his watch; it was three twenty. He walked over to the window and saw large black ominous storm clouds rolling towards Corbridge. He'd noticed the temperature going up on his walk back into town. A thundery shower, it would pass through.

The screen in the emergency control room flashed an urgent update from the Met Office, an unusually deep low was making its way down the North Sea corridor. The highest tides of the year were in the next forty-eight hours along the East Coast and the rivers were abnormally high. To exasperate the situation a second front was working across the Pennines from Cumbria and the Scottish Borders. Phones were ringing; keyboards were being tapped, little groups were standing by smartboards calculating the possible responses.

Outside rain pattered down in large drops, the wind swept the grass. A BBC reporter zipped up her coat; it was going to be a very long shift.

Copley sat in the candlelight along with the few regulars that had made it out for their evening pint. The sky was alive with lightning; the wind was screaming and the sounds of parts of Corbridge detaching itself began to alarm even Copley. The landlord alarmed by the sounds encouraged everyone to head into the kitchen. Copley had tried to contact Evelyn, but all communications were down. A loud crash and the widows blew in; the kitchen door slammed shut. Copley made his way to the steel preparation tables and along with the other six souls got down onto the floor and made themselves comfortable as they could. Not a word was said; there was a realization that this was no ordinary storm. This was a fury. A gnashing raw moment of nature sent to humble the ants that thought they were in control. A bottle of Brew Arthur was passed round. Copley held onto his pint. He instinctively put his hand over it as the ceiling caved in.

Evelyn had been sitting with four of the regulars in the Crown Posada; cordial introductions had been made by Arthur and the conversation had been light and jovial. Evelyn was as welcome as anyone through the door. The Posada had no typical customer; all life walked through the door; council for the defense, council for the prosecution; policeman; sailor; archaeologist. Everyone had gone to the iron gate; the darkness, the lightning bolt hitting the bridge high above; the torrents of water rushing down the street. The fifty-foot fountain just up the way at the bottom of Dean Street; parked cars being pushed down the road; the rescue of a girl being washed away downside. Initially there had been a fascination with the sound, the light show, the noise. But as it continued, and the water didn't recede, and the rain kept on falling and the water began to rise the fascination turned to alarm; there was no going home, no going outside. The power went off, the phones were dead, and water was making its way through the iron gate as debris was diverting the flow into the properties. With the door shut and bar towels at its base a futile attempt was made to hold the water back, the cellar hatch was discreetly hidden by matting immediately inside the door. Outside the lightning crackled and the sound of tiles falling onto the pavement mixed breaking glass as the wind swept down along the streets seeking out its reflection and breaking it. An hour passed, then two, the temporary barrier was holding, but there was an increasing sound of water coming from the back yard; suddenly the fire door to the yard was forced in off its frame; it stuck halfway across the passage directing two foot of water down into the bar, a solid flow, pouring in. Arthur and two of the men waded towards the door in an attempt to force it back, but the damage was done. Forcing his way through the doorway it became obvious that the cellar and its ale was doomed, the water was cascading down from the Castle above. Arthur waded back into the Posada.

"Evelyn. Does that temporary fire door open from this side?"

"Yes, it's got a glass bolt on it."

"Well I think we would all be safer upstairs. Come on, grab what you can because this is going to be a long haul."

The party collected the sandwich basket, bottled beers into coat pockets and waded out into the storm, around the yard and up the contractor's stairs to the decking that connected the Crown to the new hotel next door. Arthur smashed the glass bolt and slid the bar back and within no more than five minutes the party were established in the back first floor office. Two more runs back down into the water to rescue supplies and Arthur's possessions and the contents of the till after which there simply was nothing left to save. The last artefact rescued was the record player. The Crown Posada was left to its fate. The situation on the first floor was slightly brighter. Although everyone was wet the offices were warm; Evelyn had aired them and there were camping seats and folding tables and Evelyn's battery radio.

"There's a pile of clean sheets next door. I was going to spruce the place up; we can use them to dry ourselves. "

A yawning crash to the front of the building and without anyone looking it was obvious the scaffolding had given way; how long the causeway they had traversed to get upstairs would survive was anyone's guess. The darkness was illuminated by lightening, creating eerie shadows and blue purple momentary daylight. An emergency broadcast was being transmitted. Stay put. Stay calm. Emergency services would respond when possible. Listen on the half hour for updates. Evacuation centers would be announced when it was safe for people to move.

"We need to get out of these clothes and keep warm; follow me."

Evelyn led the party two doors down from the office, cardboard boxes and bubble wrap that will do; there's enough here and there's a pile of boiler suits.

Whilst the storm continued to wreak havoc the little band made themselves comfortable in their boiler suits, made a corral of cardboard boxes to keep the draughts out and arranged enough bubble wrap to sleep quite comfortably on. Not that anyone was going to sleep. It was activity, the normality; something to keep everyone sane in an insane situation. Evelyn decided not to turn on the radio every half hour. It was obvious nobody was going to be doing anything possibly for days. This was a disaster. As she sat with a bottle of beer and a corned beef sandwich, she wondered how Copley was fairing. The party were all lost in exactly the same thoughts for their kith and kin.

Copley opened his eyes; the dust had settled; he removed his hand from his pint and took a long gulp of ale. He seemed for the moment the only person alive in the room. Apart from the noise outside, nobody made a sound. Plaster and laths, floorboards lay everywhere. Eventually the dust moved, shook itself and all crawled out from the wreckage. Mercifully nobody was injured; but they were now in need of a safer refuge.

"Come on everybody. Follow me"

The landlord led the party to the door of the courtyard.

"Wait here."

He opened the door, the blast threw everyone about, the dust being swept from them. The landlord, pinned to the wall edged his way out and knelt next to a small wooden door down a set of steps; he opened the door and beckoned everyone across. With mobile phones the party lit their way along a narrow stooping passage for a hundred yards until they reached a circular full height chamber.

"Welcome to the tunnels. Never thought we would have to be down here. God help those out in this; It's a killer; I don't want to think what this is going to cost to put right."

Copley looked around him as the landlord turned on two battery lanterns, the room was stacked with wines, benches and a couple of tables; it was bone dry, not a whiff of damp or must.

"Make yourselves as comfortable as you can, you are safe down here and if you are worried about getting back to the surface there's a least two other ways to get out. Should have brought you all in here, but I never thought it was going to be this bad.

Copley just stared at the dome, the walls; they were painted; it was faded, but it was undoubtedly Roman; the tunnel had been a later intrusion but the other two arches were original; red and green, white background, panels bordered in red. Copley was always amazed at how the past had a way of turning up when he least expected. He looked around, smiled and settled down with the rest of the party, away from the furies. He could stare at vines and maidens it was enough for now.

Thirty-six long hours later after the second peak tide the message went out on the radio that the evacuation centers were open and power was being restored. Evelyn had looked out of the first-floor window frame; the glass gone; down below mud, wreckage, bodies; ill defined, but bodies. Evelyn walked back into the offices; Arthur was sitting on the floor. The others were sleeping. The constant noise, the wind and rain battered not just the buildings, it entered the mind, flooded the senses.

"Time we all tried to get home Arthur. Better wake the rest. Its hideous down below. The causeway scaffolding is just about there, we can cross to the Castle. The radio says that the road to Hexham is open; but the mobile network is going to be out until tomorrow. They're not saying how bad but there are bodies in the mud outside.

"I just hope the wife's ok. Did they say anything about Hexham?"

"No. Just that the main North, South and West routes were being opened as quickly as possible; the Army are doing their best. They've stopped all private travel except by buses, the trains aren't running."

Copley picked his way through the rubble of his room. Dusting down what he could find of his kit and rescuing his trusty rucksack from beneath a fallen roof truss, gathering his belongings felt more like gathering himself, attempting to stay calm, in the midst of all the chaos. He looked through the gap where the window had been. Not a tree not a roof stood intact

All was twisted and broken; as twisted and broken as the people. He shuddered; shoved everything he needed into the rucksack zipped and secured it and put on his back. He was going to Newcastle even if he had to walk.

Copley knew the Railway would be out of action. Too close to the river. His best chance was the A69.

As the strategic arterial route, it would be the priority of Highways or the military. The phone network was out; he was working on common sense and instinct; Copley was good at crisis, he had caused a few in his time; his task was to get back to Evelyn. Evelyn always made crisis go away; Copley steadied himself with that thought.

In the remains of the garden Copley bid his host and fellow survivors farewell, telling them all his destination and intended route.

He stepped out across the fields straight to the embankment of the A69, the fence was gone, and he made his way through clearing created by flattened and snapped off trees, the earth gouged up with roots reaching for the sun. Up onto the carriageway where his hopes of an easy passage East looked dashed. A forest covered the carriageway; West and East swathed in greenery; his morale slumped, and he sat down on the central reservation crash barrier. Copley felt a wave of fear sweep through him; the ferocity of the last two days, the shrieking crashing wrenching heart stopping noise, a noise full of dying agonized souls. He could hear them; he felt them; a whispering cry away.

Copley sat, blank, beyond unsure, the whispering got louder until it was growling at him. He shook himself out of his depression; a Land Rover was making its way towards him.

He stood, an arm waved at him from the cab, as the vehicle slowly made its way over the small branches. Copley waited, just glad to see another human being. The Land Rover pulled up next to him. A cheery round-faced man with a big grin looked out at him.

"Hello. How did you get here?"

"Up the embankment. I could say the same"

"It's not as bad as it looks, all the Newcastle side fell and snapped pretty cleanly short of the central reservation, haven't had to use the chainsaw once; just took my time. Where you heading? If it's Carlisle things are pretty bad beyond Haltwhistle.?"

"Newcastle and onto Tynemouth"

"I can get you nearly all the way, could be a bit of a long haul for us, but get yourself aboard"

Copley made himself comfortable in the passenger seat.

"Fred Partridge, land agent."

"Copley. Archaeologist."

Fred put the Land Rover in gear and slowly moved forward along the central reservation.

"Take it you were in Corbridge? How bad?"

"Not a roof left, I didn't venture towards the river, but I anticipate it's bad"

"It's horrendous. I was up above Haltwhistle on a call when this all kicked off, hunkered down with the farmer and frankly I was glad to get away; lost all his stock. Same everywhere, just wiped out; blown away. Tried to get down to Haltwhistle but turned back and came along the Wall and dropped down to check on what's left of some of our property above Corbridge. Might as well not have bothered, but I bet you're glad I did?"

"I certainly am. I really didn't know what I was going to do. I think the last couple of days just suddenly caught up."

"I know how you feel. I've no idea what I'm going home to."

"Nor have I"

The Land Rover ground its way out of the woodland and onto an empty carriageway. Nothing, the emptiness seemed to create a sense of unease. No cars, signs lay flat, no fences, walls gone; then it became obvious that the emptiness was in fact scattered over the fields to their right. A jumbled mass of animals, cars, stone and broken timber.

"As if somebody had a giant broom and just swept it clean. God help them"

Copley stared at a wrecked car some distance away, tumbled into the mud, barely recognizable. There was a large black red streak, wide across the yellow paintwork.

The two travelled in silence, crawling past wrecked cars, fallen road signs; dead animals.

Copley sat doing what he did best, observing, he knew Evelyn was safe; he felt her presence and he knew she would make it.

Copley was heading home.

Chapter Two

Copley stood outside his Tynemouth home, he had nothing against Tynemouth; he just liked being in the City. He'd wanted to come back to a charred wreck, an unfortunate electrical fire perhaps, caused by the lightning? He stood and looked, not a window, not a sheet of copper roofing touched by the storm. Not a scratch. He fumbled in his pocket for his keys.

"Copley"

The words came from behind him. He turned.

"Evelyn"

They embraced; kissed; Copley stroked Evelyn's hair. Her touch everything go away

"I knew you'd be alright"

"You too."

"How was it. You were at The Posada?"

"Yes."

Evelyn paused, looked at Copley. in a way that let the fear of the previous two days drain out of her

"I've seen things I never want to see again. Let's get inside. Copley, I was worried terrified, even though I wasn't alone. The sounds, I'm never going to forget them"

"It's alright darling; we've made it, were bloody lucky to be alive and the house seems to have been equally so."

Copley may privately wished the house wasn't, but even he realised they were extremely lucky still to have one. Everything was just as Evelyn had left it; water and electric were working. According to the security alarm the mains had only been off for five hours.

They headed to the bedroom stripped off and both headed for the shower, the steamy water refreshing their grimy bodies; Copley liberally applied shower gel to every part of Evelyn and she reciprocated. The sheer joy of being together and being able to wash some of the last two days away was a sheer joy, a relief.

Shaved and down in the kitchen, Copley prepared them both a bacon sandwich, the aroma wafted through the house.

"Copley, you've noticed what state the rest of the street is in?" Evelyn had walked into the kitchen in a well-fitting boiler suit.

"It's better than a lot from what I've seen."

"Well I think we should offer a helping hand where we can; not every house has bullet proof glass and a reinforced roof."

"One advantage of buying an ex drug barons gaffe; very good security and a quality bit of workmanship; no skimping on the quality and thickness. Let's have a look at what the cameras picked up."

Copley went to turn on the cctv replay.

"Not now Copley, let's enjoy a sandwich and go and see if we can help."

"My phone's working again, is yours?"

"Yes, it hasn't stopped beeping with incoming messages. I haven't time right now. I've sent out a message saying we are ok and are in

Tynemouth Odd; I'm sure they said the mobile network wasn't going to be up and running until tomorrow."

"Well it's good that something is getting back to normal. Now have your sandwich. If we are to help out, we need building up, apart from a mint in the Land Rover I've had nothing today."

They sat at the breakfast table and smiled at each other.

"How bad was it Evelyn?"

"The Crown Posada flooded; the water cascaded in from the Castle side; we escaped upstairs using the fire escape. We had food and no shortage of water, beer and whisky. The lads all pulled together and we were warm and dry, but the sounds in that first twenty-four hours; terrible. There were bodies in the mud outside on Side; the whole area is one twisted mass of carnage. We got out via the fire escape up to the Castle. You saw the state of the City?

"I got a lift with a land agent that had been out near Haltwhistle; we made it along the A69; I've never seen anything like it."

Evelyn was looking at her phone.

"The railway to York is open, limited service; they hope to have the line open to London open tomorrow; if we need, we can always head to London; this is going to take months if not a year or so to sort out."

"Any news from the University?"

"I suspect some of the messages are from the department. They know we are ok. We should help those we can here. Where did your lift drop you?"

"Haymarket. It looks like a bomb site, the University has taken a hit, glass and rubble everywhere. I got a lift from a truck driver as far as North Shields. Bit grim."

"Grim?"

"He was delivering a truck load of body bags"

The atmosphere chilled. They eat their sandwiches in silence; the recent past was raw. Copley stood and walked around the back of Evelyn, hands on her shoulders, he leant forward and kissed her head. She smelt of spring pastures, of sunshine; he kissed her neck.

"I'll get changed into my digging gear"

Evelyn looked up at Copley; they smiled deep into each other, they were alive, that was all that mattered.

The pair stood in the road outside their house, intact, amongst torn down windowless wrecks; they were the only people in the road, passable on foot, trees, hedges, fences all scattered, tossed about; ripped like weeds from their beds by a malevolent gardener. The two houses to their left had spray painted telephone numbers on their walls, obviously the occupants had gone. Within twenty minutes it became clear that they were the only occupants left in the road; there was nothing to do; Copley surveyed the destruction with a critical eye; the worst destruction was from the North, the chimneys had toppled over the garages rather than the living quarter; he mused that the hideous conservatories were gone, not one trace anywhere. Lost as to what to do they wandered back home and sat on the front step.

"Just us then."

"Yes Copley. Just us. I'm not surprised; once one chimney went, I suspect everyone could see what was going to happen and took their

chance to escape. Did you see the area code on number four;
Glasgow. I wonder if they made it in one piece?"

"I must admit I'm still taking it all in. I've just spent two days in a
Roman subterranean dining room."

"I spent it in the Crown Posada, or should I say over the remains of
it"

"How many dead Copley. How many?"

"I have no idea Evelyn, but we are talking thousands. We've just
lived through a particularly brutal bit of nature"

"As far as I can tell we're still in the midst of it. Extreme like this,
people need shelter, food supplies; that leads to looters, disease."
Before Copley could respond there was the sound of heavy
machinery at the end of the road. Men in uniform wielding
chainsaws, a bulldozer and several army trucks started cutting their
way through the vegetation and woodwork. Copley and Evelyn
stood up and waited to see how long it would take for them to make
a path; it was a matter of five minutes. An officer jumped down from
the truck and approached them.

"Professor Copley"

"Yes."

"Captain Smith, Intelligence. I have orders to request you and your
partner accompany me to headquarters."

"Might I ask why?"

"Sorry. My orders are to get you safely there as soon as possible.
Don't worry the house will be safe; these lads will be setting up a
field unit in the garden of next door."

At which point the bulldozer started shoving the remains of the hedge and garden of next door away.

"Do you mind if we get changed."

"Not at all."

"How did you know we were here?"

"We turned your phones back on; I'm afraid we limited the number of messages."

Copley looked at Evelyn. Evelyn knew the look.

"Right. We will be ten minutes; come in and make yourself comfortable"

Copley ushered the Captain over the threshold and Evelyn followed."

Up in the bedroom Copley wrote Evelyn a note.

RADIO SILENCE.

WHAT IS THIS ABOUT?

WHY US?

ANY IDEA?

Evelyn shrugged her shoulders.

They changed and headed downstairs. The Captain was waiting in the hallway. They stepped outside to find most of the house next door gone and soldiers preparing to erect a very solid temporary building, from the back of a wagon, where it had stood.

"The REME don't hang about do they"

Copley watched as the last of next doors remains were levelled.

The Captain smiled at the efficient demolition.

"Don't worry your property is safe. Orders have been issued. You will be back later today I assure you. The vehicle is waiting. You will have new neighbours for a while"

Copley and Evelyn walked to the Panther that had stopped by their gate; a soldier held the door, and another helped them aboard. Captain Smith sat in the front. The road had been ruthlessly cleared. Soldiers were busy erecting a barrier and fencing.

Copley sat looking out of the window as the Panther hurtled along the streets; two military motorbikes making the way for them. As he stared at the ruins, he realised for the first time what they both had lived through, no ordinary storm. Nobody spoke. Evelyn looked out of her window, equally aware but more so. Copley was about to be embroiled in something. God alone knew. At least she was with him. Whatever it was.

The Panther hurtled passed broken houses, shops, lives. Huddled groups kneeled by blankets with shoes sticking out from the bottom. The wind had played a deadly game and won. The Panther swung into City Hall; the adjacent park and churchyard was covered in military tents; the Captain ushered Copley and Evelyn in through the main entrance and to the military reception. They were directed straight through and into the lift. Down they went, at least three storeys.

"We're using the nuclear bunker, as a precaution; it's systems are unaffected by the storm."

"Yes. Make sense It feels as if we've been hit by one."

Copley was somewhat puzzled as to what awaited them but just took it all in. Plus, he had Evelyn, doing just the same. Out of the lift, through a double set of doors an along a corridor; to a door, with armed personnel either side of it. The Captain knocked and entered, Copley and Evelyn followed.

"Prime Minister, Professor Copley and"

"Hello Evelyn"

Evelyn smiled.

"Prime Minister"

"Thank you, Captain."

Smith withdrew.

"How are you both? Can I get you some refreshment?

"A pint would be nice."

"I knew you would want something more than tea Copley; its bottled but I'm sure you can manage. Evelyn. Tea?"

"Thank you, Rosemary."

"I suppose after we have been through the niceties you are going to tell us why a military camp is being built around our house. Box Social Brew; well at least your taste in local ale is better than…."

"Copley."

"Sorry Evelyn, but let's face it we've just been through three days of hell, the region is a war zone with God knows how many casualties and we find ourselves in a nuclear bunker with the PM. I might just for once have liked to have taken a back seat and got on with some archaeology, when the place isn't upside down; which at the usual rate of progress by politicians will be never."

"Copley"

"No Evelyn, let him rant. He's got a point. But not for the first time he's got it wrong; it's not you Copley we want. It's Evelyn. You set out on your most recent enquiries deliberately to include Evelyn; the project is being led by her at your behest."

"How do you know that? More to the point considering the little matter of a devastated North East, why are you bothering to bring us here regarding an archaeology project?"

"Ever since you were contacted by Toby, we've been keeping an eye on you. Actually; for the record, Copley, we always keep an eye on you, but you know that. Thirty thousand dead, twenty thousand injured and two years to get everything back to, well it never will be for some, what it was before. That's the present estimate. It's wrong, of course, the figure's closer to sixty thousand dead, but we put an estimate round and that allows us to manipulate the figures. Your house needs protecting, looters are rife, the Army is busy with putting the basics back together; it's an ideal place to station those responsible for the entrance to the Tyne."

"Sixty thousand"

"Sixty thousand; whole communities washed or blown away; our North Sea platforms; harbours, gas pipelines; power stations. I need Evelyn; I need you Copley; but you are here because of Evelyn. Remember that. Evelyn; I would like you to work for me, for the Government; we need your local knowledge but more importantly your logistical experience, especially as we will be requiring International assistance and I know you have global contacts and can get things done in ways I don't need to know. One advantage of being the partner of Copley. In brief Evelyn the regional authorities are on their knees; they have more than enough to cope with. I need you to act on my behalf; you will answer to no one but me; I've known you all my life; in this emergency I need you to be my eyes and ears and drive things forward. I will give you everything you need; it's a case of moving things through on the ground and you know the ground. I'm appointing you to head my Northern Recovery team and I'm appointing you to my Emergency Cabinet; the Queen has graciously approved your elevation to the House of Lords; with all party agreement. I hope you will accept."

Copley choked on his beer.

"Rosemary. It's a bit much to take in."

"Don't be modest Evelyn you can do this, and I mean it"

"There Evelyn, even Copley agrees. He should know, you've got him out of more scrapes than any of us would like to mention or remember. I need you onboard. The country needs you"

"Yes. I accept. I will do my best."

"We know you will. Now I need to speak with Evelyn alone Copley. I promise you, only a little while; you both deserve some rest and what I require of you both is frankly daunting, but you have a major task of your own Copley. We may not ever see eye to eye, but I do respect your ability. The officer will take you to your quarters. "

The door opened; an officer waved the direction in which Copley was required. Copley kissed Evelyn on the cheek. He looked into her eyes; he felt lost for a second. She really was more than capable of putting things back to normal thought Copley. She'd had more than enough experience with him. As he walked down the corridor he looked back and he noted a small woman with a bright hat heading into the room he had just left, along with a small entourage. So. Evelyn had beaten him to a title. Not exactly the way Copley had imagined things would work out, but Copley was remarkably sanguine. They were both alive, unharmed and he had a beer. Something would turn up for him in the way of a title, sometime, probably; he was quite happy being a Professor. The corridor seemed to go on forever. Eventually the officer showed Copley into a side corridor with a reception desk and clerk.

"Professor Copley."

The clerk smiled. Copley was instantly on his guard.

"Please follow me; we just need to process you and get you a pass." Two hours later a medically examined, photographed and security cleared Copley stood back at the door to the PM's office. His pass checked; he waited. He waited. Copley knew the game. Rosemary was one of Evelyn's oldest friends; he knew where he stood in the pecking order. He mused to himself that Evelyn had beaten him to the House of Lords. He was puzzled by the presence of the monarch; there were enough grandchildren to go on walkabouts encouraging the masses; why had the dear old queen been dragged up North? Odd. Very. The door opened, Copley's thoughts evaporated; he was beckoned in; Evelyn was standing with Prime Minister and several high-ranking military officers; they all looked at Copley.

"Sorry to keep you Copley, I see they've supplied you with your passes. You now have access and authority covering combined military and civilian services; ask and it will be done!

"Fine. Exactly what am I doing, or is that too much, to ask?"

"For a start off anything Evelyn wants; but specifically, you are responsible for rescuing historic artefacts and sites within the region, documents, securing historic and archaeological sites. Whatever it takes to protect our heritage. I know it's a huge task, but the local authorities are going to struggle keeping the basics going, let alone worry about their wrecked heritage; looting is an issue; you will be allocated resources to rescue what you can. You set your own agenda. I leave the details to you. Now I'm sorry Copley but I have to take Evelyn away for forty-eight hours, to London. Formalities. Gentlemen I think we can head for our transport, if you would like to follow us in five minutes."

The Prime Minister and the officers departed. Copley was left looking into Evelyn's eyes, he drew her close; kissed her gently on the lips.

"Take care my love; I wanted you to lead this project; didn't quite expect this to happen. Still, you deserve …"

"Copley, I never ever expected to be in this position. I will do my best"

"Evelyn, you do fantastically all the time; you have me to experiment on; anybody that can keep me on the straight and narrow, well, this is a walk in the park"

"It isn't."

"No. It isn't, its huge, it's awful, terrible. But I know you can do this."

"We can do this. We didn't make the wind blow, but we can gather up the leaves."

"Yes. We, can. I love you. Be careful and don't overdo it."

"Copley. I love you. Now let me get on. I will be back a soon as I can."

"Lady Copley. You got there before me. I will remember that. You can be certain I won't let you forget."

Copley held Evelyn close; he kissed her, losing himself in her; just as he always had as he knew he always would. He'd wanted her to lead a project, now she was leading an even bigger one.

Evelyn left the room.

Copley stood looking at the closed door, as if waiting for her return. Perhaps, thought Copley; his strange feeling on the train had been some sort of warning, or perhaps an awakening; he was unsure. Ever since Toby had told him of the inscription his world had been slightly askew; now it was at ninety degrees. He looked down at his pass, his face looked back at him, it was as sad as he felt.

The door swung open and a military officer strode in,

"Professor Copley. Good to meet you sir. Clive Haverigg I'm assigned to provide you with logistical support; firstly though, I better show you your office and team. If you would like to follow me.

"Lead on Major."

Copley followed the Major down the corridor and through another set of double doors to a large open office space filled with desks, screens and ten personnel in military uniform. Everyone stood up as Copley entered the room.

"This is your team; I've arranged a meeting of the heads of sections for tomorrow at 09.00 hours. With your permission I will provide a quick general overview now. We've done our best to find, engineers, logistics, transport, storage experts.".

"Excellent. Carry on Major I'm all ears. All I know is it's a mess out there."

The Major nodded and the lights dimmed, and a screen dropped silently from the ceiling.

"On Tuesday last the remains of hurricane Justine hit the Borders and Cumbrian coast at precisely the same time a deep depression was driven South through the North Sea, combined with the highest tides of the decade. Flooding was expected, especially as Cumbria and the Borders had seen a month of rain in the week before Justine arrived. Coastal communities were extremely badly hit, Tyne port is out of action, assessment is ongoing; the airport should be operational just about now; casualty figures are currently standing at an estimate of seventy thousand dead and a hundred thousand injured, All the immediate regions hospitals are damaged, so that death toll will rise. A State of National Emergency will be declared in the next few hours. Remarkably some of the local councils and the City are managing to operate rest shelter centers and get the main roads operational, a basic bus service is already restored in the city and volunteers are assisting in myriad of ways, which shows morale is holding up. Now why are you here and not assigned to the general clear up? Because there are priceless and unique documents, artefacts and exhibits lying in destroyed buildings; looting is an inevitable consequence of chaos; a United Nations World Heritage Site runs right through the area and we have a duty of care to protect the site as best we can. Professor Copley, based on his knowledge will assist us in prioritizing the securing and rescue of materials. So far, he is the only member of his department that has been located,

I'm sure our ranks will be strengthened in the coming days. Our first task is to identify how big a task we have, and we will have the satellite link in place shortly, allowing us to make a quick assessment before we visit on the ground. Any questions?"

Copley stood trying to comprehend the numbers; he had walked through seas of glass, tiles, slates; broken cars. He had looked ahead, avoiding the hazards, deliberately removing any suggestion of bodies beneath the rubble; blanking everything out was a survival technique he'd learned through life, a grim determination and purpose was being offered to occupy him. The bodies could remain numbers in the dust.

There were a few technical questions of the Major, Copley took no notice and he was aware that he was the only nonmilitary person present, leaving him feeling very exposed. There, thought Copley, was that feeling of doubt, that desire to flee; where was his self-assured confidence? It seemed to have deserted him. Copley pulled himself together. They needed him, he was the leader, he would lead from the front and he could do so because he knew the patch and they didn't.

"Thank you Major. I will be very brief. I've just lived through hell; surviving by sitting in the remains of a Roman subterranean dining room that its present owner thinks a Victorian folly which he keeps his wine collection in. My point is, firstly, I'm exhausted and will be going to bed as soon as possible. Secondly. In these circumstances we are faced with accidental damage to sites and artefacts, because they don't know what they have before them and more worryingly, deliberate opportunistic looting. Buildings can be put back up.

Artefacts, documents can be lost forever. There is millions of pounds worth of material lying in the rubble, the nations, the regions, heritage and treasures need rescuing. It falls to us to sort it out. Now if it's all the same to you, I work best when I can stay awake, so I shall see you in the morning"

Copley lay in the bed; the landscape was flat; Evelyn was missing. They had texted, it wasn't easy for Evelyn to phone, suggesting she was with Rosemary; staying at the PM's residence. Evelyn knew the drill; Copley knew the code words; their secret tokens of love and devotion; they knew to be careful. Yet Copley was near to tears just seeing the text; knowing Evelyn was there.

Copley looked at the shadows on the ceiling; outside the Army were making themselves at home, vehicles were coming and going, a rumble of what sounded like a tank seemed to come perilously close to the house. Copley reached for headphones and settled back to a little Bach to ease him to sleep. Evelyn was on his mind; how lucky they had been to survive. Seventy thousand hadn't been. Seventy thousand. Seventy thousand. Copley tossed and turned, his headphones pushed against his ears, the music slowly overcame the numbers; only Evelyn was left. He could feel her presence, her perfume; her scent on the sheets. He was nothing without her; a team of two halves, except Copley was at best a quarter. The bluster and the front. The real star was Evelyn. Lady Evelyn Copley of? That was a point. Copley mused, smiled to himself and eventually fell asleep with the permutations of Evelyn's ennoblement blanking out all else.

Six thirty. Copley was up, showered, dressed and hunting the kitchen for bread for his toast without success. Frustrated he decided to see what his new neighbours might offer in the way of sustenance, he popped out of the back door and noted the fragrance of bacon and sausage wafting its way into his nostrils from the large marquee where next door had been, he duly found himself in the queue for breakfast. Nobody questioned his presence and he was soon sat at a long table with a very substantial breakfast and a mug of tea before him. The atmosphere was congenial; some of the troops were talking football, others about holiday plans; the reality outside was on hold. Copley realised they all knew who he was, he couldn't be inside the fence otherwise; but he took to heart the fact he was just part of the team. For the first time, in a very long time, Copley didn't mind being anonymous; just a cog in the machine. He would do his bit. He had slept well but was still not clear in his mind where and what to start with; structures would have to wait; clearly documents and paintings would deteriorate and therefore should be rescued first; then artefacts, especially as they would be easy prey to looters, if made of precious materials. As to housing and immediate preservation that would require space and experts working under extreme conditions; transport and co-operation from other unaffected areas. Copley realised he didn't know how big an area he was responsible for; the map suggested the Tyne valley and the coast from Berwick upon Tweed to Scarborough, an impossible task, he could only deal with Newcastle and a radius of about twenty five miles at most, he would need to find the curators, the archaeologists.

His mind pondered the scale. He finished his tea, placed the mug on his tray and placed it in the rack with all the rest, exited and was back in his kitchen in less than two minutes; with ideas bubbling away. Copley sent a text to Evelyn, he kept it short, just to know she was fine, that he was coping; for a second he felt lost, missing her. A tear began to well.

"Pull yourself together Copley. It's going to be fine."

Copley still felt lost, but he had to believe in himself and Copley knew how to rise to his own challenges. As long as Evelyn was there in spirit, he was fine.

Collecting his notebook and jacket he headed to the front door; there was no point locking up he thought; he stood on the front doorstep from where a veritable town of tents and portacabins now occupied the street. His presence having been duly noted a Panther drove up and stopped at the gate. Copley duly obliged and even managed to get aboard unaided, his driver giving him a cheery

"Good morning Professor"

"Good morning. How goes it out there?"

"Well, the lads at Hexham have got a temporary bridge across the river; the old ones nigh on intact, but the river has shifted onto its old course; there's no sign of the supermarket or the sports centre; station's gone too. They say there's a trawler in a field at Fourstones, or what's left of one."

"I was at Corbridge. I didn't venture down to the river."

"Same story, the rivers moved South; I suspect it will have exposed the Roman causeway to the pontus."

"Are you interested in archaeology?"

"Yes Professor, always been an interest of mine, done a couple of excavations; did a course at Vindolanda."

"In that case Private Matthews"

"Bob"

"In that case Bob, I hereby make you my driver; please tell whoever your sergeant or officer is that you are assigned to me. Can you do that?"

"Yes Professor. Delighted to do so."

"Can you find something a little more car and a lot less tank"

"That might be a bit difficult Professor; we have orders to keep you safe and only a few roads are absolutely clear; this really is the safest way to get around. How did you get back from Corbridge"?

"Land Rover, I was up on the A69, it was a forest, or to be precise a fallen one; I was contemplating a very long walk back to Newcastle when this land agent comes along the central reservation and we make our way back from there; so I've seen how bad it is."

"That's the North bank, you should see what it did down the coast and on the South side of the river. I did an early morning run; they are trying to get the reactor under control at Hartlepool and needed some engineers shifted, more fool them. It's chaos down there. I'm grateful to you. I didn't fancy the idea of going back there again; further away the better."

Copley made a few private decisions; he sat quietly as Bob made his way into the city center.

"Good morning Professor."

Good morning Captain. I've assigned Private Matthews as my driver and can you arrange for his security clearances to allow him access to my office, I want him on my team."

The Captain looked passed Copley. Private Matthews looked straight ahead. There was the merest pause and then the Captain smiled.

"I see your fully rested Professor. Yes, no problem; Matthews is assigned to you. Matthews park up and follow us."

Matthews parked neatly on the only blades of the park unoccupied and joined Copley and the Captain. The party walked into City Hall and headed for the lift.

Down they went.

"There's a video conference with the PM in ten minutes. Matthews when we get out of the lift, head to the security section, wait there; I'll be along after the meeting"

Copley noted a slight strain in the Captains voice, something was up, and it wasn't Copley wanting a driver that was causing it.

Matthews departed and the two proceeded to the PM's room. A large screen descended in front of the desk.

"Good morning Copley"

"Good morning PM. How's Evelyn?

"Very well. Rested. I apologize for having to ask her to come down to London; I assure you it was vital. You will be aware that a state of national emergency has been issued; we have problems at Hartlepool power station and Sellafield in the West. Depending on the next few hours I may have to order mass evacuations."

"That gives me a priority, I've been grappling with the scale of the task; I will concentrate on the irreplaceable artefacts of national importance."

"I just hope and pray the technicians can get things under control. Evelyn will be back with you tomorrow, whatever the situation. I need you to get as much as you can either up to Edinburgh, or down to London as you can. Now I'm afraid I must go. Good luck Copley. Evelyn will be in touch; she got your text."

The screen went blank.

"Right then."

Copley spoke to the empty screen. He turned to the Captain.

"Looks as if it's going to be a busy day."

The Captain half smiled; they both were fully aware of the impending crisis, what else was there to do but just get on with it.

Half an hour later and Copley's team were assigned to tasks. Communications were an issue; Copley was desperate to contact University colleagues, curators and experts. Copley decided that The Scouts were his best hope, details were being issued that museums and art galleries were to be protected by armed personnel.

Copley had just organised a team to investigate whether the Lindisfarne gospels had survived the storm; the Captain was summoning up a helicopter, when Matthews entered the office.

"Ahh. Good. Matthews, duly passed and ready for anything. We have a mission. This shouldn't take too long. Up to the University and one other stop." Copley gesticulated his departure to the Captain and was out of the door before anyone could stop him with Matthews in pursuit.

"Up to the University and as close as we can get to my department; have you got a screwdriver set and we will need some carrier bags."

"No problem on either Professor; I take it time is of the essence?"

"Certainly is Matthews. Certainly is"

They emerged into the daylight and the organised chaos of the City. Although the University was but a very short walk from the Civic Hall, Copley needed Matthews expertise with the panther to make their way through the rubble of fallen roofs, the razor sharp steel and glass, up the steps, pass the wrecked students union, the gatehouse and into a choked garden of tile and fallen masonry. It was obvious that no one on foot had attempted to get to this point and having surveyed the perilous angle of timbers above them they got inside the door as quickly as possible. They made their way up the winding staircase to the second floor; partly open to the sky. The corridor half blocked by roof timbers; Copley led the way to his office.

"Bit of a mess in here; have you got those screwdrivers, can you take the hard drives out of the computer and do the same in Evelyn's office next door; I will get to work on the safe."

Matthews duly started on the computers and Copley keyed the code for his safe; the contents of which duly fitted into his jacket pocket. Matthews had moved into Evelyn's office; the neat and tidy room was a rubble field, the desk covered in bricks. As Matthews worked on the computer Copley forced the drawer open, inside was a small silver photo frame; it was a picture of them both on their honeymoon. Copley smiled at it and held it close for a moment; then, seeing Matthews had the hard drive handed him the picture to put in his bag.

"I think were finished here Matthews, thank you. Just one other call to make. Might be a difficult one."

They made their way back to the panther; Copley could rest easy. Nobody was going to pilfer his work; whilst he never kept his finished research on any University system, he wasn't leaving any clues either. He thought it odd that no one had attempted to get to the department; not a soul; nothing had disturbed the dust before their arrival. Perhaps everyone had evacuated, or were dead?

"Where next Professor?"

"The Crown Posada, Side"

"We can have a go; it's petty hairy down by the river. Hold tight Professor"

Copley strapped himself into his seat and stared at the onboard screen; there was a better view from it than the slits of light through the armour covered windscreen. They made their way back down the steps and turned right; a military policeman stopped them.

"Where are you off to?"

"Side. I've got Professor Copley onboard."

"Let's have a look at your passes."

They were duly handed over.

"It's a mess down there. If I were you Professor, don't stay long, it's a biological hazard. Have you got some kit onboard?"

"Yes. Couple of suits and masks."

Matthew nodded over his shoulder into the back. The policeman was satisfied.

"Good luck and don't linger long."

He returned the passes, turned and stopped the traffic, waving the panther onto the pavement of Northumberland Street. There were people, slowly but surely, beginning to clear shopfronts, walkways through the rubble. The panther edged its way very slowly down the paved street; outside Fenwick's a canteen had been set up for workers. Matthew pulled up.

"Let's get a brew. Golden rule. Never miss the opportunity for a brew."

Copley smiled and followed Matthew to the queue.

Everyone was patiently waiting; the mood was quite upbeat; out of the adversity the people were pulling together, and a resemblance of order was returning. Copley had never met people quite like those of the North East; they were as tough as nails, yet gentle, polite and caring; a certain something he could never quite identify; but whatever it was it made him proud to be, if only by location, part of. His colleagues had told him he was mad, that he was throwing his life away. Quite the opposite; it had been the making of him. He moved forward as the line was processed by the counter. Hi eye was taken by something glistening in the dust; he bent down to see what it was. As he did so there was a rumbling sound and a plume of water passed over his kneeling body. The queue, took the blast; Copley scooped up the object and deftly stepped out of the jet. As soon as it had started the jet turned to a dribble, the queue reformed without comment. One water main being repaired somewhere close by, a bit of water wasn't going to do any harm; not now at least. Copley took his mug and cheese bap and leaned on the panther alongside a damp Matthew.

"You were lucky Professor"

"Yes. There was something in the dirt. I just bent down to pick it up and you lot got a soaking."

"What was it?"

"I don't know. Hang on I'll have a look"

Placing his tea and bap on the panther, Copley extracted the object from his pocket. Matthew stopped eating his bap. Copley realised what he had in his hand. A large single diamond ring; it was not the quality of the cut that Matthew had been so struck by, but the remnants of a finger severed either side of it.

Taken aback Copley examined the cuts; a knife wound; somebody had cut the finger off to gain the diamond and had still not been able to extract it so had cut the other end of the finger leaving a stump of bone and tissues still stuck fast to the ring.

"Looters"

"Yes Bob. Looters."

Copley threw the ring onto the rubble next to the vehicle.

Copley sipped his tea; Bob finished his bap; a silence fell; which Copley broke before it became painful.

"When you're ready Bob."

"Ready Professor; we can have a go; we might have to go on foot, doubt we will get down Dean Street."

"Well in that case we will go to the Castle and we could access via the construction walkway; the way Evelyn and the others got out, if it's still standing."

"Good idea. Right. Off we go"

Back in the panther, Bobs comment regarding Dean Street was soon confirmed; the tarmac and much of the road surface of Grey Street had been eroded away; a mixture of room beams, shop fronts and brickwork had cascaded down the hill to meet the remains of the two buildings at the beginning of Dean Street, creating a mountain of debris. They turned right passing St Nicholas's a roofless shell left into the street and under the railway bridge to Castle garth. They parked under the railway arch."

"Look at that, not a scratch."

"Yes. The Normans knew how to build Bob; they had to; they kept on getting burned out of the spot. The Vermont is not too bad, minus a few windows; the courthouse looks nigh on untouched, which hopefully means we can get across to the Crown Posada."

"I think we should put our biohazards suits on Professor. I don't think it's going to be very pleasant down there."

Above them a diesel locomotive was grinding it's way North; it was a reassuring sound. Copley nodded. He wasn't exactly looking forward to the prospect, he could smell a rancid putrid oily stench.

"Here we go. Mind the boards."

Bob was leading the Professor out onto the walkway, testing it as they progressed, even with the mask on the smell was obnoxious. They entered the Crown Posada on the second floor and the cardboard encampment that had kept Evelyn, Arthur and the others warm for two nights; crossing towards the front of the building Bob put a cautionary arm out, the ceiling had gone through from above and gone through the floorboards; the sky was showing through where the roof had been; they made their way to the staircase, at which point Copley took the lead. Reaching the first floor it became obvious that the front door leading off the street to the staircase had been forced open by the tide. It was just possible through the tangled debris to step outside. Copley beckoned Bob to join him; the sight that met their eyes was one of utter devastation. Everything on the opposite side from the Crown Posada was gone, just the great pillars of the Tyne Bridge with its carriageway above and the steep slope to the Church of St Willibrod; all else was gone, they could see the Free Trade Inn. Copley stood utterly stunned, he fumbled for his phone only to realize it was inside his bio suit. He turned to see Bob, with a camera in a plastic cover snapping away. He raised a thumb in appreciation. Copley knew he had a good reliable chap, he would have said so, but saying anything with the mask on wasn't easy. There was activity on the river, barges were heading up and down; he could see troops and vehicles going upriver. He wondered where they were heading and what state the locals were in. He wished them all luck. The ensign on the barge was Dutch; so, it really had become a serious emergency, it had to be for the Government to take aid from anyone. A helicopter droned overhead; it paused Copley and Bob waived; it dipped its node and carried on its way.

Copley turned to face the Crown Posada; there was mud and rubbish up to the windows. The stained glass had survived, protected by its plastic covering; the gate was open as was the door, forced in by the flow, Copley went to step into the bar, but something inside him stopped his next step; he looked down, nothing. Nothing. A hole. Copley knew that the cellar ramp was by the door, he subconsciously knew it was there and likely to have been broken. No this wasn't the cellar ramp; this was the floor, all of it. Bob was by his shoulder and holding Copley back, but turning him towards the back of the pub, it became apparent that this nothing went the full width and length of the pub. Copley couldn't believe it; the cellar had gone, dropped into a void. Copley stepped back from the edge and gesticulated to Bob. A torch. He needed a torch. A thumbs up was the response and the resourceful Bob unzipped a side pocket and took out a torch he then pointed at Copley's shoulder pocket. Hey presto. Two torches. Bob stepped forward and eased himself to the edge of the void and took photographs; in the flash Copley was aware there were very large cut stone blocks at about six meters depth, on both sides of the pub. Bob waved Copley to join him; Copley got down on his chest and peered round Bob to the back of the pub towards the toilets; he shone his torch down into the depths; the beam of light caught on stone. Bob shined his next to Copley's; in the glaring ice like light an arch appeared. A blocked arch; a tunnel mouth; to the riverside of the arch a block was missing from the masonry retaining wall. At that moment Copley knew, beyond any doubt; it was the tunnel of Cerealis.

Chapter Three

"Bugger me."

Copley stood in the doorway, Bob at his side; he couldn't agree with Bob more. He pondered. How the hell did Toby know it was under the Crown Posada, or was it just sheer luck?

"Well Bob; that was a surprise."

"Was it Professor? I mean why are we here? In the Crown Posada, or what's left of it. Least the ceiling is still there. Suppose the record player's gone along with all that lovely beer. That record player."

"Dated from 1942, American if I remember rightly. I know this bar like the back of my hand; given lectures here, got merry; got dragged out by Evelyn frequently. Sat and listened to the crack; joined in. Sometimes. Just sometimes, I'd sit in the snug and let the place talk to me. I'd listen, the stories, the laughter, the tragedies, war and tempest. Nowhere on earth quite like it. It will rise Bob, it will rise again."

"Is this the old harbour side?"

Bob had turned and stared out of the gated entrance, he could see straight to the Free Trade Inn, that stood seemingly, from a distance, impervious to the storm.

"Yes. In Roman times the ships would dock along the Eastern side of this part of Side. The safest place to be, out of the currents running in the main river. A sheltered spot long before the Romans; after they departed it gradually began to silt up and eventually was filled in. That's only half the picture, Dean and Grey Street didn't appear until much later because most of it was a gorge. There was a bridge across it just outside the Wellington on appropriately named Bridge Street."

"Yer kidding"

"Not at all; the town rubbish was piled down into what became the Lort Burn."

"Lort?"

"Shit"

"So Grey Street and Dean Street is built on shit."

"Precisely and a great deal of it. For centuries it was the only part of the overcrowded city that wasn't built on. In the eighteenth century a lot of topsoil was brought in and the area was gardened; even then they knew it would have to be left for a while."

"Might need a bit of work right now"

Bob looked up the street to the tangle of cars and the contents of offices and restaurants, piled up under the railway arch. Copley viewed it with a strange wonder. The colours the tangle of chrome and steel, paper and wood, plastic and glass; a monument to a moment in time. An archaeologist's field day.

"Yes. That will take a while to shift. Let's get back.

Somebody will probably realize we are AWOL by now, not that anybody is really bothered about us. I think they have slightly more important things to do."

They made their way along the front of the Crown and up the stairs and across to the Castle. There was quite a lot of activity outside the Vermont hotel and the magistrates court; the police were busy taping off both buildings. Bob approached a policewoman with a large roll of Police tape.

"What's going on here then?

"Emergency reception center in the court and the Vermont to be used for essential personnel dormitories."

Above a diesel locomotive hooted as it headed North. The policewoman looked up as the train passed by.

"I wish I was on my way out of here right now; I've seen enough over the last two days."

"You got family?"

"Two boys. They're alright; they were away in Birmingham at a school football festival. Thank God. They haven't got anything to come home to anyway."

"Get yourself allocated to the Vermont lass."

Bob nodded at a couple of suits making their way into the building with briefcases.

"Excuse me gentlemen"

The suits turned towards Bob. Bob beckoned them over. Bob winked at Copley

"Gentlemen can I see your passes."

The suits showed their access passes.

"Thank you. Now gentlemen are you by chance responsible for allocation of rooms in this new government dormitory?"

The suits nodded.

"Well be so kind as to take this wpc with you an allocate her a room. On the orders of Professor Copley"

"We can't just allocate rooms on a nod."

"Yes. You can. This is Professor Copley"

Copley showed his pass; the suits looked suitably impressed.

"Please provide this young lady with suitable accommodation. I need her to conduct work at the Castle."

"Certainly Professor."

"Thank you. She will be along shortly."

The suits departed.

"There you are lass. A bit of comfort."

"I'm grateful to you but I didn't say I was homeless."

"You've been sleeping on the floor and those eyes tell me you haven't done much of that. Anyway, the Professor wants you to do a job for him."

"I'll have to clear it with control. Sorry sir. Professor. If you could talk to my Inspector."

"Name, rank and service number"

Bob smiled at the wpc. The wpc smiled back.

"Henderson Jean, wpc Newcastle Central; what's left of it."

"Leave it to me Jean."

Bob tapped a number on his arm mounted radio.

"This is Whisky Kilo Alpha Zulu can you patch me through to the Police at Newcastle Central. Priority One for Copley."

Copley looked at Jean. Her uniform was dirty, her eyes were sunken; hair covered in dust, hands scratched. He really could find something for her to do. It was standing next to them. The Castle. Somebody had to retrieve, record and protect. Bob passed the mouthpiece to Copley.

"Professor Copley, this is Inspector Chivers. How can I assist?"

"I'm assigning one of your wpc's to my team. WPC Henderson. I need her for the foreseeable future for protection and general duties. I have arranged suitable accommodation for the officer, and she will be under my command. I hope that is in order?"

There was a slight pause at the other end of the line.

"No problem Professor. Off the record give her my best. You've got a good one there; I want her back when things get back to normal. If you can hear this Henderson, keep safe"

"We'll take good care Inspector"

The line went dead. Bob smiled at Jean.

"Better get the best room in the house; then meet us here by that vehicle, the panther; we need to get your new pass."

Jean went into the Vermont.

Copley turned to Bob.

"Well you seem to have a good judge of character; how did you know I was thinking about the Castle?

"I didn't. I just saw the lass and those suits and decided I'd do her a good turn. She looked all in poor lass."

"And I could give her a job?"

"Well you need people and she would be right next door to the Castle. Sorry I made the rest up"

"And I went along with it. No harm done Bob. It is ideal to have somewhere as a base and I will need somebody close by."

"For the Crown Posada"

"Precisely. I have no intention of that find coming to any harm. Here comes our new recruit."

Jean re-joined them with a pass key and a smile.

"Thank you, both of you."

"It was Bob's idea; I merely run the show; which won't be going anywhere if we don't get back and you will need a new security pass, so if you are ready Bob, let's get going. Back to sunny Tynemouth."

The three made their way through Newcastle. Jean was asleep within a mile; Bob turned to Copley and nodded. They'd done the right thing. How many more poor souls were dead on their feet. But they could only do so much. Copley thought of Evelyn. What decisions she was making. He knew she could make anyone sit up and take notice. She could save lives. The panther stopped. The road was temporarily blocked whilst a building was demolished; the dust rose up as it fell. Copley distinctly saw arms; legs and torsos in the dust. He instinctively turned to make sure Jean was asleep. Strange he thought. How protective he was. Yet Jean had probably witnessed worse in the last couple of days. What nightmares awaited them all for years to come. The rubble cleared sufficiently for traffic to pass they travelled on. Queues of people stood waiting at the canteen stations.

"What a bloody mess Professor"

"Yes Bob. Bloody indeed."

"Yer know they had a warning. They knew this was going to happen and they did nowt."

"What do you mean they had a warning? Of course, they had a warning, it was on the weather radar. Just they couldn't move the whole population. Not enough time."

"Well that's not what I heard."

"Go on then. What have you been told?"

"Weather bomb"

"Weather bomb"

"Yes."

"Bob. A weather bomb is a natural phenomenon. "

"This one wasn't."

"So, your telling me all this is the result of a deliberate act.

"Yes."

"Your proof?"

The panther entered Copley's new compound; it could hardly be described as a suburban street anymore.

"Now then Jean wakey wakey. Time to get you to our pass office; then you can spend a happy morning at the next one at the Civic Hall in the morning. "

Jean shook herself awake. Smiled at them both.

"Thank you. Both of you. I won't let you down."

"Right lass, follow me. I'll see you in the mess later Professor."

Copley suddenly realised Bob had brought him back home. Not back to his Civic Hall office; he smiled to himself as Bob accompanied the wpc into the portacabin. He had definitely made the right choice in Bob. As he was at home he would see if he could raise Evelyn. He made his way across the lawn and let himself in through the back door.

"Copley"

"Evelyn. How did you?"

"I contacted Bob, had him bring you home. You have a good man there and I see you have a woman police constable onboard."

"How did?"

"I looked through the window."

"Am I glad to see you."

"Likewise, Copley. Now sit down and have a beer. I have something to tell you."

"If it's about nuclear power plants I'm not sure I want to know."

"No. The good news is we have saved the sites. Touch and go, but no evacuations."

"Good. I've seen the state of things; grim"

"Believe me they don't get any better all the way down to Scarborough and North to Berwick upon Tweed. That's supposed to be your patch, but we don't expect any great recovery of material. You've sent a team to Lindsifarne. They can't find it."

"What do you mean, they can't find it?"

"The storm swept the entire archipelago clean; there's nothing but bare rock"

"Nothing left?"

"No."

"My God."

"I'm sorry Copley. They will be beachcombing no doubt; but there is nothing, no causeway; nothing standing at all."

"Nature and time wipes everything clean. I just didn't want to be around to witness it."

"Copley lets go upstairs and go to bed."

"I'm supposed to be in charge of recovering our heritage."

"The world can wait a few hours"

"I couldn't agree more Evelyn. I could do with a hug."

"Come on Copley, I think we both need a little more than that."
Evelyn took him by the hand and led him upstairs.

She stood facing Copley at the foot of their bed.
He held her face in his hands and kissed her lips softly.
She closed her eyes and savoured his tenderness.
Copley moved his lips down to Evelyn's neck, below her ear.
She sighed and slowly tilted her head back, his mouth moved slowly and lightly down towards her cleavage.
His hands moved to her breasts, he gently brushed them with his fingers. Such lightness of touch and yet her nipples hardened and pointed through the lace of her bra, quite visible through her silky blouse.
Copley undid the blouse sliding it over her shoulders it fell to the floor. Her bra followed it.
He caressed Evelyn's breasts taking her nipples into his mouth he sucked and gently nibbled them.
He knew how to arouse her, how to make her feel wonderful.
His hand slid under her skirt and smoothed it's way to the inside of her thighs.
Her knickers were damp. He felt his cock strain harder against his trousers. He lightly fingered her through the satin. Slowly, then as her breathing quickened so did his fingers. Parting her cunt lips and rubbing her clit.
He fell to his knees and pulled her knickers off, he gently pushed her back onto the bed. Her legs wide apart Copley buried his face between her thighs and licked and flicked Evelyn to orgasm.

She lifted herself up onto her elbows and smiling took in the vision that was Copley.

He smiled back licking his lips.

Evelyn crawled over to Copley and as he stood upright she stroked his straining cock and then carefully undid his trousers. Lying on her front she took his cock and slid him into her mouth.

Deep and long, running her tongue over his helmet, licking the trickle of pre cum.

Evelyn, pulled Copley onto the bed.

She sat astride him and slowly slid his cock inside her.

Copley smiled. His hands cupped Evelyn's breasts once more.

" Evelyn, it's bloody good to be home."

Copley dressed slowly, he looked through the window, the slatted blinds broke up the view of green tents, masts and myriad large vehicles.

"You were going to tell me something, before we came up here. Love in the afternoon, most certainly clears the woes of the day away."

"You know I can't tell you anything; you know that."

Evelyn pointed to the notepad on the bedside table and the bathroom.

Copley hummed to himself as he wandered into the bathroom and turned the shower on and pulled the blind. He sat on the loo and

Evelyn made herself comfortable on the dry side of the bath. She wrote on the pad.

ITS NOT WHAT IT SEEMS.

Copley wrote in return.

SO, WHAT IS IT?

A WEATHER BOMB

Copley looked at the ceiling. He looked back at Evelyn and scribbled.

THAT'S ANATURAL PHENOMMENEN

Evelyn replied

THIS ISNT NATURAL WE WERE ATTACKED.

Copley stood up and pushed the flush. Leaned over to Evelyn and spoke all but silently into her ear.

"Who by?"

"We don't know"

"Bloody typical we can't even work out who hit us."

Evelyn turned off the shower. They walked back into the bedroom.

"I better be going dear. Or should I call you Lady Copley?"

"Baroness Copley of Miterdale."

"Miterdale. How did you manage that? I thought you had to have an association."

"We do."

"Since when? Since I told the PM you always wanted the title. The rest was down to her."

"Did I see HMQ in the bunker?"

"Couldn't possibly say."

"That explains it. There's hardly any point in secrecy; all the troops know it."

"Doesn't surprise me. The media are under a D notice. We are holding our breath."

"In case something else happens. Don't tell me, you can't tell me."

"Have you found somewhere to hold the artefacts?"

"Give me a chance Evelyn, I've only just got a team. No. I haven't."

"Well you have one. Manod"

"Blaneau Ffestiniog. Deep storage. The nuclear option. Figures. At least I know what I'm dealing with. Thanks, my love. I'm not going to ask anymore. I know you are busy doing whatever it is your're doing; just stay safe."

"You too. You seem to have a sturdy chap in Bob."

"He certainly knows the system. He's a good lad. Rescued that wpc. I'm going to set up my other office, the one where I can get things done, in the Castle. Those two can keep the World out and get me what I need."

"You've been down to the Crown Posada, haven't you?"

"The transponder on the panther. Is there nowhere to hide?"

"No."

"Yes, I have been down to the Crown Posada and yes I have found the tunnel mouth. Toby was bang on. Which worries me. How the hell did he know exactly?"

"Research. You do it. It's most likely the John Tradescant the Younger and Ashmole; which is what Toby suggested. I agree there is something unusual in the fact the inscription seems to have been lost; especially as it is highly unusual. Perhaps that's why. Perhaps they thought it was fake?"

"I suppose your right; well done Toby that's all I say"

"I must be going Copley. You keep close to Bob and be careful."

"I promise"

Evelyn kissed him on the forehead and left him. Copley felt the immediate loss of Evelyn's presence. He shook himself, continued dressing and pondered. He still couldn't get over Toby's accuracy and why was the inscription hidden away. But there was no time to waste; there was work, hard work, to do.

Copley made his way out of the house and back into the ordered world of the military. Bob saw him coming.

"Jean's being tidied up by the quartermaster; I've organised her security clearance for tomorrow at nine"

"That's something for her to look forward to. God help her"

"I warned her. She'll be fine."

"Can we get on Bob. I take it Jean's safe to get back to the Vermont?"

"No problems Professor, all arranged. She can get her head down. Poor lass."

"Come on Bob, no time to waste."

They settled themselves into the panther.

"Where first Professor"

It's a tough one Bob. We are going to Lindisfarne"

"Christ"

"I take it you know. By the way. I know about the Weather Bomb"

"Right Professor; understood. I will have to contact control as to our destination."

Bob radioed through the coordinates. A voice crackled back.

"Advise against unless absolutely necessary"

Copley yelled at the mouthpiece from his seat.

"I have a team out there. I know how bad it is Thank you very much"

The line went dead.

They travelled in silence through blasted scenery, dead cows, dead people. Lost souls walking from where to where, Copley knew not. Ragged souls in need of rest. The further North they went the landscape had absorbed the fury; less settlements. Roofless cottages; caravans and chalets lay crumpled in the flattened woods. They reached the level crossing of the East Coast mainline. The lights were at red. A sign of normality. They waited. Copley broke the silence.

"Here we go."

"Not looking forward to this Professor."

"Nor me."

A train rattled by; Copley counted the carriages. Twenty. You never saw that under normal circumstances. But these were not normal anything. All the usual, the predictable had gone. The lights stayed red as a train headed South, Royal Mail vans.

"Coffin carrier; they're moving the dead up to Edinburgh and down the Waverley line; mass graves."

The lights stopped flashing and the barrier lifted.

Silence resumed.

The panther bounced over the crossing and gently eased down the road towards the coast. The hedgerows were flat, scrubbed away and that was all they saw. No road, no causeway, just dark rocks hardly above the water line of the placid sea; no buildings at all, nothing. To their left was three vehicles and two large tents. A group of four men were looking at something on the table.

Copley and Bob pulled up and joined the group. It distracted them from looking out to sea.

"Gentlemen."

A sergeant replied.

"Professor. I'm afraid there is nothing left. Absolutely nothing, it's as if it's been wiped clean. We've had a look along the shoreline, most of the material seems to be out in the North Sea, very little on the beachline. We can carry on, but I really don't think we will find anything."

"No. I think we can safely say all has been lost. Can you and your colleagues break camp and head to Berwick upon Tweed. If you can rescue any documents that you can from the museum; the standards, anything you can with your limited resources. I don't want us to get in the way of the rescue services, if you can get the empty coffin train to stop and load it; I leave that to you then head back into base. If you find a church safe enough to enter, feel free. I think it appropriate."

"Yes Professor. The lads found these two bits of roof timber."

He pointed to a makeshift cross just down by the tent. Copley nodded. Two of the men picked the cross up and walked down to where the causeway had commenced. A hole was already dug; the cross sank into the hole, deep and sturdy. The hole was filled, and the small party stood before it in silence. A silence that seemed to last an eternity. The sun shone; the waves rippled on the shore. A distant train announced the World again.

Copley walked back to the panther.

"I had to see for myself. I simply couldn't take it in. Now I have. Sorry Bob. I had to see it. Those poor souls."

"Can't take it in. Completely vanished"

They retraced their route, over the crossing. Copley looked at the roofless station and the debris in the yard.

"Pull over Bob I could do with a pee."

Bob pulled into the station road; the main station was intact saved for the roof; it was no longer used, the few trains that stopped deposited their passengers at a glorified but practical bus stop. The station stood, whilst the bus shelter had vanished in the wind.

Copley alighted from the panther in somewhat of a rush and fell on the deck. He went to right himself and noticed the rear of an upturned car hidden by the collapsed roof. He attended to his immediate need. Bob taking the same opportunity. Zipping himself up Copley brushed himself down and walked over to the car. The smell caught him in both nostrils; rotting bloated flesh. Somebody hadn't made it. He moved closer. He knew the smell, but he also had a concern that somebody could have survived. A thin chance. He was soon proved wrong. The upturned cars front seats were smashed near flat by a beam from the stations roof.

"Poor bastards"

"Yes."

Copley turned away. He suddenly felt a hand on his right shoulder; it swung him round. Copley was in total shock. There was nobody there. Bob looked at Copley as if he was about to have a seizure.

"You ok Professor?"

"No. I'm definitely not. Somebody has just got me by the shoulder and wants me to look at that car."

"You stay where you are Professor, there's fuel all over the place."

"Look in the back. There's something there."

Bob crawled towards the cars back seat, just visible under the fallen roof. He vanished under the remains.

"Bob, be careful."

Copley began to sweat profusely. What the hell turned him round? Bob remerged with a large plastic box with straps on all sides.

"It's bloody heavy whatever it is. You ok there, you gave me a hell of a fright"

"Not just you. I have no idea what happened."

"Well let's see what's in the box then."

Bob laid the box on the ground and unclipped the straps; he carefully opened the hinged lid. A white plastic sealed cover. He lifted the bag out of the box; took his knife and gently worked it down the seam and pulled the plastic away. What met his gaze had him fall backwards onto his backside; he clutched at the book.

"Professor."

"Yes Bob. My God it is. It's the Gospels. They must have realized they were under extreme threat and tried to get them away, sheltered behind the station and the roof got them."

Bob clutched the book tight. Tears began to flow, the two of them wept.

"Sorry about that Professor."

"Not at all. I was as amazed as you. Well done Bob, you have certainly made everyone's day." There was a crash behind them as part of the retaining wall fell onto the roof below, a sudden powerful cloud of flame and the petrol tank exploded.

When the dust cleared the two men gathered themselves up and putting the Gospels into the plastic box put them safely in the panther.

"Bob. I would prefer you don't say anything about what happened back there."

"No problem Professor. I honestly have no idea"

"I think you can send a message that the Lindisfarne Gospels are saved, that two brave souls lost their lives saving them and whomever they were they deserve the credit. We merely found them and the Gospels."

"Absolutely. Even if it was bloody odd."

Bob radioed in the news. There was a good amount of noise in the background. The news had lifted spirits. Not all had been lost.

"I didn't even need a pee. Very odd."

Copley felt a presence, warm comforting it passed through him and away. He looked ahead trying to ignore it.

"You ok Professor? Whatever that was back there, you just let it go. Believe me, when you've seen what I have you have to. You'd go potty otherwise."

"Sound advice Bob. I'm just glad we rescued something. The lads on the Lindisfarne search will be over the moon."

"Everybody is. It's what we need when things are tough. A bit of good cheer. Hey up, we have company"

A chinook circled them, dropped its nose and nodded to them in salute and went upon its way.

"The news is out."

"Good. You're right it's a morale booster. All I have to do is to persuade the authorities to let it stay here in the North East."

"They aren't taking it away; we fought for years to get it back from London."

"I have a suspicion it will be heading for Blaneau Ffestiniog and deep storage, unless I can come up with something fast."

"The Castle. It could withstand anything,"

"Good idea Bob. I think we will have about twenty-four hours before they will want to whisk it away. If I can delay things whilst you get Jean and a team of your chaps to sort out the security and any reinforcement of the building, you need. I leave it to you; you're the one with the initiative."

Copley scrabbled behind him and amongst the papers strewn over the seats he found the one he wanted and scribbled his signature on it.

"Here you are. My signature gets you anything you need. Now drop me and this parcel off at the station at Alnwick junction. The Press will be tracking the panther so do what you need to do and keep it quiet. I'll meet you at the Castle mid-day tomorrow. Get Jean out of the Civic HQ as soon as you can. I want the Castle working like the fortress it is. I have to convince my wife and others the Gospels stay put."

"Provide the holder with whatever assistance and means required. Those signatures should do it."

"Yes. Just don't overdo it, I will have to pick the pieces up later and as it's my wife and her best friend I will be none to impressed if you go overboard."

"Understood Professor. Leave it to me."

Copley scrabbled around again in the back.

"Bob. I don't have any authority over military rank, but I do have the authority to tell people to do things. So here you are. My authority. You are now an acting field Colonel appointed in the field by me. That should shut any jobs worth up."

Bob brought the panther to an abrupt stop.

"Rank is earned Professor. You can't just promote a feller like me just like that."

"Yes, I can, and I just have. My family has a long and distinguished military history and I know talent when I see it. I've no time for rank or title; it just comes in extremely useful for getting things done; use it to your advantage, or to be precise our advantage. If I want to put a spanner in the system, I can think no one better than you to wield it, so you might as well have some of the benefits. Now drive on and get me to the Junction."

Copley held the paper out and Bob took it, a face of half surprise and shock.

"It's a field appointment. You earn it; secure that Castle."

Bob looked straight ahead; taking it in. Copley pretended to be interested in some of the paperwork he had dragged forward. He wasn't; he was quietly smiling to himself; Bob was quite capable of reaching a senior rank and he had what it took; Copley was plotting a smoke screen; Bob's rise through the ranks would create a minor stir. Bob had broad shoulders and could cope with it. What Copley intended was to keep the PM and her suits thinking Professor Copley was as eccentric as error. A small pebble in the pond perhaps, but Copley had two tasks on his mind; getting as much in the way of documents and artefacts away as possible and get into the tunnel beneath the Crown Posada; neither would be easy, but he didn't want interference and the more flak he could put up, the more difficult it would be for the suits to know what was truly going on. Keeping the Gospels in the North was the first task.

The panther crossed the bridge to the station.

Copley checked the straps on the box. The platform was quiet; the buildings lay crumpled in a pile in the car park, the platform was empty.

"Right Bob. Here's the plan. You head back to Newcastle. The Press will be all over you. The priority is to get the Gospels to the Castle; you do your bit. When they know I've got them they will forget all about you and you can get to work at the Castle. We have to prove it would be safe to store them there. I will get them to Newcastle my way; I'll be in touch. Now get it stirred up."

"Understood and thanks Professor. Leave it to me I will. You stay safe."

Copley carried the box in his arms onto the station platform and waved Bob goodbye. Waiting until he was out of sight, he walked off the station, back up to the main road and turned left for Alnmouth. His phone rang.

"Copley"

"Hello Evelyn."

"What are you up to. You are not with Bob."

"No. I'm heading to Alnmouth"

"Why?"

"Because I need to check something out. I knew you were tracking me. Don't worry everything is fine. Bobs heading down to Newcastle."

"Alright. If you need any help; just call. Well done regarding the Gospels"

"They found us Evelyn. I'll explain later."

"Take care"

"I will."

Copley strode on. The buildings along the road were ruined. Having seen the destruction of Lindsifarne, Copley didn't expect too much of pretty little Alnmouth; he was right. His twenty-minute walk brought him into the one main street. The whole shoreline had changed, centuries of dunes swept away, and the golf course was sea again; the ruined houses and hotels, broken teeth in the face of a brutal punching sea. There was activity; the locals were busy securing a tarpaulin to the café, which remained reasonably intact. Nobody took any notice of Copley. Just another soul going about whatever mission they had to survive. Copley made his way to Sun

Cottage, just off the street; the cottage had no roof, the door was off, and the contents was a jumbled mess. He picked his way carefully through the ruin to the kitchen. A large fitted cupboard stood proud; Copley opened it; the shelves were still full of pots and pans; plates and glasses. Copley set down the box on the washing machine which was sitting on top of the upturned table; he then removed everything from the shelves, stacking as he went; then removed the shelves and pushed hard on the back timbers. It sprung forward revealing a door. Copley picked up the box and with the torch hung on the back of the door lit, proceeded down the steps. Down he went, initially through cut stone, then into solid rock; down ancient worn steps into a natural cave. Copley lit an oil lamp, illuminating the scene; rows of steel cabinets and a desk; which soon had the box upon it. Opening the desk draw and turning the eight disks in the security box Copley sized up the keys and chose one. The cabinet squeaked open and Copley removed a box nearly identical to the one on the desk. Undoing the straps, he opened the box, lifted out the plastic covered package and carefully pulled the plastic seal apart. Copley was standing looking at an identical set of Gospels. He studied the covers of both; then randomly turned pages left and right. An hour passed. Copley smiled; his copy was safe; number three of six and the one he had rescued was number two; he mused that he did not have to sacrifice his copy to the benefit of all; but he had to check the one he'd rescued was real and it most certainly was. Copley knew the secrets of the texts, but that was a long time ago and another lifetime. Content that no personal sacrifice was required, his contemplated benevolence was selfishly relieved that he could calmly parcel up his copy and stored it safely away. He made his way up the steps and carefully put everything back on the shelves and made his way back onto the street.

"Hello Professor, need a hand there?"

"Fred Partridge. What a surprise. What are you doing here? Glad to see you are alright."

"Likewise. We've property in Alnmouth. This is the first opportunity to see how bad they were hit"

"If there anything like ours it's a bloody mess"

"Aye. It's going to take a bit of sorting. Anyway. Can I give you a lift with that box?"

"If you could drop me at the Junction?"

"No problem. I'm on my way to Edinburgh."

Copley made himself comfortable in the Land Rover and was soon waving Fred goodbye at the Junction, but not before surreptitiously dropping his phone into the door side pocket.

Copley stood on the platform waiting for anything heading South. Bumping into Fred had saved him the bother of putting the phone on the Northbound train. A distant honk indicated a train was coming; it dragged itself into the station.

"Sorry mate this isn't a public service"

The driver cheerily informed him.

"I'm not public."

Copley showed his pass. The driver honked his horn once. This attracted the conductor's attention and that of a soldier in the first coach. The soldier stepped out of the train; looked Copley up and down and examined his pass. His reaction changed reading the detail. He smartly stepped back and assisted Copley aboard. The conductor waved the driver away and the train rumbled forward. Copley found himself in a sea of uniforms.

"Make room lads. One of us"

A general shunting of kit and Copley found himself sat next to the window looking at the blasted scenery. The speed wasn't great; the engine was roaring to keep the long train moving. Copley mused that it wouldn't be diplomatic to ask if the buffet car was open. Nobody said a word.

"Sorry Professor. No first class on this one. Thought it best just to get you on; the whole train's like this; these lads are on the way to protect the ports and airport. What's it like down there?

Copley suddenly felt a great number of eyes upon him.

"It's a mess; for example, to give you a sense of scale; Lindisfarne is gone; not one stone left; just bare rock; the same blast hit Tynemouth, the City, the entire coast. At the same time a storm blew in from the West; the weather had been bad over there for two weeks, so the river's were high. Result. Destruction on a massive scale. Death toll, well over forty thousand; no idea on the injured. But the people are resilient and pulling things together; but they are all in need of your support; the Police are exhausted; all the emergency services are on their knees. Having the railway operating has been a God send. I won't lie; I doubt if you've ever seen anything like this unless you've seen action in the Middle East."

There was a silence.

"Thanks Professor. You heard him lads. The people need us. A lot of people in shock, so don't expect them to react normally and lots of exhausted emergency personnel. Take this onboard and spread the word."

An hour passed and the train arrived at the roofless Newcastle Central. Copley blended into the huge number of soldiers disembarking; on the opposite platform the entire length was full of people with what was left of their lives in suitcases, backpacks and black plastic bags. The soldiers were waiting to cross the bridge so face the population on the other side. Copley's summary had spread down the train. The truth of the situation struck home.

A soldier summed it up perfectly.

"Fuck me"

Exactly. Thought Copley. He kept in the midst of the throng, the backpacks creating screening from the prying cctv. Copley needed to disguise the box; he saw a black plastic bag, shiny, new, neatly machine folded lying on the platform. He picked it up and the box was duly hidden away; anonymous amongst all the others on the platform. He knew that Bob would be back, everyone would want to see the Gospels and be somewhat disappointed; Evelyn would be ringing him, and Fred would undoubtedly be delayed. He owed Bob for that.

Copley made his way out of the station. His destination was Summerhill and he reached it by dodging the rubble strewn remains of the Science Museum. The archive section was open to the sky. Copley made a mental note. Reaching the park, the full extent of the damage hit him, the trees were uprooted, and the roof of the bowls club lay on the children's playground like a blanket. His hopes of a resting place began to sink, but undaunted he pressed on into

Summerhill Street, where a line of roofless house met him to his right and the noble church tower lay in the street, a great rubble pile. To its left, unharmed the houses appeared intact; the pavement had been swept. Tidiness confronting utter carnage, flowers swayed in the breeze and a cat sat on the gatepost.

The door was, as ever, ajar; a smell of fresh baking exuded from the porch. Copley entered, the smell of a good Irish stew hit his nostrils, no, it was Turkish, or was it Hungarian. Whatever it was it was good. The cook was a broad lady of retiring years with the tenacity of an enraged rhino. Sharp, abrupt, intelligent, gentle and kind. Nobody's fool.

"Hello Beryl"

"Piss off Copley I'm busy"

"I love you too. Smells good"

It's amazing what produce is just rotting out there, the community garden; I haven't seen a soul; they've all gone. Evacuated to God knows where."

"But not you."

"Why. We survived the storm we can certainly survive the aftermath. Water and power. What else do you need?"

"Beryl. Can I ask a favour?"

"The beers next to the fridge but hands off my Wylam."

"Thanks."

Copley helped himself to a bottle.

"What brings you here?"

"A bed for the night. I offer a special treat in exchange."

"Let's see."

Copley cleared some space on the overflowing dining table. He unclipped the box and wrapper. Beryl looked over his shoulder, then pushed him aside. Reaching into her voluminous pocket Beryl extracted a magnifying glass.

"Where did you get this from Copley?"

"I found it"

"Copley"

"No. I really did. Lindisfarne has been completely eradicated from the planet. I'm in charge of saving what I can of the region's relics. I found it in the back seat of a car. Some poor souls were trying to get it to safety when they were crushed. I'm supposed to send it to Blaneau Ffestiniog for storage"

"Over my dead body. That stays here"

"I quite agree, and I have a plan. I'm going to secure it in the Castle; I'm making the arrangements and as Evelyn is now some sort of North East supremo for the PM, I've got to persuade them to let it stay as a symbol of defiance."

"Well I think that's wonderful. How I can help other than giving you a meal and a bed?"

"Is this the real one?"

"Of course, not"

"How do you know that?"

"Because you've got the real one hidden away at Sun Cottage."

"How did you know that?"

"Copley it's the worst kept secret of the century. Everyone knows you've got God knows what down there."

"Then how come everyone knows and no one has done nothing about it?"

"Because nobody believes it. They believe it's blarney"

"So, I have the real one and this is a copy; is that what they think?"

"Yes."

"Now this is going to sound ridiculous, but it found me. Something physically turned me round so I could see where it lay."

"Why does that surprise somebody like you"

"But it's a copy"

"Yes"

"There's six copies that I'm aware of."

"Nobody is ever going to admit it are they? Everyone sees the real one. And there is only one because the others are hidden away. They were produced at the same time and were kept apart, not that anyone would ever admit it, an insurance policy against loss."

"Can't disagree Beryl. I predict they produced twelve copies. I also don't think any of them have been lost. They have a strange way of surviving everything that's thrown at the humans that possess them. Sometimes I wonder how it was done."

"You know exactly how. Mirrors; time and patience, of which you are capable of the first as long as you are standing in front of one but none of the latter. Tracing lines are found in all of them, plus the same hand. It must have been a life's work. Dedication of a profound nature. Hence they are blessed."

"Problem is, if this goes wrong, I can hardly come up with another copy."

"No. It certainly wouldn't help the cause. The original, or should I say this one has to stay here. Another beer?"

"Yes please. There is something else"

"What?"

"Toby"

"Little prick of Oxford. What's he been up to?"

"He led me to find the tunnel of Cerealis."

"Under the Crown Posada no doubt"

"How the hell did you know that?"

"He contacted me a couple of months back saying he could prove that the tunnel existed and its location."

"Why you?"

"Because he was frightened."

"Frightened. What of?"

"Copley. You have seen the inscription. Why would an engineering marvel of great use to the Romans be sealed up; one that they had probably just completed. Ever stopped to think of that?"

"Well I take your point. I personally think the tunnel is much older than the Romans and they merely upgraded it."

"The coracle burial at Corbridge. Plausible. But why seal it up and more to the point why did somebody want to hide the inscription, especially in the age of the enlightenment when every bit of Roman script is being fought over; why throw it away. Makes no sense?"

"You have a point"

"Toby has played you for a mug. Being feeling a bit odd, recently have we? Not your normal pompous self- opinionated self; getting panic attacks?"

"Yes"

"Thought so. You started feeling like that after being near that inscription didn't you; even before you saw and touched it. You read the script out, loud didn't you?

"Yes"

"As I suspected. Toby has passed the curse onto you. Nice of him"

"Curse?"

"I have no idea what it is, but anything and I mean anything to do with that tunnel is wrong. Oh, I have no doubt it is all still there; it's by no means the longest Roman engineering project; it will undoubtedly be the find of the century, but no good will come of it."

"So why hasn't it affected you? "

"I had the cat check it out"

Copley looked at George lying on the couch, George eyed Copley with disdain.

"George didn't like it, so I cut it up into pieces and tried it word by word. I can't see any effective resonant celestial rhythmic pattern. No code. No actual curse formula. But George is adamant, and George is always right. They sense things"

Copley looked at George and George at Copley.

"So, I can pass this curse onto some other poor soul?"

"Yes. But knowing you, you won't, you will go trampling around and create chaos. You are very good at it Copley. It might well have met its match with you. Perhaps you are meant to solve the puzzle. It is really why Toby gave it to you. If anyone can. You can. A cantankerous, conniving, ill tempered.

"Yes I get the message. Yes. Now all I have to do is work it out."

Chapter Four

Copley woke to find George looking straight at him. At close range George didn't look any happier than he had the previous evening; the beer and food had gone down well; the conversation opinionated yet erudite; fuelled by good wine. He made a mental note to have the street secured for Beryl and generally tidied up. He decided, as George observed him with the eye of a cat about to pounce on it's prey, that he'd better do better than that. George was demanding not only security but an active part in the proceedings. Copley decided to make George part of his rag tag army. Beryl and George could be very useful, and Beryl was a renowned expert on many subjects, of which Copley only knew of a few; archaeology, manuscripts and textiles. That was enough to get her in. She certainly would give security a run for their money. George agreed terms and departed. Not before shaking his bum at Copley. A deal of sorts.

Copley asked Beryl to join his team which she refused. Changed her mind on George's instructions and was duly dispatched with a form to the Civic Centre. George was travelling with her, I his plush cat basket.. The authority clearly stated that George was to be included. Copley was left in the house with the Gospels; Evelyn and everyone would know where he was within thirty minutes, the moment Beryl walked in with her piece of paper and George.

He had to move fast. With Evelyn's mobile phone he tapped in a number, the number rang. Bob answered it.

"On my way"

Copley put the phone down. He had less than thirty minutes to get to the Castle. He grabbed one of Beryl's voluminous raincoats and a hat, closed the front door and made his way with a large object in a string bag down through the back alleys onto the Westmorland Road, down to the junction, across and to Central Station; blending in with the other walkers, the City was strangely calm, the lack of traffic; only buses and emergency services could operate in the City. Deliveries came in at night. People walked or rode bikes, pushed prams loaded with whatever they could find. Copley melted into the throng. Only the cctv cameras could trace him; the hat helped. How he was to get to the Castle was the main problem. The public thinned out a bit beyond the station, it would be easy to intercept and stop the few that would be going that way, once he got to the high-level bridge the traffic would increase, but he was right of the edge of the restricted area. Nobody was allowed near the river or Side because of the health hazard. Copley began to feel very nervous as he passed the wreck of the Mining Institute, he looked across at George Stephenson buried up to his neck in the frontage of the old Liberal club and the student flats next door, fallen as one; revealing the contents of wardrobes, shirts flying in the wind, barstools on the brink; a chaotic jigsaw of lives, memories, all blowing in the wind. He made his way passed the Lit & Phil and saluted it in his mind. Its portal stood proud. He could see the roof was on the ground floor. Another one for his ever-growing list he thought. His mind was brought sharply back to earth with the sight of the Police stopping pedestrians from passing the Sleepers Inn. He instinctively went to cross the road. No traffic, but no easy passageway to the Old Post Office, the way blocked by rubble. He began to panic. As he resolved to walk away, he heard a vehicle; a panther, coming toward him; coming straight at him. It stopped between the Police and Copley.

"Get in Professor"

Bob dragged Copley in and sped round and back the way it came. The Police did nothing to stop them.

"Am I glad to see you Bob."

"Looked as if you were in a bit of a pickle there."

"How did you know where to find me?"

"No other way to get to the Castle unless you could fly. The river is crawling with my lot; no go zone, all the bridges are manned; I figured your only chance was the shortest one; you caught the train down. Bit later than the one I set you down for."

"I had to check something out. I note your rank; does the Quartermaster keep that sort of thing in stock?"

"Oh yes. I can tell you it's caused one hell of a stir, but you have the written authority of the PM so that was that. The Army does as it's told, we obey orders."

"Then get us into the Castle now; I've been slinking about trying to stay invisible."

"You bet Professor."

The panther rolled right up to the Castle steps on either side four soldiers with weapons ready were standing at the door. Copley stepped out.

"Pass please sir."

Copley showed his pass

"Professor Copley. Sir. Proceed"

Copley climbed the steps to the door with all the solemnity of a newly appointed monarch; the door was opened as he approached, and two more soldiers stood to attention as he passed through. For a moment Copley truly felt King of the Castle.

Bob had been busy. Most of the staff from the bunker were now in the Castle. A white wall took up one side of the Great Hall and desks and screens the other. The place was a hive of activity.

"Incredible."

"No. Just bloody hard work and your bit of paper.

"Well here it is. One Lindisfarne Gospel. My instruction is under no circumstances is this to leave this building without my written permission on pain of death"

The Great Hall went silent. Everyone looked at Copley.

"I mean it. That Gospel does not leave this building under any circumstance; not even the archbishop of Canterbury or the Monarch is to move that Gospel without my permission.

Colonel can you arrange for the Press to be invited to see the Gospel this afternoon. Select two representatives, one from the BBC and one from whoever for live transmission. No flash photographs and the usual screening. Have you arranged for a display cabinet?"

"Yes. It's being installed in the chapel. I thought it appropriate."

"Well done everyone. I repeat this Gospel is the property of the people of the North East; in these dark hours it is a symbol of the future. It survived against all odds, as will the people of this blessed spot."

Somebody started to clap, the whole room started, the sound rang out. It was a moment. Copley had become a moment in history. He enjoyed it.

"Now can we get back to the task in hand. The Science Museum and the Archive are both wrecks. I would appreciate a report on the Hancock and no doubt my wife will be here telling me what to do. Make it difficult for her and any suits to get beyond the front desk. Only the PM's signature or the Crown get in until I say otherwise."

Copley called Bob over. Whispering in his ear.

"I want the place visibly bristling with armoury and preferably and North East lads on the trigger end."

"All in hand Professor"

"Where's Jean?"

"At the Civic Hall. I'm a bit concerned. The lads haven't seen her."

"Don't worry Bob. I have a suspicion I know where she is. With my wife. The problem is Evelyn is only to aware of my schemes, mostly because she has to usually extricate me from the mire, I've got myself into. The difference is, this time I have the people of the North East on my side. I need Jean here, local lass, well respected law enforcement officer. Keeper of the gospels. A practical local guardian." She's got the right credentials and the right smile"

"She has that. I think you've sold it to me Professor. Now all we have to do is get her back here
In front of the cameras"

"Give me a phone please Bob. Listen in if you will."

Copley tapped in Evelyn's number.

"Copley. What are you playing at? Why is Beryl being security cleared? That cat is lethal. What the hell are you doing?"

"My job dear Evelyn. Can I have Jean back please; I have work for her"

"Where's the Gospels Copley?"

"You know where. Can I have Jean back now and then we can talk."

"Alright. But I'm not happy. Beryl. Why do you need Beryl? Why have you promoted your soldier to Field Colonel?

"I need Beryl, we have thousands of documents and she is the best we've got. Bob deserves his promotion. His skills are many fold and numerous."

"Well you better have the Gospels ready because they are going to Wales."

"Just get Beryl processed and sent over here and Jean right now. Thank you darling. Bye"

"You're truly in for it Professor."

"Possibly. But there are more important things to think about. Please get the Press sorted out. Also, can you possibly find anyone from the Universities that are willing to work with us. I haven't dared ask."

"Not good Professor. Hancock took a massive hit when the ground subsided along the motorway; two walls caved in and took the roof with it. We can do our best but initially not good. I'm ordering heavy lifting equipment, but everybody wants that, plus I've been told we are to hold some national reserve"

"Why?"

"Just in case it happens again"

Copley stood silent for a moment.

"Have we no idea where and whom?"

"None. So, we prepare ourselves, just in case. My new rank allows me some privileges; there are movement orders for some of the troops just assigned to the North East; we might be managing a national issue."

"We've got enough to cope with here. Not a word about the Crown Posada. Beryl knows. I will brief you and a few others, but you are not, under any circumstances to read the inscription in its entirety. Understood."

"Understood"

"Now I need to get ready for Evelyn. "

"The Press are following her every move; camped outside the Civic Offices; so, the moment I announce a press conference here they will be swarming like flies."

"Go for it. Maximum show of force. Now, what facilities have we got for storing artefacts in and around the region that could withstand another event?"

"According to Gerry over there, the major problem is that all the mines have been closed for so long that there's nothing left in the way of deep storage. For some items, the best we can do is cover them up; I mean we can't easily move Turbunia from the Science Museum, but we can shield it."

"What's the situation like at Segedunom?"

"Buildings gone; there's a team of volunteers and a couple of archaeologists doing their best to rescue small finds, the bathhouse survived, just a couple of tiles come loose. Amazing."

"Good design Bob, good design."

"They are using it as a base. The Metro will be up and running today, so I thought, once everything is sorted, we could pop down and see how they are doing; once the Press have gone?"

"If that's your way of saying can I have a go at rescuing something hands on, be my guest and if you want to take Jean along feel free; she'll want to escape the Press Pack after today. You've got the gist of the plan, make sure everyone is right on the nail."

"Will do."

Copley patted Bob on the shoulder.

"You never expected to be doing this did you Bob?"

"Well to be honest the first time I heard I was going to be driving some Professor about I did think; what plonker have I got here; when I found out it was you; well I had a feeling it was going to be different, but not quite as different as it has been so far."

"As they say 'You ain't seen nothing yet". On a serious note. Any news on any of my department?"

"Evelyn's staff have been onto it. No fatalities as far as we know."

Copley suddenly became gloomy, suppressed the thought and replied.

"Good. Very good news. But none come forward?"

"No. Most of them have gone South. We're relying on archaeologists that live here, volunteers. Most are just getting themselves on their feet. It's early days"

"I just hope we don't have another event."

"You and me both Professor"

A member of the white board team approached Copley and Bob.

"Excuse me Sir, Professor. We've been contacted by Beamish; they're asking for assistance in storing some large equipment and vehicles."

"Excuse me Professor. I better see what I can do. Everything is in hand"

Bob moved away leaving Copley to survey the scene. Quietly and efficiently and a result not of his own hands, the situation, if not under control, had a resemblance of order and direction. One thing about the Army; tell them what to do and they do it. Pity he couldn't get his department to do the same. He looked at his watch. He walked down the steps from the Great Hall and waited by the doors to the Castle. It didn't take long for a vehicle to get from the Civic Centre to the Castle. The soldiers seeing Copley by the door opened it; as predicted a panther pulled up and Jean got out, along with Evelyn. Formalities of passes approved, they walked up the steep steps, Copley making no move to walk down towards them.

"Jean. Good to see your security clearance has been so thorough. Evelyn."

"Copley"

They walked up the steps into the Great Hall.

"Jean, Bob's over there he will bring you up to speed. Evelyn, follow me, we are off to the chapel. Evelyn followed Copley up another flight of stairs and across to the chapel where the display case lay with the Gospels secure within. Four armed guards stood, one on each corner.

"It's not leaving this building Evelyn."

"I have my instructions Copley"

"Stuff your instructions. This stays here. Where it belongs."

"It's Government policy that such relics are securely stored in case of.."

"Nuclear attack. This isn't a nuclear attack. It's a weather event. It's not in the instruction manual. I agree to storing documents and other artefacts; but these people need something to hold onto and you don't get better than this. Now sell that to the PM, because I'm not shifting on this."

Evelyn looked Copley in the eyes. She knew when the red mist was about to come down and Copley had a point; the people did need a symbol of hope.

"I'll call the PM. The Castle is secure against attack; it can withstand the elements and I agree the people do need a symbol of hope. Give me a few minutes."

"Take as long as you like Evelyn; give her my regards."

Evelyn walked up the narrow winding steps onto the roof; she looked out over the blasted scene. Life was scurrying about below; order of a sorts, amongst the ruins. Of course, Copley was right, she agreed; but having to see a wider picture and knowing the actual scale of the potential issues made Evelyn painfully aware of how many other people, in other parts of the country would need symbols of hope. The suits would need policy documents and guidelines. She tapped a number into her phone.

Copley waved his hands in the air. A technique he knew of old got people's attention, often this would lead to questions as to whether he needed psychiatric treatment, but on this occasion one of the soldiers merely crossed the room and asked if he could be of assistance.

"Can you please prepare a list of all the breweries between here and Durham, as far West as Alston; names of head brewers or owners. Then contact them if possible. Where you can, identify if their plant is operational and if not, what is required. Use your initiative, but I want beer to reappear in as many outlets as possible. Only one condition in return for us assisting them, they get Lindisfarne into the title of the brew. Then I want you to contact the Co-operative and Ringtons; if possible if the Ringtons plant can be salvaged we require tea bags with Lindisfarne on them; likewise, the Co-operative. I leave it to all of them how they go about branding and distribution; but I want to see local brands in vans back on the streets as soon as possible; people need to see the return to normality and the Ringtons and Co-op vans are part of it. If anybody says we are interfering with food distribution tell them Copley says it's a heritage matter and vital to public morale."

Another soldier approached with a folded note. Copley dismissed the first soldier and read the note.

Current situation: Durham Cathedral, Durham

Looters intercepted at Durham Cathedral.

Casualties: five dead, twenty injured. No military casualties.

Rioting in Durham city centre

Looters shot attempting to steal the Cathedral silver; additional incidents of looting has caused the town centre to be set ablaze. Cathedral not secure; troops have recovered majority of church artefacts. Request you assist with storage as priority. Additional troops required.

Colonel Smyth: Acting Commander Durham

"Bloody hell. I wondered how long it was going to be before things unraveled. Ok. Our job is to secure the artefacts; others have the nasty difficult problems to solve. Bring it all to the Castle; we can work it out from here. Contact this Smyth, get a small low-key party together and get everything back. Liaise with Army command, but you remain under my command; if you're not happy, or safe, withdraw. Use your initiative. Good luck, off you go"

Copley had a chill down his spine. This was the first major sign of public unrest. The need to broadcast that the Gospels were staying was now vital. It might not stop the rioting, but it might assist. Evelyn came down the stairs and noted Copley's frown.

"Copley. What's happened?"

Copley hand her the memo.

"I see. This makes things difficult. Well, you have permission to keep the Gospels. I can overrule you if the situation deteriorates. This will be all over the media. Can you bring your announcement regarding the Gospels forward?"

"Yes. I don't think we have any choice. I've just issued orders for a team to rescue what they can. Let's get the Press in."

"I've already got my team on the background, the Government perspective"

"Your friend in the limelight you mean"

"She's under pressure"

"She's under pressure. What the fuck do you think is going on outside here?

There was a commotion on the staircase.

"George come back here this minute."

Copley raised an eyebrow. Evelyn half smiled.

"Beryl."

"Not forgetting George."

Evelyn grinned broadly. Copley looked heavenward.

"God help us all."

"Copley, you wanted her."

"I wanted her but not the bloody cat."

There was a blur of cat fur heading for the top of the white wall. George made himself comfortable on a knife edge and glowered at the personnel below. Any attempt to remove him led to a razor shape swipe. Retreat and acceptance was swiftly established.

"Copley. Evelyn. How lovely to see you my dear? How you are still with this little shit is beyond my understanding; must be a good quality gin and plenty of it"

"Beryl. Good to see you; Copley was just talking about you"

"I bet he was"

"Good to have you both aboard Beryl. Now we have an urgent task for you and George; you are no doubt the Archive Office is badly damaged; I'd like you to head the recovery team."

Copley waved a hand in the air in the general direction of the white wall team and an unwilling volunteer responded, knowing their fate. Basic introductions done, Beryl was soon surrounded by four personnel, earnestly taking notes and avoiding Georges attentions.

"Well that's one thing sorted."

"You are brilliant Copley."

"I know"

"Right person right time and never the expected."

"That's me. So, don't let the suits interfere with my beer and tea idea."

Bob reappeared and gestured the Press were being admitted. Copley pointed at the route to the chapel and Evelyn and Copley made their way up the stairs. The soldiers manned the bottom of the staircase as well as four on the corners. In the tiny chapel it seemed excessive, but the show of security was essential. Copley had a broad message to impart, whatever Evelyn said, words meant less than image. The Gospels were very safe in local hands.

"A beacon of hope. If you say it that's fine Evelyn; but if you don't I will. Because people are having it really tough out there and that's the message they need."

"Don't worry Copley; I'm with you on this. I just hope we can get Durham under control"

"Well this might help."

"The cathedral is safe, but the City is a mess. We could do with a little heavenly intervention."

Copley remembered his shoulder being touched and him turning. Something had intervened with him. He was sure that it would again; how he was not so sure. His team was slowly working its way through the region; wrecked museum; church, archive, private collection; documents, recipes and goodness knows what else. All the small but inextricable parts that made up the heart of a place. He was sure he was missing things, but history was like that, as random as his approach. It gave work to historians through the ages, putting the bits and pieces back together. His musings were cut by the sound of many feet on the staircase. Bob appeared with two media crews; the look on the crews faces suggested that Bobs team had given them a thorough frisking before they had got beyond the ground floor.

"Here we Go"

Copley turned and smiled at Evelyn. Evelyn just looked ahead and put her camera face on, but he saw the wink. All was going to be well.

The half hour passed without incident; the interviews were crisp; all the emphasis was on the remarkable survival; the spirit of the North East rising out of the devastation; a beacon of hope; much of the time was spent on getting the best possible shots of the Gospels. Off camera the reporters and crew proved to be genuinely interested in the importance of recovering artefacts and a short interview with Copley requesting archaeologists and experts to contact him was recorded.

"That went rather well. "

Copley watched the party being escorted out.

"Yes. No problems there; at least that was two media crews not filming Durham burn."

"Is it that bad?"

"It's just about under control. Emphasis on the just. What seems to have eased the situation was a distribution of army rations. The problem was hunger. The riot started in the Refectory; it wasn't the contents of the Treasury, simply people needing food. The whole bloody business; all for the want of empty stomachs. Desperation. I think we've sent out one small message of hope. It won't be enough, but it's something. You were right. I completely agree with you on this, you know I do; just the way things are the PM and the cabinet are jittery. You can understand it"

"I can. Any developments that you can tell me about?"

"No and no. Nothing. Absolutely nothing. Our satellites; our intelligence have drawn a blank. Interestingly some of our enemies seem equally baffled."

"The Russians and the French then. Uncle Sam?"

"Absolutely no idea; but it's absolutely clear that it was no natural event."

"The storm in the Atlantic, nothing about that surely?"

"No. Likewise the rainfall, nothing that unusual. The metreologists suggest that someone waited for the bad weather in the West to compound the situation in the East. Somebody physically generated a massive low in the North Sea. The pressure dropped over a wide area as an instantaneous event; no reason, no pattern leading up to it. It just appeared and swept South and vanished completely by the time it reached Cromer."

"It could just be a quirk of nature"

"No. It's absolutely ruled out."

"Why?"

"Because any low-pressure event has distinctive markers, causes, as signature."

"No signature"

"Nothing."

"So how can you generate a massive physical event and not leave any trace?"

"There you have it. No idea. Nobody has. Hence the term bomb being attached to it. As if it just dropped on us out of the blue. Which of course it did; except it did it from nowhere."

"Do they know exactly where it started?"

"They're working on it. Oddly everyone is working on it. I think everyone is thinking the same way, where and who is next. It was a provocative planned attack, somebody waited until everything was just so."

"Well I wish your metreologists luck; but do let me know where you think it started; odd place the North Sea."

"Copley. What are you thinking?"

"Nothing Evelyn. Merely interested. Just let me know."

Evelyn stared hard at Copley. Copley smiled back, a soft easy smile. He genuinely had no plan or idea, but the whole matter attracted his instinct for research.

"I've got to attend a meeting in fifteen minutes. See you at home tonight."

Evelyn kissed Copley him on his forehead and was away.

"Odd. Very odd"

Copley let his words hang in the air. Outside in the City work parties were clearing rubble; the grim business of removing the dead continued and the first attempts at defining the new course of the river were being made. No quayside as such, survived, the river had taken back what had long been taken from her; the ballast of ages swept away in a grey green steel coated tumult. A thousand years of restricting her course undone; revealing a long-forgotten past. A small fleet of rigid inflatables were edging up the river, along the crumpled shoreline, looking for bodies; taking depths as they went; facing the Castle they approached the exposed stone quayside topped with ages of and yesterday's tarmac as a topping. Side was truly Side again.

As they worked their way along the quay's length, towards the Crown Posada, a black oily film began to rise from the depths. The crews took little notice, as the river was full of vehicles, burst sewers; every form of rotting, exploding, bubbling, foul filth. The black film began to thicken, the last of the boats cut its way to the edge and carried on its way; behind them the mass solidified into a black crust. Down in the void; beneath the Crown Posada, a single bubble rose to the surface; it rose, formed and gently lifted into the air, rising out of the depths. It caught on a broken beam; sharp, it burst. The sky above darkened, the wind began to blow; the surface of the river rippled; a squall whipped Side, blowing dust and rubbish into the air. The crew look back to see a miniature tornado fly up and then fall away; all was quiet. They shrugged their shoulders and carried on their way; compared to the last few days a puff of wind was just that, a mere puff.

Copley was pacing. He was good at pacing; he paced with purpose. An empty mind soon filled with thoughts; a few more paces; these were replaced with hypothesis; a few more; these were knocked down. More pacing and the first mutter. This Copley knew meant he needed a beer; several beers in fact. Where to get one; what was actually open? The reality of Newcastle was suddenly clear to him.

The last few days he had been in a bubble. Outside in the derelict mess people were trying to survive and here he was worrying about a beer. Where could he try that might have escaped? Where was Bob? In time honoured fashion Copley waved his hands in the air and a minion came running. Copley rather enjoyed the attention. It was a technique he had learned as a child, it worked then, it worked now. On occasions it had nearly had him arrested, but in general it worked. People stopped and looked at least. Even if they thought he needed psychiatric help.

"Anybody know where the Colonel is?"

"He's waiting down in the vehicle for you."

"How did he know I wanted to go out?"

"No idea Professor"

Copley made his way out of the Castle to meet Bob. The panther had been replaced with a Range Rover; with no military markings. Copley looked at the vehicle.

"Get in Professor; I decided this was less obvious, where we are going. It's fitted with radio and one or two extras should we need them."

"How did you know I wanted to go out?"

"For a beer."

"For a beer."

"Simple. When was the last time you had a good pint of ale? A real pint, not from a bottle?"

"Ok, you got me. Guilty."

"You've just had a real success and the Gospels are staying here. Great news for everyone."

"No. We've all had a great success. A team effort and the whole team deserves a drink."

"And they will get one. You and I are going to pick it up for them. We might just have to test the quality. So, as an officer we are being driven. Bob stepped out of the car and got into the back seat as a corporal stepped in to take his place.

"Free Trade Inn, Peters and step on it."

Copley sat watching as little of the world as possible, he squinted his eyes, hoping that everything along the way had magically got better and when he stepped out at the Free Trade the view was of old. A grand vista of a proud welcoming City.

They were waved through the Police checkpoints; the route pre planned and the blue lights hidden in the radiator grill acting as a passport. They crossed the bridge and Copley opened his eyes and looked to his left, just in time to see a metro train crossing the bridge, a moment of normality, before gazing at the ruin of the school to his right and the remains of the flats to his left. The boarded turn was a rubble mound which had been cleared enough for a vehicle to get through, below to their left stood The Free Trade, a tarpaulin roof, two boarded windows, but the plate glass view of Gateshead and Newcastle remained. The door was open, and the cat sauntered out just as they pulled up opposite the front door. The view was not restored. The City looked as if it had been redesigned with a big hammer; bent, twisted; jagged. A distorted vision, the robustness, the refinements, equally torn away. Most of all, the open water between the Free Trade and the Crown Posada, the quay gone;

nothing left, all swept away. Whilst Copley was taking the view in Peters was busy filling the back of the Range Rover with polybins.

"Mike"

Copley suddenly realised that the landlord was standing by the door. He was overtaken with relief.

"Copley, good to see you."

"Mike, I hope the team are ok? My God what a change down there."

"Yes. Everyone survived, that includes the regulars, some near misses and a few knocks but yes we made it."

Copley kept staring at where the quay had been, and his eyes looked over to the Crown Posada.

"It's hard to take it in, so much gone; yet look what it's revealed, the Roman quay."

Bob finished assisting Peters and the vehicle was duly sent on its way back to the Castle.

"Come inside both."

Mike ushered them both inside.

All was as it had always been; the bar festooned in pumps the nicotine walls and the plank of wood perilously holding up the ceiling that had survived the onslaught remarkably well.

"Mike. I'm not sure if you have had the message yet, but I've instructed that breweries should produce whatever they can and where possible celebrate the Lindisfarne Gospels being saved. I have people contacting every brewery to see what we can do to get production and supply back up and running along with distribution. I'm doing the same for the tea drinkers. All helps with morale."

"Yes, we got the message; the major problem is water and the basic ingredients; if you can get that sorted, I reckon its feasible, some of the breweries are wiped out; it's been luck of the draw. A few micro-breweries are operational. We've got barrels from pubs that are physically flat; we know where they came from, some haven't anyone to pay at the moment, but we'll see the families right when things are back to normal. We've rolled barrels here; no other way in some cases. We'll keep going if you can get the basics to us. I see the Crown survived."

Mike finished pouring three pints, which he duly passed to Bob and Copley and supped the third.

"Well. Externally it did. The cellars gone, a void."

"A whopping great hole"

Bob helpfully advised.

"That's a tragedy. Arthur kept a magnificent cellar."

Copley sipped his beer; it was a taste of normality. Like his journey, he just wished it all would be as it was. But it wasn't; the reality was raw. He was living in history; he was so used to excavating catastrophic events, he now was in one himself. Mike and Bob noticed Copley's faraway gaze.

"It's going to be ok Copley. We feel it just as bad. Not easy but we are here, and we survived, and we can make a difference. Last week I was planning my cycling holiday and worrying about a couple of beers not settling. Now I don't even know where my bike is under where my house once stood, and the beers sorted itself out."

Copley turned from gazing at himself in the long mirror and faced them both.

"Aye Professor. It will be ok; things get knocked about, but it's the people that matter and were doing our best for them. Ok we might not be feeding and housing them, but we are looking to their future just as much, because we give them their past. Their treasures."

Copley suddenly felt as lost and frightened as he had in the café at Fenwick's, a desire to run and hide.

"Something's going to happen chaps. I'm feeling very strange, odd; lost. This happened not long before the storm; I was in a meeting with the Fire Service to get access to the Crown Posada. A terrible desire to flee; panic, it's not me, not my style. It's quite overpowering"

Copley began to shake.

"Sit down. Here Mike take his arm"

The two of them took the suddenly frail Copley to a seat. Copley was ashen.

"Is he having a stroke Bob?"

Bob squatted in front of Copley

"Can you look at me Copley, that's it, smile. Good. Your face hasn't dropped. Let's just check your blood pressure. Mike take my phone. Press six and turn the speaker on"

Mike did so. A voice crackled at a distance.

"Control. Confirm identity."

"Staff that Taffy. It's the Professor. Code twelve and have the resuscitation team ready. Repeat code one two, you have our location"

"Help on its way Colonel. ETA 5 minutes; airborne unit. If you can hear me Professor, we'll have you safe and sound in a jiffy"

"You hear that Professor they will be here very soon. Mike, the tarpaulin, is it really well secured?"

"You mean, will the helicopter take the roof off; I doubt it; its nailed down."

Copley began to froth at the mouth and attempted to scream, desperately trying to stand up. Mike held him down.

"Not long Copley. Can you hear that, they will have you sorted in no time? Stay with us. You are going to be ok. There's nothing going to harm you"

The helicopter roared overhead and the tarpaulin held in place. Copley was winched aboard, oblivious of everything having passed out as he was secured to the stretcher. Seven minutes later he was being assessed as he was being trolleyed into a resuscitation bay in the RVI. An hour later a heavily sedated Copley was lying peacefully in a side ward with a military guard at his door. Evelyn arrived with Bob at her side.

"You say he spoke of being frightened at the café, wanting to flee. He certainly was acting strangely; he's been acting odd ever since he went to Oxford. Talking about a curse."

"A curse?"

"The inscription is the curse, that's why it was hidden away. You mustn't say the whole thing out loud, not even under your breath. It travels from one person to the next only being released by giving it to someone else. It's rubbish, but to Copley, any archaeologist, rubbish is fascinating; even myths and curses. There's always some kernel of fact in there somewhere. Now look at him. If he's right we are in trouble within thirty-six hours, that's roughly how long it was between him acting odd in Fenwick's and the storm hitting."

"I hope he's wrong. We hardly have the situation under control now. I'm not sure how we would cope if we got caught again."

"Well I have a decision to make. I either tell the PM that Copley has had a premonition of disaster and I remove the Gospels, or I wait and see."

"The Castle can withstand anything that's thrown at it."

"It better, because I'm going to risk it. But just in case Bob, you prepare to move to the nuclear bunker. Get your teams somewhere safe, preferably bring them back to the Castle or somewhere similar."

"I've already requisitioned Bambrugh and Alnwick for storage, being as they have cores as strong as here at Newcastle."

"Good. Whatever you think will withstand another attack."

Copley stirred, slowly rocking himself from side to side. Before anyone could stop him, he sat up, pulled aside the bed sheets and sat himself cross legged on top of the blanket. He had a blank look on his face. Che opened his mouth and a voice echoed out, not Copley's tone, nor did he move his lips; Copley was a mere vessel. Evelyn and Bob stepped back in horror.

"Now hush. I'm going to tell you a story. A very old and odd story. Are you listening my friends? For all that call at the Crown are friends of mine. As long as they pay, and I know you all will in time my friends; all will pay in good time. Now settle yourselves one and all, here's my tale.

Now many a fine ship has left this port and I believe you would agree that there was none finer than the Commonwealth; such a vessel as the Dutch did say it alone created a friendship between our two countries, a ship, to our credit that no King ever built. Well my friends, the Captain of the Commonwealth was often to be found in this very spot, enjoying my hospitality; these rooms have seen the likes of which you can hardly imagine. A man has to enjoy this life and the Captain certainly meant to live every minute that God gave him. Not that he was not a pious God-fearing man, but he enjoyed the services of our upper chambers for his rest and solicitude; often on his knees in earnest prayer accompanied by one or two the lasses in congregation that would oft as not end in glorious alleluias. The Captain would be on the eighth floor and we could hear him singing praises out on the street above the noise of the town. He would chase the building round, along the passages to and fro, in anticipation of catching a maid unawares. What a devil he played. He was best of friends to me and silver flowed to me in generous amounts, so I kept the Captain a room at all times no matter how far he be from town. One night he asked to join me in the cellars. There being no part of the Crown he did not know I considered he wished to discreetly hide some valuable amongst the casks, or in the walls, they are being so old and deep. He was earnest upon his task; asking me to stay at the cellar steps whilst he went alone into the deepest and oldest part of the cellar. He did this for three weeks, night after night, whilst above the noise hid his digging. I never dared to ask what he was hiding; but one night he emerged with a sack and whatever was in it was extremely heavy that I knew it was stone, the coldness, he swore me to secrecy that he had such an unusual prize; for my part he paid well for my silence and as no harm was done to my cellar nothing more was said. It was past Michaelmas before I saw the Captain again; what a change in a man; whatever had befallen him he was a poor wretch; sunken with ill health and pious too; always at the church and never went near the women, not once. He left on the Commonwealth and the crew were ill at ease seeing their Captain so altered; rumours began coming to my ears that he was cursed by some written rock. He had taken the stone from my cellar and sold it to a learned gentleman who had insisted that he read the lines on it; the Captain being schooled in the Latin. He did so and from that point he was a cursed. Some of his crew deserted, not daring to serve with him e'er they would be likewise cursed. And as you know the Commonwealth sank beneath the waves with all drowned. They say the sea boiled round her. Those poor souls all gone because of a stone from these very walls. Now I don't believe in curses, but I do believe in silver and gold. So, when the Captain was about his business, I went about seeking out his treasure; only to find he had found a deeper cellar than I ever knew and a great blocked arch, where he was cutting a block with the Latin from the wall. I may not have the Latin but I copied the letters everyone and knowing that the Captain saw worth in them, for when he removed it there was naught but stone behind, I ventured there was some special meaning and thus set about asking customers of mine of the mason trade to make me copies; which they did; two fine cut copies from stone lying down there, as you would have believed they were the Captains. Finding learned men to buy was simple; the girls are popular with the men of God and so I sold one to Cambridge and one to Edinburgh for a fine amount. They didn't keep them long, fire, drowning and death followed the stones wherever they went. But I profited and am as hale and hearty, for I never had the Latin. Now don't be disheartened by my tale, education is a great thing if you profit by it. Ha haaaa. I tell you one last thing. That place, you never wants to be sent there by me, not that any of you lads would ever cross me, all of you be God-fearing law-abiding types. That place, that blocked arch, what was beyond it I don't like to think, but it sounded, as if the devil was trying to make his way out, a bubbling in hell. The stone and lots of em, holding him back; unless you has the Latin; then he comes for you. Now are you ready for another drop; of course, you are. What's that you say Elias? Yes. That's my copy of the Latin, makes a fine fireplace and I keeps the last part covered by that here cloth to stop anyone from cursing themselves unless I wants em too! I carved that on that fine piece of oak that washed up myself, I did. Those that read it all never leave; they go below to join the Captain and his clever friends. One of the lasses curious like went down there; I forbade any to do so, but she went; I found her poor wretch a convulsing on the floor just there where you sit and all she said in her dying breaths was.

"I touched the devil. risen from the depths, the words, waiting their time.   Into the mouth of, the waves take me, into the darkness." Poor lass. Those were her exact dying breaths, no calling out to her maker. She said no more. She had the Latin, maid to a fine lady once; thems that has it are doomed.

Ha. I have you. My word I have. Only jesting my friends. Only a tale as would get you a trembling and loosening your bowels; a jest, a tale to make you tingle and look over your shoulder on this dark night. Drink my friends enjoy the hospitality of the Crown, let's have no more of this dark humour."

Copley woke from his trance like state to find Evelyn and Bob and the medical staff, who had joined the pair unnoticed, staring at him in sheer disbelief.

"Where am I? Evelyn. What are you doing here?"

"Copley"

"Evelyn. What happened. All I remember is I was at the Free Trade with Mike and Bob, then getting the shakes and feeling terribly frightened."

"Just rest Professor. Take it easy. You've had a shock Evelyn and me, we are just going to pop out and leave you to the doctor here, he needs to examine you"

Bob led Evelyn from the room.

"Clearly he's had some form of seizure or breakdown, I've never seen or heard anything like that."

"I have Bob. You know nothing of Copley. Frightening thought that was, it's not that unusual for Copley. You have to take it from me; Copley isn't like you and me. It's what makes him who he is. It is simply horrifying, and it never is any less for me, but something was sending us a message. They won't find anything wrong with him. I was shocked at how fast it came on, but the content is what struck me; the curse is in the stone; it's the stone that's the problem. It's physical contact within the stone. Whoever that was thought I was the words, but he had a wooden copy; not stone from the tunnel. We need to know more about that Innkeeper.

The pair were interrupted by the doctor.

"You can go in now. I can find absolutely nothing wrong with him, other than he's overweight and wants a beer; he's clearly had a terrifying experience, but who hasn't. There are hundreds if not thousands out there in shock. He can be discharged as long as you keep an eye on him. Any further recurrence and straight back here."

"I leave him in your care Bob. Find out what you can. I will have Toby found. Leave that to me. I know the Quay is off limits but have an additional exclusion zone put around the Crown Posada. I've got to head South. The situation at Durham has caused considerable alarm in the Cabinet. Water contamination; food distribution; emergency accommodation. The list is endless."

"We'll get through it; we've done it before. We don't give in."

With that Evelyn smiled, looked Bob straight in the ye.

"Colonel Matthews. You have no idea what your sudden promotion did in the Ministry of Defence, but Copley was right; don't tell him, but he often is. Keep close to him and whatever he says to do in a tight corner, however mad it may seem, do it. You'll learn about Copley. You'll see."

"I think I already have a fair idea."

"Now I must be away. Take care of Jean."

Bob smiled.

"I will"

Evelyn left Bob standing in the corridor. The last few days had certainly changed his life completely. Jean was on his mind, that worn-down soul; what a difference some food and sleep made; a lovely lass and very competent. Not frightened to stand her ground. He stepped back into the room. Copley was sitting on the end of the bed looking lost.

"I take it something happened at the Free Trade. It's got something to do with me feeling panicky"

"Yes Professor. It seems touching the stone has some sort of effect on your metabolism. The voice that came out of you sounded as if he was the landlord of the Crown and I'd say as the ship was the Commonwealth, it was during the reign of Cromwell. He talked of a Captain digging the stone up; of the bad luck that befell the Captain, but also of the fact he, the landlord had made two copies from stone from the entrance to the tunnel and they were equally unlucky."

Why do you think it's the physical stone that's the problem?

"Because the landlord made a copy onto wood. He played on the notoriety of the words; reading all of it would curse the reader. Kept part of the message covered. Sounded a nasty piece of work"

"Tobias Gurndy. Landlord of the Crown until the ending of the Commonwealth and the coming of the Restoration, when he vanished. Probably went to the Netherlands. Oh, I know of Gurndy; innkeeper, definitely, brothel keeper, definitely; mass murderer, no doubt. No doubt whatsoever. Newcastle surrendered during the Civil War; they could have held out; even brought in troops from the continent, but like everywhere else the picture wasn't black and white; the King hadn't exactly been popular the further North in the kingdom you went; in fact wherever you went, opinion had been pretty divided. So, one Tobias Gurndy saw opportunity; in smuggling the Royalists out of Newcastle whilst the place was under siege. He offered a safe passage on ships to those that could pay a hefty price and then they disappeared. No doubt, down into the tunnel mouth. The siege lifted, the Royalist supporters with money fled. Nobody would suspect anything. I think he murdered nigh on two hundred people; men women and children and I think they still lie there; hidden away until now"

"How can you be so sure about Gurndy?"

"Gurndy was a meticulous bookkeeper, he liked to know where his money was. He must have left in a hurry because he left his accounts book behind and they were found when the old building was demolished in the 1870's; behind a rotten beam, in a purpose-built hideaway. They are in the archive. Beryl might be able to find them. But I know it lists all the people he assisted, and their names never appear again in any other records here or in the rest of Europe. Gurndy isn't alone in this, there were numerous cases, not just in the English Civil War. Beryl knows the case; she will be fascinated to hear he's resurfaced"

"You really gave us a real good fright; that was one hell of a performance."

"I wouldn't know I didn't see it. I have no recollection whatsoever. But I do remember I was about to have a pint. Can you get me out of here and back to the Castle?"

"Certainly professor, if you think you are up to it?"

"I am. This bed is needed by somebody that's really ill."

Bob found Copley's jacket and within five minutes Copley was sitting in the Range Rover on the way back to the Castle.

"Sorry about that Bob. I knew something was wrong with me when I got back from Oxford. Now I know what. How to cure it is another matter. At least it's a useful barometer as to what's going to happen. Problem is what."

"If it's the same as last time I don't think there's much chance for many round here. Poor devils. Soup kitchens and tents; what the hell are we doing; these people need getting away."

They were passing Central Station and the queue of souls waiting patiently for a train to somewhere seemed endless to Copley. He was not one for easy sympathy, but he could see that his efforts at lifting morale meant nothing to these passengers. Somebody through a beer bottle at the Range Rover. The only cars were military or Police; the luxury of free movement lay in the hands of a tenuous authority, prepared to use force to maintain control. Copley suddenly felt very depressed as they drew up to the Castle keep. His experience had exhausted him, but compared to all those he had just seen, he was in fine form and he dragged himself out of his self-pity. The guards smiled to see him.

"Good to have you back Professor"

"Thank you. Good to be back."

As they walked up the steps Copley gained a little on every step. There was work to do, and it wasn't all about Copley, it was, for once all about everyone else.

Chapter Five

"Jean. Our queen of the Castle. I have an additional task for you. Might be a tad on the difficult side but I'm sure you are up to it. I'd like you to take responsibility for what remains of Side; that is the new shoreline from the railway arch to the site of Bessie Surtees house. Shame about that, but one day it will rise again. Anyway. I want you have the area cordoned off with an additional high security exclusion zone on all sides of the Crown Posada. Now I know the area is contaminated and all sorts of agencies are involved but this authorization overrides anything anybody can say stops you."

Copley scribbled his signature on a paper and handed it to Jean.

"Your empire grows by the day. The Crown Posada is to be guarded twenty-four hours a day. No one is allowed to enter any part of the property under any circumstances without my written authority. I need a plan for Bob to start draining, or at least control the flow of water in the void beneath the Crown; not an easy task; I need the whole structure made safe. Any questions"

"No Professor; perfectly ok with me."

"Evelyn was asking after you."

"That was very kind of her."

"How are the boys?"

"There fine. Bob got them to stay with his brother in Birmingham. It's worked out fine. It's really great to know they are safe."

"Well; once this is under control, we will make sure you get to go and see them. Remind me. That's a promise. Good luck and if you need anything on the history of the building speak to me."

Copley smiled to himself; Bob was obviously interested in the lady; from the moment he saw her. Good old romantic Bob. All Copley had to do is make sure they all stayed alive to reap some crumbs of benefit from this disaster. His mind wandered back to the conversation with Evelyn about the origin of the storm; something was troubling him. Instead of waving his hands about expecting some attention, Copley walked over to the white wall and asked a member of the team if they could find any record of unexplained shipwrecks in the Northern part of the North Sea known as the Witches Hole and to find out which of the oil platforms survived the storm. Somebody must be responsible for picking up those pieces; slightly more perilous than his task, thought Copley. He left the great hall and made his way up onto the roof. The team had been glad to have him back. Beer was to be drunk that evening; Mike had been informed that Copley was well and supplies to him and other pubs and brewers were in hand. Assurances were given that there was to be no increase on food and drink prices; soup kitchens were free; nobody would go hungry. Restriction on vehicles were to be lifted on a registration basis; fuel was still in short supply; the supermarket chains were planning portacabin shops; Fenwick's had a date to reopen in Northumberland Street. The good news lifted him. But there was that ever-present fear that something terrible was about to happen. The flight factor; a disturbance in himself, he was coping; everything was under control; Evelyn was managing the bigger project, as he wanted it to be. He was Copley, he was doing his bit; heritage rescue. No need to fear. The wind had gone; the noise had gone. Just something was not right in himself. If only he could pinpoint it; he knew something was communicating to others through him; something on the stones, a bacterium; a poison; whatever it was it crept into the brain. Yet Toby had suggested it was passed from one holder of the stone to another; he had passed it to Copley. The bastard. But Toby had known he was incapable of solving it; Copley was up to it. Only thing was Copley was unsure that he was. That was at the heart of it; his confidence, his drive was flat, whatever it was, was eating into him, and taking away his core, bit by bit; so, he would make mistakes, lethal mistakes. A slow killer. Copley realised Toby couldn't pass it on, he was still infected, he was deluding himself; this thing was playing with all their minds; anyone that touched the stones was at risk. Toby had been most persuasive; yet truth be known Copley had jumped at the chance of finding a new Roman inscription; everything had changed after he had. Why had Cerealis sealed a tunnel that from all accounts had probably been a trading aid; speeding up supplies to the port. As Roman tunnels went it wasn't the longest, he surmised that it was pre Roman and the combination of good geological good fortune and hard graft on the part of the locals, which the Romans just tidied up the façade of, named it after the Emperor and then sat back and extracted taxes from. So why close a lucrative route. Why announce its closure as a personal success under the circumstances it would be normally the last thing one would want to do; unless something was very wrong with it. Safety wasn't a high priority, especially if it involved locals and slaves; the goods were worth more; improvements were well within Roman engineering capabilities. No. It had to be something more serious than a few tribesmen drowning, or the loss of expensive slaves. Or cargo. Perhaps it had caved in and was impossible to unblock? Perhaps something lurked in the caverns that objected to the presence of man? Perhaps it was the earth itself? Perhaps the stone held the answer? He was going to fight whatever he had caught; he felt abused and he was going to fight back from now on; Copley never could stand bullies.

"Now come on Copley. You can do this. You. Are better than this." The sky replied with a droplet of rain, then another. The sky to the North was dirty green grey; a storm was rolling in. Was this what he had been waiting for? What the gut wrenching, palm sweating fear had been about? He didn't feel the urge to escape. Just a rain belt passing through. In the distance there was blue sky. No. This wasn't the next event. If Copley had his way, there wouldn't be one. He walked down the steps; the shower sped over; the sun shone through. His tread was lighter than his way up. The fight back had begun; the sunshine was peeking through.

"Beryl. How's it going with the archive? Yes. Fine. Glad George is enjoying himself. Have you time to discuss the Gurndy papers. Have they survived? Yes. Yes, I thought you would. Don't blame you, one of your projects I remember. Well it appears he is in some degree involved in our present predicament. Yes. Long story. Can you make time to come to the Castle tomorrow, say in the morning? Thanks. Love to George."

Copley put the phone down and focused on the group in front of him.

"Ladies and gentlemen. It appears that I am the unwitting bringer of bad timings; my sudden attacks of fear seem in some way related to the recent storm event. The role of storm warning indicator is not one I have taken on with great joy. However, it does give us perhaps two or three days until something happens.

Firstly. Can I ask what we have on The Witches Hole?"

"The Witches Hole Is a large methane vent in the North Sea, believed to have caused a steam trawler to sink vertically to the sea bed leaving it remarkably intact with no sign of damage, although this is yet to be proved it is considered scientifically plausible that a vessel could just drop as if in a lift shaft to the seabed without warning. Methane is venting into the atmosphere, both naturally and as a result of oil extraction. The witches Hole location appears to correspond with the point where the storm appeared on the metreologists sensors."

"Yet I was told that there was no known reason why this storm should appear; nothing physical to cause it!"

"The metreologists consider that it is purely co-incidental that the storm originally centred around the Witches Hole. A methane release does not cause a drop in barometric pressure."

"My arse. The Witches Hole was the cause of this. I will bet any money you like. What triggered such a massive release is another question. Didn't our satellites pick up any additional release, something abnormal?"

Old oil platforms are leaking millions of tonnes of methane every year. As to the state of the oil fields; the majority are lightly, or not damaged at all; the storm hit the coastline and hinterland harder than it did the central belt of the North Sea; we lost eight rigs and there are no reports yet as to the casualty number; although we do have reports that most rigs were evacuated to the eastern sector and the Dutch, Danish and Norwegian coasts, so we can only hope it's infrastructure's undamaged.

There is damage to platforms but no report of well heads being destroyed. But. I stress information is patchy"

"You said something about the Captain being lost in a boiling sea" Bob interjected.

"Did I?"

"Yes. Gurndy said the Commonwealth was lost in a boiling sea"

"Did he say where?"

"No. But there must be something on the ship's loss."

"Well. If it's the loss of the Commonwealth, it went missing in the Witch Ground, off Dundee. Beryl has studied Gurndy and his devious activities. Do we know who the Captain was?

There was a commotion and George made his presence known, jumping up onto the table and swiping at the nearest human just to show who was boss and announce Beryl's unexpected arrival.

"Beryl. I thought we agreed to meet tomorrow?"

"This couldn't wait. The Gurndy business and the Crown. The Captain of the Commonwealth was Josiah Premm; long story short. Premm died in 1675 in Bruges."

"He died on the Commonwealth long before that"

"Premm died in Bruges; whoever Captained the Commonwealth that sank off Dundee was not Premm. Premm was in the stone trade; the low countries use brick, no shortage of good clay; stone is at a premium; Premm exploited the peace treaty between Cromwell and the Dutch; undoubtedly he was a fine sea Captain and filling a British warship with a cargo of stone in exchange for spice from the Dutch East Indies was, if not sanctioned by the British, was at least a profitable move for all concerned. Premm wasn't on the Commonwealth."

"But Gurndy claimed the Captain foundered with the ship."

Bob sounded utterly perplexed.

"Has Copley had one of his turns?"

"Yes Beryl, I've had one of my turns as you so delightfully put it. We both know Tobias Gurndy would have lied through his teeth; he survived by cunning. No doubt a Captain went down with the stone, but obviously not Premm."

"Premm only used the Commonwealth once."

"When he wasn't on it; when it foundered; well off course for the Dutch coast. I see what you are thinking Beryl. Not quite a co-incidence?"

"The Dutch may have had a peace treaty, but the Commonwealth was a formidable warship; it's disappearance was only to the advantage of the Dutch"

"Disappearance?"

"I have no doubt the cargo was jettisoned."

"Jettisoned? But you said it was valuable, why dump it"

"Because cannonballs are rather more vital if you are going to take a ship to war than lumps of stone. The Dutch had signed a treaty with Cromwell in 1654 after the Cromwell's navy had beaten the Dutch. The Dutch were more interested in long distance trade than fighting over local coastline; trade needed protection and the Dutch were happy to settle with Cromwell so they could concentrate on attacking the Spanish interests in America. In brief the Dutch need ships and Premm was part of the commercial good will gesture; the Dutch were after the ship."

"So, the Dutch intercepted the Commonwealth and changed flags and loaded it with ammunition and the ship is reported lost in the Witches Hole."

"In short. Yes."

"The stone is jettisoned straight into the Witches Hole. Mariners know the Witch Ground; for most part it's a name, but they know to be careful; so yes, they took a risk, but they needed to make the changes in a spot that was off the main trade routes. The Dutch probably sent three merchant ships and loaded her the best they could."

"What about the crew?"

"I have no doubt most would have eagerly changed sides."

"What proof have we got for any of this?"

"The Dutch start building ships remarkably similar to the Commonwealth immediately after its apparent loss. The Dutch building programme, after the First Anglo Dutch war was delayed and the easy answer was stealing ships to make up the shortfall."

Copley thought for a moment. There was silence in the room. George licked a paw, his rasping tongue breaking the pause. "Stone drops into Witches Hole; ship gets renamed and armed; Premm and Gurndy live happily ever after. Doesn't help us in anyway. Let's leave this alone and get on with the tasks at hand. However. I would appreciate a full survey of the Crown Posada and the structure to be protected however we can. Bob you have that in hand."

"Yes Professor. I have a team of engineers on their way"

"Thank you. Now let's have an update from the team leaders"

Copley was soon embroiled in the increasing catalogue of material and sites; his mind filling with argument and counter argument over priorities. It was just like being at the University. For a moment he drifted back to his office, to Evelyn in her domain. Life was good. Now it wasn't. It was hard; he was playing at little tin God; making decisions over people's heritage; they may not have a home to go back too, but he could at least give them an anchor, a reason, a tethering point for memories.

As Copley reminisced a team of Army engineers were approaching the Crown Posada, over the scaffold bridge and down to the street level to witness the chasm where the bar had been. One of the engineers brushed the inner door as he looked down to the blocked arch of the tunnel. A small amount of dust fell from the bottom of the ridge holding the glass panel in; the dust cascaded into the depths; a fine dust, no audible plop. But just enough for a froth to appear on the water below and a bubble to rise. A small translucent globe gliding upwards; bobbing; darting, as if alive. The engineer called to his colleagues to come and see this oddity; by the time the team had gathered the bubble was hovering at the level of the bar floor. Motionless. Curiosity overcoming surprise, an engineer threw a half brick at it; the bubble burst against the jagged edge. As it did a wind rose from nowhere, swirling round the remains of the ground floor, sweeping up the water below, creating a vortex that reached the doorway in seconds, pushing the engineers out onto Side and across the remains of the road and off the ancient Quay edge. Hurling them down into the solidified black mass below. As fast as it had happened all was restored to normal. Not one of the party stuck in the black mire moved.

"Professor we have an incident down at the Posada. We sent a team to evaluate a way ahead and they didn't report in. so I sent another; just in case they were having difficulties. They were all found dead, lying in some sort of solidified fat on the old quayside across from the Posada. I've had a look at the bodycam footage. You need to see this"

Copley watched the footage with a passive near indifference; watching people die wasn't Copley's favourite form of entertainment. At least it had been sudden, and they hadn't seen it coming. No time to panic. No time to do anything. On the picture going black he turned to Bob.

"That fat. I think I know what it is."

"Go on Professor."

"The human remains of Gurndy's victims."

"What!"

"I've seen the effect before."

"Why can't it be just the chip fat from the burger bar next door?"

Copley raised an eyebrow.

"More importantly Bob; what was in that bubble to cause that? It is critical we confine the area, so none of whatever it is can escape further. The bodies; we need a full autopsy undertaken as if it's a chemical warfare incident."

"Underway Professor. Do you really think that stuff they are lying in is mushed human remains?"

"Yes. I'm sorry for the loss of your colleagues. Actually, I do want to know what killed them; allowing for being flushed out the building and across the road I would have thought they would have survived. The landing would have been soft. A bit roughed up perhaps, few broken bones perhaps."

"I agree. We will have to wait for the report. But. You are not going to like this. We are going to hospital"

"Why?"

"Because we have been down there and I'm not taking any chances. I have a suspicion that your human remains, if that is what they are, might be carrying some pretty nasty germs."

"We never saw that mush."

"Even so; we were in the building, what's left of it and you say that stuff is from it. We are not taking any chances."

"really."

"No ifs, or buts. Come on Professor."

Reluctantly Copley followed Bob down to a waiting vehicle.

"I'm sorry you lost those four colleagues."

"It's never good. They weren't part of our team, but that doesn't matter they were here doing their job; they knew the risks when they joined up; but I doubt any of them considered the risk of a bubble exploding and drowning them. Dodging a bullet out in the Middle East, but not here in a pub. You put the uniform on, you accept the good, the bad and the downright life changing, or no life. It's duty. We do it."

The vehicle drew up at the RVI and Bob and Copley were escorted to a waiting room where they were joined by an RAMC officer.

"Good evening gentlemen; I understand you may have possibly been in contact with something nasty."

"Well that is one way of putting it; considering I've been with my team and partner in the last forty-eight hours until the Colonel insisted, we come here because of the"

"The Crown Posada fatalities. Yes. Well Professor. The Colonel is absolutely correct in getting both of you checked out. Just in case. Please go through the door on the right and use the cubicles and bins; place your clothes in the yellow ones and take a paper suit from the white one. See you shortly. I'm sure there is nothing to worry about."

Copley and Bob complied. They were then scraped for samples; internally examined, swabs taken and generally subjected to a full decontamination procedure. Two hours later they were sat in their paper suits back in the waiting room. The RAMC officer re-appeared.

"Well gentlemen. At least one of you is. I'm afraid Professor, we have a slight problem. Something is living on you; but we can find no trace of it on the Colonel. Good news for you."

The officer had a broad smile as he turned towards Bob.

"What is it?"

Copley was anxious beyond mere curiosity. He dreaded the prospect of further decontamination.

"We don't know yet. Samples are being flown down to London. We do know that it only likes your body. It seems to be attached to your skin tissue; doesn't seem to like anybody else's. Odd that"

"What happens next?"

"Well you don't appear to be infectious in anyway and your body seems not to be having any adverse reactions."

"I've been feeling a bit odd, anxious, even quite terrified; not like me."

"When did these symptoms start?"

"On the way back from Oxford; when I went to see an inscription found by Toby Rutherford."

"Ah. Yes. Doctor Rutherford"

"Do you know him?"

"No. Doctor Rutherford has been detained on the orders of your wife; he's being detained in a secure facility undergoing tests. He seems to have the same problem. We were informed because the source of the problem originates here in Newcastle and your wife contacted the Colonel to bring you in"

"Sorry professor; orders are orders."

"No problem Bob. If Evelyn tells you to do something; you do it. I suppose I'm going to be detained?"

"As I was about to say, you don't appear to be a risk to anyone, other than possibly yourself; I see no reason to detain you, as long as you are supervised and I'm sure the Colonel can arrange that."

"I can go. "

"Yes. We will contact you as soon as we know what's going on. "

"And Toby?"

"They have orders to detain him until further notice"

"Oh dear. Poor Toby. What a pity. Never mind. Well done Evelyn is all I can say"

"As I say we will let you know. You can both have your clothes back; they will be sent through to you in the next ten minutes; you might like to know Professor we found a transponder in the elastic of your boxer shorts."

Copley swung round towards Bob with a look of furious indignation.

"Don't look at me Professor"

"Evelyn"

"Never let a woman buy your underpants."

Copley laughed out loud; he knew Evelyn too well. He would never escape her, and he had no intention of doing so.

The doctor left them with broad smiles.

"It's too dangerous for anyone to go near the Crown Posada; whatever it is will kill. But there just might be another way to find out what's going on down there. "

"Lovely old pub the Crown Posada; lovely ceiling. Good beer."

"The finest and most unique of places. "

"Your local?"

"One of them, but from the moment I first walked in that door I knew part of me would never leave. There is something about it. Light and dark. Its history is quite unique; I have no doubt in stating there was a structure on the spot long before the Romans. A rock face with water spewing out would have been a site of religious significance from the beginning of history. I suspect the tunnel is, at least under the Castle a natural sheering of the rock; the Lort Burn is an exposed example, least is was exposed version until Dean Street was built over it. The sight of a spring or in this case a cave would have housed deities. The Gods demand respect, administration of offerings; priests and priestess need shelter and food. Fresh water for vessels journeying across the North Sea, water blessed by the Gods. Traders word of mouth; eventually combining all the knowledge of minerals and agriculture and tribes the Romans come along and exploit the resource and with my minor alteration maximize the profit and returns. They stamp their mark by engineering; they understand water, how to improve flow; they build new shrines and grand tunnel mouths because they discover a system of chambers which allow movement free from the treacherous river. At the point where this emerges, they build a grand statement. Then something goes horribly wrong. All the work is closed up, sealed and done so with pride in doing so. A challenge that has been fulfilled. The whole site is deliberately forgotten; a quay is built across the entrance. The space is filled in and the foundations are re-used for large warehouses fronted with shops; they remain in use until the

Romans leave. The coast and the river are ravaged but trade continues under many a different hand; fire and flood come and go, and the quay continues to thrive. The Normans stamp their mark; order equals prosperity on the river and the amount of space along the quay is at a premium. The answer is build upwards. This policy remains the norm up to today, even though the quay on Side has long been filled in; space in a busy transshipment point is always expensive. All those ships travelling to far off places, all the services they need; everything, everybody crammed into just one street. Brewers, silversmiths, cheese mongers, tailors, engineers, Captains, shipping agents, seamstresses, bookkeepers, whores. Every part of life living on top of each other. The Crown as it was by 1700 was eight storeys high and reached back to the Castle mount. A warren of a place; connected to the buildings on either side; long passages with shops ran the length of Side. At street level the Crown was a plain boarded structure, no windows, just two openings; one central one to the left, which was a through passage, gated and manned by a keeper. The central entrance took you to a benched area with a pot hatch to the left and a formal central entrance door through which you would walk into a low beamed room with table and chairs either side of the central walkway. The principle feature of this room was a staircase which took you up the first floor which was a landing to the first floor shops running North to South. If we required refreshment, we would continue working our way back to another door where we would be welcomed by our genial host and shown to a table. If we required rooms, or private dining we would be shown to the fourth floor and fifth. The third contained gentleman tailors and seamstresses; shipping agents and alike. For sexual services the sixth and seventh. The rest was for the landlord and his family and staff. Basically, the street level was filthy, where you stopped for a beer and moved on, as you went up the building the delights got more varied; everything was available under one roof. You went up the central staircase and came down the one at the back; a more discreet exit; you could access the shops at any part of Side, just walking the passages that wended their way as high as the mast on the Quayside. Eventually this timber menagerie, which laterally included analytical chemists and grain dealers, falls into decline; better harbour facilities, bigger ships; decline and fall. Every generation having left its mark, the whole is torn to the ground and a sturdy modern structure is planted on the footprint. Only three modern storeys high, the Crown Posada is the picture of sophistication. A statement of sunshine, extolling Spanish heat amongst the new Baltic northern timber trade. Wines and gin as well as brewing. For the grain dealer, the chemist and the brewer saw opportunities; the brewer in particular. In the famous windows you can see wine barrels and vine; hops by a kiln and juniper berries. The Crown Posada isn't just an architectural gem it's something on a completely different scale; it's a vessel containing the essence of the past. That's the only way to describe it. The echoes are inside you, you become part of its song."

A porter delivered their clothes and they headed into the cubicles.

"What do you thinks going to happen next professor. Another weather bomb?"

"Well. Quite simply. Why not? What or whom caused the first one, so why should it stop? No motive, no apparent external cause.

Random, thus potentially repeated, or not. So. Yes I do think it could happen again based on probability, but only because it's happened once."

"You haven't a clue have you."

"Actually, I have; but I can't prove it."

"The Witches Hole. You heard the findings; a methane release wouldn't create a drop in the barometric pressure. Nobody's denying that methane seeps out. Just it doesn't immediately have an effect on the weather."

"What if, what's living on me can attach itself to the methane bubbles as they rise to the circle. If they come into contact with the stone, they might somehow react with them."

"It might help when we get a report on the engineers"

They left the cubicles; just as the doctor returned.

"Ah. Glad I caught you both. Just been asked to pass a message on regarding those four unlucky engineers of yours. They drowned. Hope that's useful. Sorry about that. Bad business. How the hell did it happen?"

Copley looked at Bob.

"Thank you, doctor. The Colonel and I were wondering that ourselves."

"Well we've all come across barotrauma, there was no sign of it, they drowned, but none of these lads were in any water, yet their lungs were full of it. They landed on some thick greasy fat along the exposed quay. Very odd."

Copley frowned and headed for the door; he deliberately blanked the doctor.

"Colonel. Can somebody get that fat analyzed?

Bob followed and nodded his farewell.

As they sat in the panther heading for the Castle Copley continued to frown; the silence darkened, the mood was sombre. Copley knew that something in that tunnel was the cause; that any advantages of speed of movement of goods through to Corbridge had been outweighed by whatever lurked deep beneath the ground. The stone for the formal structure was probably cut from the local geology. It made sense, as the Romans improved the route they would have quarried as they went and had accidently hit a very strange deposit and obviously the resulting problems had caused the closure. All had been well, the route, the entrance lost, until Gurndy and Premm saw an opportunity; even their efforts had little effect; the stone lying at the bottom of the North Sea, the sediment covering them. The Posada site had to be sealed off, but the source of the trouble had to be dealt with.

"Bob. We have to find the other end of the tunnel at Corbridge."

"Are you sure that's a good idea?"

"I don't think we have any choice. I'm positive the cause is the stone, or what lives on it. We need to know what it is that is happily living on me but will equally kill without warning."

"Aren't we going to provoke the same sort of attack as happened at the Posada?"

"Gravity. The flow is towards the coast, plus we need to analyze the stone. I haven't heard of any major weather incident at Oxford, yet that stone is a building that's ruinous; I accidentally brought the interior of the bell tower down. But no; cataclysm. Why?"

"No idea."

"Nor I. It's a puzzle. Have the Royal Navy patrol the Witch Hole? Everything is to keep out. Obviously, an exclusion round the Posada."

The panther drew up at the Castle. Jean was waiting at the bottom of the steps. Bob cheered up immediately. Copley roused his spirits.

"Jean. A welcoming smile. What news? We need to cheer ourselves after the business at the Posada"

"I'm glad you two are back; I feared they would keep you in isolation.

They climbed the stairs together.

"I'm sure I speak for us both. We are glad to be back. Tell Evelyn I'm alive and kicking"

Copley suddenly stopped mid staircase.

"That's it. Why didn't I think of it before.?"

"What is it professor?"

"Bob. I need engineers, heavy excavating equipment and probably explosives. I'm going to open up the Corbridge end of the tunnel."

"Yes. You've mentioned it I was going to get it sorted now we are back here."

"The water in the Cor"

"What about it?"

"The river was nigh on over its banks, it had been raining for days on and off, but I was able to wade along the Cor, no increase in the depth, no strong undercurrent. The water, the runoff; it isn't running out towards Corbridge, its heading down the tunnel."

They continued up to the Great Hall.

Copley requested an aerial image of Aydon Castle and a map overlay; this was duly put on the big screen. Copley was instantly back in his element, he pointed at the bank across from Aydon Castle

"Somewhere here, is the tunnel entrance. I'm sure we can find it relatively easily."

"Won't we have the same problem as we have at the Crown Posada. Which I should explain to the team is an unidentified organism that drowned four members of REME without them falling into the water; the Professor believes that the source of this organism is in the tunnel system between Corbridge and Newcastle."

"I'm also convinced that the recent weather bomb is directly the result of stone from the tunnel being dumped in the North Sea by Captain Premm. Why it should suddenly become active now, I'm not clear, but the methane vent, The Witches Hole, seems the likely epicentre."

Jean looked at the board, then at Bob and asked.

"How does accessing the tunnels assist us?"

Copley turned from the board

"I suspect that before the Romans improved the system, the locals had no difficulty with the route. Caves and water are sacred space; there may well have been Roman soldiers equally unhappy about improving this system as the locals. Water finds its own level; water is definitely flowing into a cavern, I walked the Cor burn, not above my knees at any point; yet the Tyne was bursting its banks. At the time it didn't occur to me; considering the terrain above Aydon there should have been a torrent; instead, it was flowing away on its own easterly subterranean course."

Jean pressed on.

"If this is a means of getting barges to Corbridge, that means you would be working against the flow?"

Copley appreciated this, intelligent questions. Why didn't students manage to ask ang?

"Good point"

Copley used the few seconds to consider a reply.

"The Tyne, even when not in spate, is a difficult river; shallows, rocks and temporary islands. An unhindered course with means of attaching lines to the tunnel wall, allowing haulage against the flow, is certainly more preferable to the same prospect on the surface. Knowing the Romans delight in hydro engineering, they may well have installed water powered lifts and locks if space allowed but allowing for the very brief period of operation it seems unlikely that such sophistication was applied. But one never knows."

"Won't entering the tunnel system only aggravate whatever it is in there?"

"I doubt it; the flow is towards Newcastle; the problem lies on the stone in and around the tunnel face at that end. I suspect this was quarried from somewhere between the two points, most likely towards Newcastle; otherwise we would have known about the problem with the construction of Roman Corbridge. This wasn't an instantaneous problem; the tunnel face looks complete, even signs of pediment suggesting ornamentation and completion; the reaction must have taken time, suggesting an exposure and contamination build up at the egress. In simple terms we creep up behind the source and tackle it, otherwise we are just mowing the grass; it won't be cured."

"And the problem in the North Sea?"

"If we can solve this problem here, we have the remedy for the North Sea. All I can suggest is we have as many operational platforms in the North Sea that can release methane, to do so. It's primitive, but it might just reduce the buildup. One thing is for sure we can't drop anything over the site it would only aggravate it. Any ideas most definitely appreciated."

Copley felt his self- assured self, he worked best under pressure and Jean had fired the right questions his way. He was aware she was worried for Bob's safety; the team had been shocked at the deaths. Copley was still coming to terms with the fact a mere bubble could hold such ferocious power within it. The power of Jupiter; such that could destroy all before it. Copley realised his audience was aware of his musing.

"Any further questions?"

One, two three. Thought Copley.

"Ok. Thank you everyone.

Never give them a chance when you are hard pressed for a n answer.

"I'm fully aware everyone is fully stretched, and I will be asking for further assistance. If that's everything. Colonel and Jean, can you come with me.

Copley made his way back down the steps and out of the Castle; he looked towards the new barricade between the Vermont and the court house, preventing anyone getting near to the rear of the Crown

Posada; it was getting dark and the scene was floodlit, the shadows of the soldiers large against the Keep's ancient walls. Bob and Jean stood expectantly, waiting for Copley to say something. There was a long silence as Copley looked far beyond the barricade, back into the past, before the chaos, before all of it. Was it just this thing, this whatever, that was clinging to him, was he directing him, or was he coping? Copley felt sick to his core.

"I don't know if that was actually me in there, or whatever it is that's living on me. I know that you must make the decision Bob. I need you Jean to find a way of plugging this end of the tunnel, so nothing gets out. I don't have the foggiest how you do it, I do know that nothing must fall into the water by the tunnel mouth; we've got to enclose it. What I do know is if we get this wrong, we are unleashing a huge problem in the City. We've got to solve the problem in the tunnel before we can do anything in the North Sea."

Bobs phone rang. He took the call.

"Thank you. I will pass this onto the Professor."

"That was the pathology lab. That fat. You were right. It's human"

Jean stood, a look of shock on her face. Copley half smiled.

"I knew it was Bob; I've come across this before; the human body under certain circumstances, temperature and external factors such as acidity of the soil, can melt away, bones and all. Occasionally you get a soup, quite common if the body is in a lead coffin, acts like a hay box, slow cooks everything. In this case Gurndy's victims must have been thrown into the…"

"Water. But if that's the case why didn't the water react? Surely there would have been a reaction every time he dropped another one in?"

"Good point Bob. Perhaps he just buried them under the floor, but that doesn't work, too many; he's down at water level; he's got the quay to his back and the tunnel blocked in front of him, a confined space; the bodies would have wreaked, even considering the lack of any sanitation somebody would have complained. No, he had to have disposed of them without any contact with water."

"Well that's it. The water. Gurndy's cellar was dry; I don't think there was any water in the cellar until after the stones were removed; probably the removal of them caused seepage."

"But that would suggest all the water is equally dangerous, but that isn't the case. The stone seems to be causing the infection in me and others, the water reacts after contact with it."

"Jean can you get hold of Beryl if she hasn't gone home for the night and ask her to check on the trades within the Crown at the time of Gurndy's ownership. Thank you. I wonder where Evelyn is?"

"Behind you Professor"

Copley turned to see a black jaguar followed by another two drive up to the Keep. Evelyn stepped from the centre vehicle; seeing Copley she diverted from the expected path, resulting in her bodyguard scuttling around.

"Evelyn."

"Copley"

"I only have one thing to say to you Evelyn. Underpants"

"Grow up Copley. I take it we have some idea what caused the engineers deaths?"

"It appears anything that causes the water between the tunnel mouth and the back of the old quay wall creates a miniature typhoon, enough to drown four engineers with one small bubble."

"And the Witches Hole; can you guarantee it's the source of the weather bomb?"

"It appears so. Methane naturally rises to the surface and we believe stone from the tunnel was dumped there, it's suddenly come to life. Why I have no idea. But with the Crown Posada and the Witches Hole we have to be extremely careful."

"But you think this is some sort of natural event; not a hostile power."

"Well it is a hostile power, it's nature of some sort. They still don't know what's growing on me. How's Toby?"

"Undergoing radiation treatment."

"What!"

"The scientists are trying to get whatever it is to react, or just die. Toby's not too happy about things. But there again he did get you involved, so what did he expect."

"Evelyn. Even I think it's a tad harsh to put Toby through that sort of treatment"

"Copley if it wasn't for the fact, we need you, I would have you doing the same. Toby is the guinea pig. It's imperative we find out what it is"

"Lucky Toby."

"Are you alright? Is he Bob?"

"He's fine Lady Copley; we'll keep an eye on him"

"And a short lead. Now. Do I order a commencement of evacuation for the region, or do you believe you can get this under control? Tell me honestly?"

"I can get this under control. No. We can get this under control. My apologies both. Team effort. This is going to take some specialists. Bob. Can you organize for SBS and SAS units to meet us at Aydon Castle tomorrow along with REME with heavy excavating equipment? Evelyn can you assist. Oh no."

Security men were suddenly scattering as George clawed his way passed three suits with Beryl fast behind.

"Hello Evelyn."

"Good evening Beryl, hello George; aren't you a little sweetie."

George rolled over to allow Evelyn to stroke his tummy. George watched the suits nurse their wounds.

"Your list of tenants of the Crown whilst Gurndy was landlord. Note page two."

"Butcher; pie maker; candle maker; leather worker; glue maker. You were right Beryl. I owe you a pint or three. Beryl has studied Gurndy for years; well the pathology lab has just proved you right. Gurndy disposed of his Royalist refugees by butchering them and disposing of their bodies with little or no waste; the only thing on this planet you can't dispose of is fat. That's all that was left."

"My God.   He was a monster."

"One of many; he couldn't do this alone; there was a decent profit for all concerned."

"One good thing about Gurndy"

"What possibly could be good about him?"

"His activities stopped most of the water seeping out; it acted as a liner. Jean. Can you arrange a barrage and at some distance a coffer dam? Make sure you test as you go and oxygen equipment for anyone on the job. No more drownings. Start at first light. Now then. Thank you Beryl I'm sure Evelyn's helpers will get you and George safely home. Bob; I'm sure you and Jean have things to do; but get some rest. I am taking Evelyn back to Tynemouth."

"But Copley"

"No but Copley. We are going home. I've had enough for one day." With which Copley took Evelyn by the arm and briskly marched her to her car.

Copley was feeling just fine.

"Good Morning"

"Morning Copley"

Copley lay, observing, creating and reasoning the duvet landscape into territory; Evelyn was an island, with many and varied lands within.

"What time is it?"

"Its British Army get up time; which is why I'm awake."

"Oh God."

"He might help, but any minute now your cavalcade will turn up and I will be making coffee for your suits."

"Thank you. Copley. Be careful."

"Don't worry I won't upset your bodyguard, miserable sods the lot of them."

"I didn't mean them. You know exactly what I mean. You let somebody else to do the sharp end, you do the thinking. Sometimes you are quite brilliant at it"

"Thank you"

"Sometimes. Just make sure you get it right this time. Especially as you have been having these panic attacks."

"I'm aware I'm not always myself. Whatever it is it seems relatively benign, as if it doesn't mean any harm. As if it needs a host to survive its adapting to me."

"Well the sooner we know what it is the sooner we can get rid of it. I wonder how Toby is doing?"

"I have to say it's pretty savage using radiation treatment on him."

"We've got to find out what kills it; what happens if suddenly it starts spreading?"

"You didn't think that way with regards to me?"

"We did. But we have control of the entire region, plus we could tackle it as a post disaster infection. We need you. We don't need Toby. As I say we need you"

"Thank you."

"One thing this, whatever this thing is, it's humbled you down; I'm actually missing the pompous Copley. Not a lot, just a little."

With that Evelyn threw off the duvet and headed for the bathroom. Copley dragged himself out of bed and into a dressing gown. Down to the kitchen, where he could see the cavalcade parking up. Copley put the kettle on.

The field opposite to Aydon Castle was a scene of military hardware. Excavators, trucks, tents and personnel. Copley was impressed if a little concerned, he had no idea where the tunnel was, and he could see a small party using ground penetrating radar a short way east of the main military set up. A good start thought Copley; Bob must have worked all night to get things arranged. Evelyn had insisted on making a couple of calls before Copley had dragged her to bed. This must have been her handiwork because under the present circumstances excavators, indeed, any equipment, was as rare as hen's teeth.

"Good morning Professor."

Bob walked into the tent along with two officers; one Special Boat Service the other Special Air Service.

"Good morning gentlemen. I'm not sure if you have been brought up to speed by Bob, but we have a task for you. When the ground penetrating radar team have located the tunnel which we expect to find, we want you to access the tunnel and make your way towards Newcastle; we don't know how wide the tunnel is at this end, we know that at the Newcastle end its fourteen foot wide. We have no idea of condition other than the Romans constructed it over two thousand years ago, so it should be in reasonable condition, we don't know if there are caverns, obstructions; even if it is possible to traverse it from this point all the way to Newcastle, but we must try. Something is lurking in that tunnel that has immense power over the environment, particularly weather events. We believe, inadvertently as a consequence of an historical event, it caused the catastrophe on the East Coast. We do that if you come into contact with whatever it is, and we are waiting to find out what is, I have a particular interest as its living on me, that it is relatively benign, but agitate it with the stone from the tunnel and it becomes a typhoon. A teaspoon size bubble has already killed four personnel. Your task is to get along the tunnel and record what is going on and send back samples as you go."

Bob added.

"It's a biological suit job and you will need to set up relay teams for getting samples back to the surface. As soon as we have gained access, we will need a pathfinder team to assess the best approach to traversing the tunnel."

The two officers looked at each other; the SBS officer spoke.

Why not try digging along the length Professor?

"Good point; except we don't know where the source of the problem is, the flow is towards Newcastle. We can't drill holes because if we hit the stone that reacts with whatever it is, we'd set off goodness knows what. Basically, the first time you encounter the phenomenon is the likely source."

Bob noted the alarm on the officer's faces.

"You need to consider some sort of forward probe, to give yourselves a chance."

"Understood."

"I understand that this is a highly dangerous mission; but that's why you are here; we need the best."

As Copley outlined his hypothesis as to the likely route of the canal to the officers; Jean was busy in Newcastle supervising the containment of the Crown Posada. The REME had suggested a complete structural cover, incorporating part of the hotel and restaurant on either side of the pub; these could be accessed relatively easily. The major problem was vibration. Anything that fell in the water below could cause the repeat of the engineers unfortunate demise. The REME answer was to use spray foam, creating a base for a lightweight structure without disturbing the ground beneath. The other problem was containing the human fatberg; as the troops had nicknamed it. A coffer dam was the answer, sandbags, cement and steel plate was being delivered by barge. Jean was coordinating the delivery of resources and the security of the site. How her life had changed in the last few tumultuous days; she had been dead on her feet when Bob and the Professor had turned up. Not an ounce of strength left and only now had some of the sights she'd witnessed begun to clear from her dreams. The luxury of a bed and sleep, hot food and knowing her boys were safe. That meant everything to her. The sights she'd seen; two of her colleagues washed away in their patrol car, no chance of escape; the looks on their faces haunted her; along with parts of bodies in the rubble and rows of children's legs sticking out from beneath plastic sheeting. Grim. Grim. Grim. She put the thoughts back into the box and stored them away, she had things to do, people relied on her. There was one thing that had puzzled her; how in some of the most terrible of circumstances, some things just continue as if everything was normal. Like buildings demolished but mirrors still on the walls undamaged. In her case she had been assigned to clear the Haymarket bus station when the storm had just got underway, some roof panels had come loose. By the time she had got there the Haymarket was a scene of utter devastation; cars and buses had been pushed by the wind into the Eldon bus station entrance; the glass walls of the University building opposite were being ripped off and were sailing through the air; motorists were abandoning their cars and running for cover; many into the metro station; where she in turn took shelter and directed the people down onto the platforms away from the flying debris. Taking a moment to gather her wits and using a concrete pillar as shelter she had attempted to radio in, whilst doing so, she looked across the road towards the University, the furniture being flung around, papers swirling into the air; thus distracted she hadn't noticed the Land Rover drive up on the pedestrian side of the building.

The driver slid the window open.

"Get in lass, you can't stay there, the upper storey's not safe. Come on"

Instinctively Jean had run across and jumped into the Land Rover, even now she didn't know why. As she sat down the driver moved away. She had just closed the door when there was a screaming cracking grinding noise and the whole side of the metro station collapsed onto where the Land Rover had stood; the pillar was lost in the rubble.

The driver smiled and weaving his way through the maze of wrecked vehicles drove her through the storm wrecked streets.

"Thanks. You saved my life"

"No problem lass. My names Fred. Glad to be of help."

Fred dropped her at the door of the Police station; smiled, waved and had driven away, back into the maelstrom; as calm as if it was a Sunday afternoon drive.

Jean didn't notice the number plate or even much about the man. She was in shock; perhaps part of her still was. Just a random act of kindness; like Bob's. But it was puzzling. Her phone rang. The real world was calling; there were things to be done.

Copley was looking at a laptop screen; undeniable; a void; he then looked around him; as he had predicted; the tunnel mouth had faced Aydon Castle; he had a suspicion that there had been something beneath the early medieval house; a good Roman foundation most likely.

"I think we start right there."

Copley pointed to the spot. He was in his natural environment, a field. Armed with a spray can he marked out by strides the area he wanted de-turfed. The digger got to work and within the hour a sizeable sloping trench had been opened and stonework was appearing. The tunnel was there. The digger stopped. The site was cordoned off and a small group of suitably suited personnel approached the stonework. Samples were taken. Images were taken of crisp well-cut stone creating a curved arch. Copley gave the thumbs up and a digger fitted with a hammer proceeded to pound away at the stone. After ten minutes the digger withdrew, and a camera was lowered down into the hole. There was a perfectly preserved canal tunnel; there seemed to be a gentle flow; the bore was over sixteen feet wide and the as the camera swung around the light picked up metal eye points on the wall, allowing haulage. The camera was withdrawn, and the digger proceeded to carefully remove stone until there was a fourteen-foot-wide section open. The digger withdrew and a ribbed inflatable was gently lowered into the canal; fitted with a bow light and cameras and the all-important long pole which deliberately sagged forward into the water.

"Well I have to give it to you Professor, who on earth would ever have thought that there was a canal tunnel here. It looks as if it's in amazing condition."

"It was built to last. I wish I was down there with them."

"Well you can't for once. You especially. We don't want you reacting with whatever is. We need you here. Those guys can do the graft, you do the observing."

Copley sat watching the screen as the boat eased its way forward. The tunnel was amazingly intact. The air quality was deemed breathable, but the oxygen supply was kept on. Copley wondered how many air shafts there must be for such a tunnel. He was mulling this over when reports came in of a noise; out of the darkness the tunnel opened up into a large cavern. The crew stopped the boat and swung the lamp toward the noise; forty foot to their right was a stone landing stage; water was running over its edge creating the noise. The lamp pierced the darkness, the passage vanished into the distance; there was stonework and metal lying at one end of the landing stage.

"It a quarry; that's a waterwheel, I'll bet anything you like. They would have used it to power the crane to lift stone onto the boats. The lamp picked up some graffito on the stonework

XX Valeria Victrix

"That's Agricola's troops under the governor Bolanus until late in AD71. Agricola knew this system, probably built it. Excellent we are getting somewhere."

The men reported a draft of fresh air coming from the distant quarry. They ventured on; by the end of the first day they had explored eight miles of tunnel; three caverns, all showing landing stages and equipment for moving stone, thankfully nothing had caused a tidal wave and all were full of admiration for the quality of the build; stone lined throughout, except where the caverns and the best quality stone was being extracted and transported.

The debrief revealed no great difficulties and as the bio environmental sampling gave no reason to concern the crew oxygen was only to be used in an emergency scenario; the use of a second vessel also would allow for equipment to be moved; the landing stages provided storage points; more personnel could safely be committed.

Copley was feeling very happy. He had been proved right, the canal did exist, it also was in truly wonderful condition. As he sat looking at the images, his phone went. It was Evelyn.

"Evelyn"

"Copley. Congratulations. You were right. Please pass on my comments to the team. I've contacted Jean; it appears they are making slow but steady progress at the Crown Posada."

"Slow and steady is exactly what we need right now. Have they had any results back on me?"

"Actually yes, apart from saying well done, there is progress. Apparently, microbes, if no other food is available, especially if underground; can gain nutrients from minerals. This seems to be the case in what is crawling all over you; it's become attached because of you putting your hands onto its food source and finding you a delicious alternative from its usual diet, because we excrete minerals. Interestingly these little microbes have quite a punch; they have a way of digging into the minerals and leaving chambers in them; these chambers are at incredibly high pressure for their size. It seems if they interact with water the bubble fills with hydrogen and as the microbe attempts to extract that at high pressure a chain reaction is created, if the bubble breaks the vacuum draws up vast amounts of water completely disproportional to the size of the bubble. The problem is we are made up of minerals and this little microbe feeds on them. We have to make you unpalatable to the microbe."

"Like Toby?"

"It's too early to say. Sorry to pour rain on your parade, but we are working on it."

"No. Thank you Evelyn. It's something. It appears these little microbes work in packs; they can form colonies and as we know they can protect themselves. So be careful."

"Bob won't let me go down in the tunnel."

"Quite right too. You have to stay out of it. Get to bed early tonight. I will be in London. I will keep you posted on Toby's progress if you like."

"Thank you, Evelyn."

"Behave yourself."

"I will. You be careful too. Love you."

Copley was determined to get into that tunnel, but he would do as he was told. For the time being.

Chapter Six

"The Witch Ground, or to be precise the Witch Ground Graben is a trench in the North Sea, running between the Moray Firth and the Viking Graben. The Witches Hole is a particular deep cleft of over one thousand five hundred feet within the Devil's Hole group, a series of deep straight sided clefts, which are renowned for snagging trawler nets, hence the name."

The officer looked at her notes.

"Thank you, Jean."

Evelyn turned her head to look out of the jet's window, down into the grey green North Sea; she was surveying the exclusion zone; two fighters were escorting her. The oil and gas platforms throughout the field were venting as instructed.

"How's the monitoring going?"

"All vessels are in place and the oil industry is providing sea floor movement data; there's always some seismic movement, small earthquakes; which is why the scenario of a bubbling sea is ever prevalent in tales of this stretch of North Sea."

"Let's just hope it all stays quiet. Now we need to be in Edinburgh to meet with the Scottish First Minister regarding funding for the displaced. "

"There's also the matter of the mass burial sites; we need more land."

Evelyn looked back at the Sea.

"Prepare the figures. How bad is it."

"Estimates now indicate one hundred and seventy thousand dead."

"Estimates?"

"The DWP and NHS are trying to assist, but the County records are damaged; the evacuation centres are the best we have as to who is alive, and we aren't halfway through the building by building checks. We haven't the personnel"

"I know. I will bring this up at cabinet. The truth is the feeling is that, if we commit too much of our resource and we get hit again, then we won't be able to respond. I can't understand why none of the North Sea monitoring stations picked up the initial drop in barometric pressure, because a storm needs to come from somewhere; it has to leave a trail."

"Studies on landfill sites have identified that rising barometric pressure reduces methane flow; there are coal deposits beneath us here, as well as oil and natural gas; I'm guessing there must be some connection"

"Copley says it's the result of stone from the tunnel being dumped into the Witches Hole"

"But if that's the case why hasn't it caused problems before now"

"It seems it has, but very localized; its sucked things in rather than causing a mega storm. None of the scientists have any more idea as to what created it, because they haven't got anything to go on, other than it appeared around here, out of the blue.!"

"We should be in Edinburgh in thirty minutes. I'm sure we will find an answer."

"Thank you, Jean, I just hope you are right."

The plane swung towards the Scottish coastline. The sun shone on the sea; the waves rippled and glistened silver. All was calm below.

Copley woke to the sound of heavy machinery passing his tent. He'd stayed on site, not wishing to miss anything and dragged himself out of his sleeping bag to look at the source of the noise. It was a low loader with a steel barge on it, a narrowboat. Copley dressed and wandered across the field to inspect the vessel.

"What do you think Professor?"

"I think it's brilliant."

"It's just a lot safer for the lads, lot more space for oxygen and equipment and she's electric. All we've got to do is expand the entrance hole and away we go"

"I'll go and have a shower."

"Hang on a minute. You know you can't go down there. We need you up here. You know why."

"But."

"But nothing Professor. You know why you have to be here. Now go and shower and I will see you in the mess tent."

Copley slunk away. He saw no reason to try harder with Bob. It wouldn't work. As he stood in the shower he pondered; were his thoughts his. Was, whatever was living on him, able to read his thoughts, change the? Was the very act of thinking about them being manipulated by them? How much of his mind was his own? They had induced fear and panic in him; they were part of him. He opened his mouth and the water poured into his throat. He choked. Part of him was trying to move him out of the torrent. Copley was grasping the pipework; he wasn't giving way. He wanted to die, he wanted to put an end to it. Evelyn appeared before him. Face to face. She was screaming at him. He wouldn't stop. Copley blacked out.

"Professor. Professor."

Copley found himself looking into a bright light. Was he dead? No. he wasn't dead his hands hurt. Why did they hurt? Because he had gripped the hot pipe. Why? Because he had decided to kill himself. They had gone. He knew they were gone. He had terrified them. They hadn't expected his action. They had left him. They were about. They were crying, they were frightened. Bob knelt by his side.

"Don't go near the shower. They are in the shower. They are frightened."

"Who are in the shower Professor?"

"The beings on me."

"They've left me."

"Left you."

"They've gone. I took them by surprise. I'm not going to miss out and watch from the sidelines. I decided to kill myself."

"What!"

"These things, these beings, they were in my head; in all of me. Without me they are lost. Remove myself; they had to escape; they think, they are sentient through whoever, or whatever they can live on. Being alive is the crucial part; death terrifies them."

"How did you work it out?"

"Seeing the boat, being stopped from taking part; I didn't challenge you. That's not me. I had to purge myself and a parasite needs a host, if that hosts dies the parasite is at risk; it flees to finds a new host. I couldn't think, they are in the head; I just did; they can't cope with death"

"But you could have died"

"That's the point. Look. Get the message to Toby's keepers; tell them to kill him; obviously don't; it will work. These beings will run. Point a gun at him or drown him and they will run. I can hear the screams; these things are complex beings. Isolate that shower."

Copley's hands were bandaged; they were sore and swollen. His throat was sore. But he was alive and Copley again.

The shower was isolated, the rescuers had fortunately not stepped on the frothy scum at the back of the shower. Copley walked to the edge of the tape.

"Bob; these beings are aware of Gurndy's victims; that's why they left me; fear of death. Don't harm them; they like minerals. Find something for them to cling onto. They will calm down.

"Can you understand them? I mean are they able to communicate with you"

"It's more I can feel than hear. Although I could hear them, it's more a sound in the mind now. They are happy being what they are; we are something of interest to them."

So, we have a microorganism that is sentient but obviously goes berserk when it comes into contact with methane."

"That sums it up rather well Bob. They clearly can-do things at the molecular level we can't. I could do with a beer."

"Professor you've just nigh on killed yourself"

"True. I could do with several pints. I feel much more me."

"Right. That's good news. I think. Well get dressed and I will get the local opened early, if you can dress with those hands; I'll give you a hand and leave our friends to the biohazard team."

"Keep them safe; give them a piece of granite to hold onto."

"Ok. Understood. "

Bob helped Copley dress.

"Thank you, Bob. I knew I'd made the right choice in putting you in charge of my team."

"Are you sure it wasn't our little friends pulling the strings."

"Well if they were it only proves that they have common sense. Now a pint to celebrate and then the tunnel."

"Professor I have instructions."

"Evelyn. Well, Evelyn isn't here and what she doesn't know won't harm her."

Copley sat in the back bar of Skinners Arms, Hexham, with a pint in his hand, Bob sat next to him, the pub was open by the time they had arrived, and a few regulars were chatting to the bar staff. To Copley's pleasant surprise Arthur Nicholson walked into the bar.

"Arthur. Thank goodness. How are you? The family?"

"What are you doing here Professor?"

"Having a drink."

"Well there's nothing new in that, what happened to you?"

Copley looked at his bandage hands. They ached.

"I had a bit of a problem to solve and they were the unfortunate casualties. I'll heal. This is Bob. He's in charge of my team. How's the wife and children. All safe I hope?"

"Yes, our house is tucked into the little valley out the back of the pub; well above the river and out of the worst of the blast. How's Evelyn"

"Lady Copley is in charge of trying to put this whole mess back together."

"Well you couldn't have got a better woman for the job. Good luck to her; anyone that can cope with you can certainly rebuild the North East."

Bob laughed out loud. Copley began to puff himself up; his Germanic air of superiority was about to shine forth; he felt a lecture coming on. He suddenly realised he really was himself again. The pompous self-opinionated Copley was back. His humility was froth in the bottom of a shower cubicle.

Copley ordered a round and the three sat at a table, happy to be out of their present circumstances for a while.

"I'm afraid the Crown Posada is a bit of a mess. Your cellar has gone. But the good news is that I'm sure we can restore it. You realize that the other side of the road to you is now open water; the Crown is back as a quayside pub; you can look cross to the Free Trade without anything blocking the view. More importantly is the fact we have discovered the Crown was built on the foundations of a tunnel. A canal tunnel that makes its way to Corbridge. That's why we are here today. We are traversing it."

"I've no doubt the Crown Posada will rise again; you know Copley that there is something about the place; something nobody can quite put their finger on. Evelyn said so; she hadn't been there long before it made itself known. The walls watch you; not in an evil way it's as if the place has a conversation with you. I can be in the bar at eight in the morning and I never feel alone. It's a tiny space with the landscape of a planet; you can go anywhere within those walls; you can dream, scheme, or just stand and let the thoughts of others just wash over you like a warm bath as the water reaches the edge and tips out; everything flows by. You catch hold of the plastic duck and back you are; in reality. Under the imperial ceiling, serving the throng."

"I must finish that history Arthur; it's most remiss of me"

"Not with those hands you won't and anyway you are adding to it; you, we are all part of it. And whilst I have the opportunity, I think I should add to the story."

"Go on Arthur, do tell, I need to take my mind off these hands and Bob's in no hurry. Your round Bob"

"Well. You know the alley way to the right of the pub; where we keep the barrels. I've often seen the lights of the bar from it. Impossible as the windows have been bricked up for probably over ninety years, but just occasionally I look up and see the light beaming out and shadows on next doors walls. I've never worked up the guts to look in the windows; not after what happened on the stairs."

"Go on."

"The yard's not that big and you know the toilets were moved to accommodate the ladies; well the area up to the back of the pub goes up to the Castle and you can see where there were buildings. Parts of the old Crown before it was rebuilt. Well I've walked up a stone staircase in the yard."

"There isn't one. There was, there's even a photograph claiming to be of the Crown Posada with a stone arch and warehouses to the right of the passageway."

"Well I've been up those steps. You can say I'm mad, but those steps took me up to an arch and through the Castle walls. It was Christmas Eve two years ago. You know I'm a family man, I like my Christmas, so I was eager to get away. The bar wasn't busy; just a few regulars and the atmosphere was fine; so, it was annoying to be told there was a row going on in the back yard. The doors kept ajar for smokers to stand by the barrels. I hadn't noticed anyone going out, but I went to see what was up. Well the door slams behind me and I'm in the passageway and there's no sign or sound of any argument; what I did notice was three lamps to my left; good bright glow that flickered; Christmas card lamps. Bugger me to my left was a flight of steps; I turned around and the door had gone; there was a timber wall. I was drawn toward the steps; it was snowing hard and the lights were drawing me up to the arch; I can't say I was petrified; I don't know how I felt; I just walked up the steps. To my left were stone landings and steep staircase rising up to a balconied walkway; light was shining through, the sound of laughter beyond. I kept to the stone steps. The Crown posada was tall and gaunt above me. I couldn't see the stars; it enveloped my view except for the lamps and the steps. So tall and dark; overpowering, frightening me. To my right on doors to warehouses; pulleys and ropes covered in snow; big painted numbers on every stone upright. I remember the numbers. At the top the arch and an iron gate, which was open; a lane with streets of shops, dark; their boards up; the snowflakes piercing the gap between the overhanging upper stories. Silence. Then I noticed a figure; standing against the arch to my left.

"And where do you think you are going? You don't belong here. You go back to your Crown Posada"

I was so frightened I nearly shat myself; up to that point I thought I honestly thought I was at home in bed asleep dreaming. Thing that's really odd; this figure moves into the glow of the lamp light and he's dressed like you and me. Not old dress, but everything around was sort of Dickensian if you like. Well I don't waste a moment I'm down those steps as fast as I can go and when I get to the bottom, I hit a cask. Swing round and fall through the open door. I tell you I have never been more scared in my life."

"Was it this man?"

Copley fumbled in his pocket and Bob helped him flick through the images. Bob held the image up.

"How the hell could you have a picture of him. I've thought it was some sort of dream; that I'd had an accident, fallen over the cask. You've got a picture of him; that's impossible."

"Thanks Arthur. Don't worry you are not going mad. You just walked through worlds a bit; the Crown Posada obviously allowed you to see a little more of itself than most. Don't worry; it will rise again, as you saw it was a very different place two hundred years ago. As for the figure, he won't harm you. You can rest easy. Believe me, what you saw was real, but leave it at that. One for the road methinks"

The conversation lightened and talk of the future cheered all. Eventually Bob looked at his watch indicating it was time to depart.

Farewells said and arrangements to meet again duly agreed Bob and Copley sat in the back of the Range Rover.

"Who is the guy in the picture?"

"Good question Bob. He turned up and recused me at Corbridge; then he turned up at Alnmouth. Once is fortune, more than once and I instinctively get suspicious; so when I waved goodbye I took a few pictures; the wonders of the digital camera, you can put it on auto; pop it in the top pocket and away it goes, hopefully you get one good shot and I did."

"How can it be the same person. Arthur's obviously seeing things; he said it was Christmas Eve, he could have been drunk as a skunk. Hallucinating. You show him the picture and he just goes along with you. Like a lot of people. He's in shock"

"I Know Arthur, he never drinks more than a half on duty and that will be tasting a sip of beer for quality, never; if he says he saw Fred Partridge at the top of those steps, he saw him; I've no idea what or why, but I'm sure we are going to find out."

Copley was utterly confused by what he had heard; he felt better in himself, the beer had worked, eased the throat and distanced him from the experience in the shower. He had frightened himself, he had no choice, taking himself by surprise, an inner instinct to survive, beyond what the parasite could reach within him. He had been lucky; but that was Copley; the real Copley, the self-assured Copley. Whatever was in that tunnel it was of interest to more than one party; just like the parasites, they needed Copley.

Back at the excavation the narrowboat was being lowered into the hole; fully equipped its eight personnel were ready to take equipment to the second and third landing stage; Copley waved them goodbye and watched as the silent craft disappeared into the tunnel. He wasn't going to make a fuss about the boat. He would bide his time, purely because Copley was convinced that nothing of any consequence would occur until the sixteenth mile; the outskirts of Newcastle; in the meantime, he could observe, and others would record this most magnificent feat of Roman engineering.

"How are things progressing at Newcastle, Bob?

"Jean says it's an infuriatingly slow process, but the dam is in place; putting the cover over the whole thing is proving extremely difficult."

"I bet it is, they can't afford to create a ripple on that water. That aside can you get this image of Mr. Partridge circulated; don't have anyone intervene; just he's to be watched; all movements. I've sent you the image."

"Will do. It will be interesting to see what turns up."

"It will indeed."

"How are our parasites?"

"The shower base has been transferred to a biohazard container and we've given them some rock to cling onto. We haven't done tests; as you say if they are sentient beings, we probably need to wait until they calm down. No news on Toby."

"I bet somebody questioned the order. Go in and shoot the patient. I bet that went down well."

Copley looked at the progress in the tunnel; the barge was just right for the task; it arrived at the first ancient landing stage. Whilst no supplies were to be left; battery lights were erected, and the full complexity of the site was revealed. The remains of a waterwheel, collapsed water trough to feed it and four passages, two above the water, two actual canals for bringing out stone.

Bob looked intently at the screen.

"I bet this is just a honeycomb of workings; they were mining it out and building tunnels with it."

"One thing is for certain. You don't abandon a resource like this unless you have no choice."

The boat moved off, on its way to the second landing stage. Copley twiddled his thumbs. He began to feel impatient. Definitely his normal self.

"Bob. Things are going well here. Can we go to Corbridge? I need to go to my B&B.

"Yes, no problem."

"Bring a couple of hefty lads along.

"Right you are; any particular reason?"

"We might need them. I'm not sure, but you never know they might come in useful."

Twenty minutes later the Range Rover drove up the drive of the wrecked B&B; there was nobody about; the owners had gone.

Copley made his way to the outhouse and the passageway.

"After you gentlemen. Torches at the ready"

The party proceeded down the passageway into the underground dining room. The racks of wine were now just racks.

"We need to get these racks and everything else out of here, we need to clear it all out."

They set to work; the easiest method was to break the racks up. Copley carried the garden furniture out; the broken racking slowly piled up in the yard; eventually the space was empty.

"Gentlemen, this is a room dining room; its underground, which is not that unusual; these wall paintings have survived two thousand years because the conditions are just right; that's why the wine was stored here. The strange thing is there should be a mosaic floor. There is but its possibly ten feet beneath our feet. Our passageway is in fact a shaft for light. Why I think this is the case is the size of the images and the perspective. They are meant to be viewed from a relining position and from a distance. Now then. This space is sound for four people to work safely; can you organize teams to work in here and take out all this fill. Golden rule. Don't damage the sides and the first sign of the floor you stop. How will you know you've got there? You've seen mosaics before?

The men nodded.

Small tesserae, small pieces of stone, usually squared off. Good. I need this emptied within two days, no full barrows no injuries. Get it done If in doubt, stop send me an image. Understood.

Colonel, with your permission let these men choose their teams. Just remember that it's vital you don't damage the walls or the floor."

"Yes, professor came the reply in unison."

The party walked back into the yard.

"Well you have a good pile of firewood. Let's get back so you can get yourself started properly."

An hour later Copley was on his way to Newcastle. He had left Bob in charge of the tunnel and his working party busy at the B&B. he was also behaving himself. He was nowhere near the canal boat or the tunnel. Whilst he had passed through the west end of the City with the suspicious Mr. Partridge, it was only now he really saw how bad it was. Tensions were high; forced evacuation was taking place. He thought of Beryl and asked his driver to divert to Summerhill; he instructed his driver how to enter the enclave, much battered by the storm. The great tower of St Matthews lying broken. It was a miracle that the houses had survived. He made his way to Beryl's house; George was sitting on the gatepost, so she was home from the Archive. He knocked the great knocker and let himself in. Beryl was cooking her dinner.

"Oh, it's the little shit himself. Prey what do you want of me? Pour yourself a beer and one for me."

Copley duly opened two bottles.

"What do you know of Fred Partridge?"

"Fred Partridge; Frederick Partridge; bar man at the Crown Posada long before you turned up, vanished. One morning, gone. Nobody knew where he went; nobody at his digs knew him, left his wages. Gone. Reported to the Police. Nothing. Nothing that he could be hung for."

"He was a wrong un?"

"Thing about Partridge is nobody knew him; he turned up, did his job well enough and that was it. Except it wasn't."

"Go on."

"You know that a pub is a hub for gossip; a place to be someone else for an hour, just escape from living. You can rile against life, join in with any debate, or keep your own company. A variable feast that we dine on as and when we please. Partridge was oft as not a topic of conversation, often low and hushed. He didn't fit in. As I say, he I did his job, was polite and would pass the time of day, but there was something odd. One or two of us did a little poking around; Partridge came from a family of butchers; he never told anybody; now the opportunity for him to make a few quid from orders would normally have come to the fore. But the fact he wasn't in the trade suggested a rift with the others. He was no more than twenty-two; it was no surprise that he moved on, but the fact he vanished leaving his wages and his family never attempted to find him; well that's why he sticks in the mind. That and three years after he left, the Police started finding meat parcels; human meat; wrapped up in newspaper dated from before Partridge disappeared. Now the meat had been wrapped, frozen then dumped years later to defrost; two pieces turned up at the Castle, another two on Side and another piece on Dean Street; they say there was one outside Bessie Surtees, but they never caught the dog. At least four young women. "

"You suspect Partridge?"
"I do. There was an air about him; cheerful but somehow detached; that quintessential difference between real and acting; the Crown Posada was a smoke hole in those days; a cloud of grey smoke; a noisy busy pub, a lot tougher than it's today. With no lady's toilet. I lie, they did give us an indoor loo; but the whole place is virtually

unrecognizable; the fireplace has gone, the piano. It started up; nobody took notice of the ceiling; you couldn't see it for the haze of smoke. Anyway; Partridge didn't socialize in the Posada; but he did in The Trent; in those days it was heaving with students; he would have been a little older, so I reckon he went there to pick up victims."

"That's a big leap Beryl"

"Because Frederick Partridge was the witness in a missing persons case down in Cullercoats when he was fifteen. Two girls went missing and Partridge was the last person to see them. They never found them. The police had no reason to suspect Partridge, so nothing more came of it. Except when "Arthur "Plod" started using the Posada that was the moment Partridge left; "Plod" had been a copper down at Cullercoats before being transferred into Central. "Plods" off the record comments made it clear Partridge had questions to answer. When the human meat turned up "Plod" reported his earlier suspicions to his bosses. Partridge was moved from a dormant missing persons case to an active one, but that was it; nothing. It sticks in my mind, because there was something about him that just wasn't right."

"Is this the man?"

Copley showed Beryl the picture.

"It's a very much older version of him, but that is Fred Partridge. Why?"

"Because he gave me a lift twice in the last few days. Once is just chance; the second time I was suspicious. Firstly; on a tree covered dual carriageway; secondly in a wrecked Alnmouth; says he's a land agent. Then he turns up in a most bizarre way with Arthur Nicholson of the Posada; Arthur claims to have walked the steps from the Posadas back yard and met Fred telling him to go back at the top."

"Impossible."

"I would have said so Beryl; but I believe him. Everything Arthur said was accurate; he saw the balconied walkway; the stone landings and the warehouses and the numbers on the pillars and the three lamps."

"Which date it to before 1666."

"Precisely; immediately after the great fire in London the two public brazier lamps on the stairs were removed; when gas lighting was installed there were four lamps. Arthur somehow stumbled on Christmas Eve, into the past and Fred Partridge was there."

"Christmas Eve?"

"Why. What's important about Christmas Eve?"

"Gurndy murdered the majority of the Royalists on Christmas Eve. He was a devious sod. He initially did smuggle Royalists to Europe, but his motive was to provide genuine proof of his escape route. Plus, beneficial trade for himself through the contacts made. He then disposed of individuals who had little or no contact with Europe; they wouldn't be missed. Then he got ambitious and on Christmas Eve he disposed of at least fifty souls. Fresh meat for the Christmas festivities. Horrendous but a perfect disposal route, the meat festival of the calendar; no shortage of buyers. His butchers must have been busy. His butchers!"

"Partridge."

"First thing in the morning. I will see if I can find out who had the butchers shop in the Crown whilst Gurndy was landlord. You think Partridge is related to the butcher at the Crown."

"It's looking likely, or we have someone whose researched the Crown Posada; or the Partridge family and are emulating them. Is the record of archive passes still legible; find out if Fred Partridge had a pass and when and what he accessed."

"How can Partridge have stepped back to the mid seventeenth century and how did Arthur end up there?"

"I have no idea; why he seems to want to help me is a mystery. He seems a perfectly affable individual; what I'd call settled. He could easily be an estate manager; in fact, I will get him checked out, see what we have on him."

Copley tapped a number into his phone and whilst Beryl opened another beer and attended to her dinner preparations Copley provided what little he had to Evelyn's office.

"Stay for dinner."

"Thank you Beryl I will. Better let my driver know I will be awhile."

"We can feed him too. There's plenty"

Copley stepped outside to his car. He waved for the driver to come in.

"Don't stand on ceremony; I'm Beryl, have a beer; its Moroccan lamb and couscous; plenty for three."

"Thank you very much Beryl; it will make a pleasant change from the mess. It's such a pity about the tower; a real landmark. I hope it gets rebuilt. It's very nice round here; bit of a maze getting in, I wouldn't have managed without the Professor."

"He knows it like the back of his hand. Don't you Copley"

"Except it looks like a war zone."

"Where doesn't Professor; it's amazing anywhere survived"

"The whole place felt as if it was going to come apart when the tower came down, but it seems to have imploded on itself with only part of it falling into the street. The Army have been brilliant."

"I didn't see any personnel when we arrived"

"You won't Professor; the whole area has been cordoned off; Beryl and George the cat are the only people here. We just followed your orders; everyone else has been evacuated."

"Ah. Yes. Well done. I did. Just forgot about it. Lots on my mind at the moment, as you can understand. This looks delicious"

The three of them eat and discussed life, whilst George sat on the gatepost standing guard. After dinner the three walked to the bowling green orchard and sat under an apple tree; the sound of bees filled the air; there was a deep silence.

"Sounds like early Sunday morning. Except it's like this most of the time now everyone's gone; you appreciate the silence when it happens, when it's constant it gets wearing. When can we get back to normal Copley?"

"When we sort out what's in that tunnel and causing the problem in the North Sea"

"If you will excuse me Beryl and Professor, I will take the opportunity to contact the wife."

"You do that. I'll see you back at Beryl's in, say twenty minutes."

"That's more than enough time, thank you Professor"

The driver walked away, phone to ear.

"How many thousands of people are displaced by this; how many lives ripped apart, ended. I tell you Beryl; I could do without this Partridge business."

"He's part of it."

"How's it going in the archive?"

"Slow but sure. I think half the archive survived; because enough of the roof survived. Alas the brewery records took the brunt; they've never been catalogued. Now they are gone."

"Like the Posada. A hole in the ground."

"Nonsense, it's just the floor, the rest still stands tall. Don't be so dramatic Copley. The Crown has risen and fallen and risen again over two thousand years, this is but a moment in history. We just have to see it through."

"How the hell did Partridge get anywhere near me in the first place?"

"He tracked you. I wouldn't be surprised if he was watching you in Oxford. It was Toby that invited you to look at the inscription and he'd sat on the information for years; academia closed ranks, no surprise there, but I wonder if Toby knows Partridge?"

"It's worth finding out. I'm a bit narked I left my second phone in his door pocket; I always have a spare phone. Thankfully he didn't notice me taking the pictures. I wonder if we can find where he is, if he hasn't found it?"

"Course they can, they thought you were heading to Edinburgh. I know that, but Evelyn knew better; we know you to well. Get on your phone and find out."

Copley tapped Bobs number into his phone.

"Bob. Can you get someone to find where my phone is, the one I sent to Edinburgh with Fred Partridge? This character Partridge is suspected of murder and worse; have him arrested. Make sure Evelyn knows I've called you; she can get any clearances to find him. My second phone was in the side pocket of his Land Rover. Good. Thanks."

"Well that's a start; mark you, we are working on straw here; nothing was ever proved in the Cullercoats case."

"I don't care the idea of him shadowing me gives me the creeps. Let's get back. Thank you for dinner."

"I will do what I can to find out what Partridge was studying. But it's going to be a challenge"

The pair walked back to Beryl's house; the silence was extreme.

"Are you ok here? I can get you housed elsewhere?"

"No, you don't. I'm at home here; you've made it safe and I intend to be here to welcome people home."

"Good for you Beryl"

The driver was back at Copley's car.

"thank you again for a lovely meal Beryl"

"Come again young man. You are always welcome."

"I will if I may, absolutely delicious home cooking"

"See you at work day after tomorrow Copley; it will take until then, I assure you. But we will make it a priority"

"Thank you, Beryl. Anything you need just ask."

"A bit of luck might help."

"Excuse me Professor, Beryl. Text message. States Fred Partridge has been found dead in his Land Rover; apparently he has been dead for some time."

"How long?"

"Doesn't say."

Copley was about to ring Bob when his phone rang.

"Professor. Your phone was still on. We found it in the Land Rover in the ditch with Partridge attached to the steering wheel by a fence post. Skidded off the road and nobody found him until a farmer went to fix his fence. He's been dead probably since an hour after he left you at the railway station. Interesting thing though. Jean saw him"

"Jean?"

"He saved her life at Haymarket metro station the day the storm hit; just called her over and the roof caved in, he then drove through the mayhem and dropped her at the police station. All he said was his name was Fred. I have to go now. See you at the dig"

"Thanks Bob. Yes. See you there tomorrow."

Copley turned to Beryl.

"So, he's in Newcastle in the midst of carnage and two days later after the worst conditions possible he's on the tree strewn dual carriageway at Corbridge with me. This doesn't add up."

"Nobody could have driven anywhere in that weather Professor; it would have been impossible; suicidal."

"Somebody that is such a good driver ends up off the road in a ditch after what he's been through in the previous few days. No. there's something not right about this."

"Perhaps there's more than one Fred Partridge"

"What!"

"What if there were identical twins; they share the same job, at the Crown Posada; they don't get close and friendly because that way somebody would realize, they stand off; which makes us think twice about them, but as one person we don't notice the subtle differences."

"They could do anything; they could commit the Cullercoats crimes. No, it's impossible; they would be known as twins at school; the Police would have checked the records. It doesn't stand up. I grant you it is a good idea; but it still doesn't explain why Fred Partridge was interested in me; Jean wasn't working for me when the Metro incident happened; that could be sheer fluke."

"Have him checked for those parasite things you are covered in."

"I'm not. They decided to jump ship."

"How?"

"I decided to kill myself and they decided living in the scum at the bottom of a shower was a better bet"

"Well they showed excellent taste in the end."

Copley ignored the comment and smiled.

"I will Beryl; I will have the body tested immediately."

Copley stepped into his car and the driver and Copley waved goodbye to Beryl.

Copley tapped his phone.

"Evelyn. Yes. I have heard the news. Can you have the body checked for the little devils that were living on me. Only a theory. Also, can you keep the search going. Yes. There is a possibility there is more than one Fred Partridge. I know. There really is a possibility.

Something very odd is going on. No. I'm not going in the tunnel. I'm in Newcastle. Yes, I've just had dinner with Beryl. I'm popping into the Castle then heading for Tynemouth."

The car wove its way out of Summerhill, back into the dereliction; waived through the checkpoints, passed the endless queue at the station and back to the Castle. Copley was up the steps and inside as fast as he could, an idea had occurred to him.

"Is Jean still here?"

The answer was in the affirmative and she was up in the chapel. Copley made his way to the chapel. The Gospels sat in their case; the guards on the door to the chapel. Jean was inside, kneeling at the small altar. Copley waited patiently until Jean rose.

"Jean. Sorry to disturb you."

"It's about Fred Partridge isn't it. I told Bob he rescued me."

"Had you seen him before?"

"When he picked me up and rescued me; no, I didn't recognize him, not even when he said Fred. It didn't seem to be the same person. It was a long time ago. Can we go to your office"?

Copley took Jean up onto the roof, they sat looking at the lights coming on; like broken teeth, there were gaps; it was just reassuring to see any at all.

"Tell me about Partridge."

"I was fourteen; my best mates were killed by Partridge. Oh. I can't prove it. They couldn't then; but he did it alright. He butchered them. He did for those other lasses, they only found bits of them; he'd kept them frozen for two years."

"How do you know it was him?"

"The Partridges had a butcher's business out at Ashington, they traded under the name of Browns, the family had bought the shops and kept the brand name going. Fred went to our school but was in the trade from about eleven. He would be out doing deliveries; he liked photography; well by the time he was sixteen he was getting the lasses to pose nude for him; there was no shortage; he had the gift of the gab. He used to stage pictures, proper props. On Sundays he'd take the girls to the butchers' shop and get them to pose as if they were lumps of meat. Thing is they went along with it; I said it was sick and told Partridge where to go when he suggested I posed for him. My mates, a bottle of vodka, a butcher's shop; Partridge did them there and then. Some sick fantasy. They were never found. I reckon Ashington ate them."

"Didn't the Police question you about any of this?"

"Yes. I told them Partridge took nudie photos of schoolgirls and that he took them back to the shop; I wasn't the only one to tell them either. They checked it out; found no cameras, no photographs and nobody would own up to be a model for him. Anyway, Partridge senior gets really upset with the Police harassing his son and my Mother gets banned from the Brown shops and we move to Whitley Bay; as troublemakers. It was an absolute travesty; there we three families that ended up moving. Nobody believed us. No evidence. Where did the girls go? Partridge actually gave evidence that he was the last to see them when he was questioned by the Police. There was one young copper who believed us; he's still with the force."

"Arthur, better known as Plod" yes, I know him; Beryl agrees with you; she remembers Partridge as a barman at The Crown Posada. As soon as Partridge sees "Plod" he ups and vanishes. Are you sure he posed them at his Dads shop?"

"Yes."

"Are you sure he killed your friends there? Where else could he have done it. He killed them there. In those days' butchers slaughtered animals and processed them on the premises. Browns had a yard at the back and it scrupulously clean; you could smell the clean-down fluid, strong stuff. I didn't know the girls were with Partridge the day they vanished but there was strong smell of cleaning fluid coming from the yard on Sunday afternoon. I told the Police that, but nothing came of it."

"Well he's dead now. It's not justice for any of those poor souls."

"Why did he save my life?"

"I don't think he realised who you were; if he was being predatory, he could have found any number of victims and got away with it under the circumstances. No doubt some have done, we will never know. No. I think he saw a wpc in trouble and just did the decent thing. He was an exceptionally skilled driver."

"Yes. He managed to get me to the police station through absolute mayhem."

"Which is why it's odd that he ended up dead in a ditch in a car crash with nobody else involved."

"Well he's dead. I hope he rots in hell."

"I'm sure he will Jean. I'm sure he will."

They sat in silence as the stars rolled out of the black blanket of night; there were more stars, because there was less light. Jean sobbed and Copley sat with her. He was certain that there had been more to Partridge than a serial killer. Arthur's experience on the steps worried him the most; Partridge had ordered Arthur back to his Crown Posada, not the one he had stumbled into; the one where Gurndy was busy slaughtering the refugees at. It led Copley to consider there was a link between the Crown Posada and Partridge beyond being a bar man. One thing was clear Partridge could not have slaughtered anyone and not been discovered in the modern confines of the Crown Posada.

Copley handed Jean his handkerchief. They sat, looked at the stars.

"Thank you, Professor."

"No problem. I do think you should talk to Bob."

"Bob"

"Yes. If you haven't noticed I think he's rather keen on you."

Jean blushed.

"Bob"

"Yes. Bob. I think you should tell him whatever you want him to know. He knows you work very hard, have two children in Birmingham and that's about it. I think he would like to discover more."

With that they walked down from the roof. Newcastle was silent. It slept tattered and torn, but it slept with hope.

Chapter Seven

"Morning Professor"

"Good morning Bob. How goes it in the tunnel?"

"Well we have a surprise for you. Have a look at this image; we recorded it at fourteen miles; we've passed six more landing stages; there is no problem with oxygen; the quarries are connected to the surface and the runoff is incredibly well controlled. "

"We are getting close now, we need to be careful!"

"Don't worry Professor the crews know that. Caution is the watch word."

Copley looked at the image. A large inscription set into the wall of the tunnel.

In English it read

Imperator Caesar Nerva Traianus Divi Nervae filius Augustus

This section of tunnel repaired by the Legio IX Hispana

Marcus Appius Bradua Governor of Brittania

"This puts the cat amongst the pigeons. Oh dear, oh dear. Bugger me. Yes. Ahhh. Mmm; yes indeed. Bugger"

"Go on Professor enlighten me."

"The Newcastle end of the tunnel states its was sealed by Agricola, he left Britannia in 85AD; Bradua was Governor until 117AD. The tunnel was still in use when Hadrian was busy trying to get the North back under Roman control. Supplies to Corbridge. Makes perfect sense. The inscription is wrong."

"Agricola didn't block it up, so why put a stone in place saying that he did?"

"Well it's pretty obvious to me."

"Enlighten me."

"The inscription didn't come from here."

Copley thought for a moment. The Oxford inscription was real; it was certainly in the sort of condition that suggested it had been exposed to the weather; but it wasn't in its original location. Gurndy's story was mostly fictitious; the supposed timber copy over the fireplace was merely part of the story. Captain Premm digging out the original; the copies. All of it was bunkum. It was possible they were quarrying out stone and selling it.

"My whole theory has just turned to dust. I assumed Agricola closed this canal down; instead it's in use into the reign of Hadrian and very useful it would be too. I was thinking it had been blocked by Agricola because of what lies in the waters. Stop it up and abandon it; the danger outweighing the usefulness. The Romans clearly didn't have a contamination problem with this route. I'm wrong"

"Well it happens to everyone, but it doesn't make much difference; we still have something nasty to tackle which buggers up the weather and crawls all over Professors. By the way. Toby has been cured. He shit himself and you can guess where the little devils ended up."

"Ha. They should have done it when he was in the shower. More to the point. Did Toby know Fred Partridge?"

"Yes."

"Bloody hell. How?"

Fred Partridge drifted down to Oxford after he was recognized by your policeman friend and worked as a barman; eventually he took a degree in Archaeology at Oxford; Toby was his tutor."

"Good grief"

"Partridge got a 2:1 and found work as an estate manager in the Home Counties. Did very well for himself. There are reports of his name being provided when missing female cases come up; seems your friend kept an eye on Partridge. There is no criminal record, not even a driving offence."

"Yet Jean is convinced he murdered her two best friends and others. Then we have Arthur's story, what was happening there? Forget what happened to me; Gurndy is just covering up his activities. None of this is related to the microbes and the weather. Least I don't think so"

"Well put that out of your mind. You are going with me in the boat today. You aren't contaminated and I'm not going to stop you seeing this structure for yourself."

"Thank you very much Bob. I appreciate that. I take it Evelyn doesn't know. "

"No. She doesn't and let's keep it that way. Let's get you into some kit and we will be away we are going to be underground for most of the day."

Copley was readied for his trip and the two of them joined six boat crew. Into the tunnel the boat silently moved along; the stonework was truly magnificent; there were distance markers and iron hauling loops, occasionally there were side channels with water quietly adding to the flow. Copley noted that every half mile there were slots for boards, suggesting that maintenance was built into the design. They entered the first cavern; the stone quay to their right; the lights illuminated the space; two tunnels with water to the right of the main channel. Copley wondered how far they went. His mind followed the lamp into the next section and so it went on; after four hours they were at sixteen miles, the air was pure, the crew were now quiet, concentrating on the probe at the bow, the speed was dropped.

"Two miles to the Crown Posada, it gets hairy from here. Right oxygen at the ready, suits on and seal up now."
Bob assisted Copley; the crew assisted each other, it was hand signals from now on and the boat crawled forward, every ripple was one ripple closer to whatever it was. The propeller had raised bubbles all the way and not one reaction; now, every rotation was scrutinized; the tension was rising. The one-mile mark was a tap on everyone's shoulder with a thumbs up; half a mile; quarter of a mile. The engine was stopped; the flow seemed to be enough to move them forward; Copley moved to the bow. The big lamp suddenly picked up a shape, the tunnel opened into a wide vaulted space; there were large arches on either side; to their left and right the water was edged by stone. Ahead was a blocked arch; there was the remains of a wooden bridge connecting the quay on either side of it.
A check on the air got a thumbs up, as nothing had happened regarding the water, everyone relaxed. Bob signalled masks off; much to everyone's relief. Copley looked left and right; it was a typical Roman harbour complex, Copley estimated they were under

the Castle keep and the Court House. The boat moved towards the centre of the open water; the lamps illuminated storehouses, row after row of them. Bob turned the electric motor on and steered to the right; as they moved down the arches one of the crew saw something odd and waved to his left, Bob turned the boat towards it. The outer arch holding the roof up, was intact but the stone beyond had been robbed out.

"Gurndy and Captain Premms quarry; the Crown Posada must be nearby. I suggest we put our masks on and get the oxygen ready. This stone is the likely source of the contamination."

"What's that then?"

To the right of them Bob pointed to an ornate wide tunnel archway facing Bessie Surtees house.

"The end of the tunnel was right next to the bridge. I understand it now, the road goes up the middle of the quay; boats from the North Sea dock across from the Crown Posada and offload, transship to the barges waiting in this facility. Having the direct exit takes valuable space up for both sea going and canal trade, so the inscription was right."

Copley cheered up. One mystery solved at least he thought.

"What worries me is our bubbles. I'm stopping the motor."

Silence reigned. The crew looked around; the empty warehouses, the water was clear; there was signs of timbers; the outline of barges still along the quay. The boat gently arrived at the quarried-out warehouse; two crew members stepped ashore and tied the boat up; the party came ashore; each with their emergency oxygen supply;

they stood looking out across the water at the sheer scale of the works.

"Well Gurndy wasn't quarrying stone from his cellar, he was taking it from here; how was he getting here and getting the stone out, that blockage under the Crown Posada is intact?

"Through here I think."

One of the crew had walked into the remains of the storehouse, the wall between it and the next had been cut leaving enough of the arch in place to keep the stone roof in place; the far end there was a rough-cut wide hole and rutted floor. The stone had been put off a wagon; there were chippings of stone and broken stone on the ground.

"They cut the stone on the spot, by candlelight."

The party moved on. Bob raised a hand, and everyone stopped; his torch had caught a glimpse of something not made of stone. The light shone on a bone; bones; clothing and two skulls; side by side.

"I have a suspicion we are looking at the remains of Jean's friends, Bob; these aren't ancient bones. Look at the clothing it's from the seventies; this is a crime scene; how they got here; well lets, go on."

"Professor; look at the floor; its moving!"

To Copley's right the floor was gently waving.

"Move. Now!"

Copley ran for the exit, followed by the others; they ran to the boat, cut the lines and pushed off.

"What the hell was that?"

"It was the bigger version of what was living on me. That's not microbial life, that's a species and believe me you don't want to mess with them. Are they following us.?"

"No"

"Don't turn the motor on"

"If we don't, we will drift back."

"These are highly intelligent life forms; where they came from, I have no idea, but they do like minerals, anything else is a curiosity to them. Believe me I know. They are terrified of death, of extinction, they fear. Those bodies, they must have stayed away from them, but whoever put them there, well he was fair game, he was interesting to them."

"Partridge"

"I guess so. They infected him. They enjoyed the ride; they were in his thoughts they just helped him; they found Jean in his memories; they found you, because Toby knew you; they even got inside the head of Arthur Nicholson; I'd bet any money you like Partridge infected Nicholson and the microbes did the rest. He just carried them in, and they found their target."

"Why Bob? Why go to such elaborate lengths?"

"I don't want to worry you, but we are going to be in the shit unless we turn that motor on."

Copley flicked the switch and pointed the boat straight back at the jetty.

"What the fuck are you doing Professor"

Copley swung the tiller, so the stern came close in and he jumped ashore, the boat veered away.

"Professor"

Copley picked himself up. Brushed himself down. He started to address the space.

"Now then you lot, you know what happened recently, you can hear the screaming. It's alright they are safe. None of these people with me mean you any harm; you've encountered lots of people haven't you; found us very complex; our behaviour; our emotions. You found out I have the ability to walk through worlds; Toby told Partridge, no doubt in one of his drunken moments; that's why you constructed that charade with Partridge and Nicholson. You like to put things together; you send out tentacles, you plan, you experiment.

The covering on the floor moved back, Copley stepped forward, it moved back further.

"It's alright to come ashore, we have an understanding"

"What?"

"I've had a chat with our friends, and we are quite safe to continue."

Bob brought the boat back alongside. The crew came ashore.

"It's alright they won't come near you. They know we know their weakness. Just follow me."

The party retraced their steps to the skeletons; the floor covering receded; Copley strode on and turned left, a blind entrance, an apparently solid wall had a wide passage to it's left, the ruts proved the route; it was heading towards the Crown Posada, behind the store houses; towards the blocked of short length of tunnel. He stopped in his tracks. Before him blocking the passage was a wall of water. As if some invisible wall was holding it back. The crew's torches shone through it into an inky depth"

"What the hell."

Copley looked at the water.

"Trust me"

He stepped straight in and vanished.

"Professor."

Copley put his hand back into the passage and beckoned the crew to follow him.

"Don't be alarmed; you are walking through them; we've thought it water; it isn't it's a colony; they've been here a very long time. They caused nobody any harm; but they became part of Gurndy's slaughter; they'd infected all his refugees in the cellar and of course Gurndy had butchered them. They avoided him, but he knew he was at risk, he got as far away as he could leaving his accounts behind. He would never do that unless he was truly terrified. They let him go because they were still reeling from what he had done; Gurndy saw them blink and he ran. Then Partridge finds his way into Gurndy's lair, he brought more bodies and they had an opportunity to travel and enter our World, through him; they had learned much, they understood terror, deceit, death; they used Partridge and of course me; they set this all up; including the show of strength; they are capable of wiping us off the planet. Except for the fact they cannot accept self-harm. Partridge killed himself; his way out."

"What are we going to do Professor?"

"We stay calm and we talk to them; their experience of humans has always been traumatic; they've witnessed the World through the eyes of a psychopath and two academics; it's not what I would call a very extensive menu."

"What is this place; I mean it's empty; there's nothing, I can't fathom this out."

"Somewhere up there is Jean and crew trying to put a top over what they think is water; I think if we explain that if a nut, or, bolt, heaven forbid, falls down here, it doesn't mean we are being aggressive."

"I think we begin with introductions. After you Colonel; keep it homely, interests, hobbies, lifestyle. Everyone please follow the Colonel's lead; they know me, intimately. That's why we are here."

Evelyn had finished her meetings in Scotland; sixteen hours of solid negotiation. Little sleep in the interim. Her phone bleeped. A text from Beryl. An odd occurrence.

IRIS

Evelyn, looked at the screen and tapped out a reply.

STYX?

A reply of

SMHL

Evelyn called for her secretary and ordered a car to Newcastle.

When they were well on the way Evelyn, who had remained quiet with her head in paperwork looked up.

"Give instructions for the remaining population of Newcastle, Gateshead, Tynemouth and the surrounding area for radius not less than for thirty miles to be evacuated immediately."

The secretary looked startled.

Evelyn was stony faced, not difficult after sixteen hours of negotiation with the Scots.

"Tell them Code Red, immediate"

"Code Red. Forty Miles, Newcastle. Yes, Lady Copley"

The secretary tapped out the message and sent it; within seconds her phone rang, and the screen filled with email messages.

"Yes. Code Red. Immediate."

The secretary looked at Evelyn. Evelyn looked calm, resolute and unmoved.

"tell the PM I will contact her as soon as possible, that I have things under control. Keep her off my back for the next four hours. Understood"

"Understood."

"Good. It will be alright."

"Yes, Lady Copley."

Evelyn's cavalcade sped South with blue lights flashing. Within an hour they were approaching the City.

"Gordon; we are heading for NE4 6EJ; it's a rabbit warren; it's in the secure zone. Get as close as you can"

Gordon nodded and the cars were duly informed, and Evelyn had a firsthand view of the state of the West End, solidly built Victorian houses were ripped facades of rubble. The population had been forcibly removed; those that had survived.

Down into Summerhill and the cavalcade crawled into Summerhill Street and stopped.

Evelyn got out of the car before her security could get to it. They followed her towards Beryl's front door; George was on guard on the gatepost.

"You can stay here"

Her personal protection team were unimpressed; George glowered at them at gave the closest a quick introductory swipe.

"Beryl"

"Ahh, Evelyn, there you are, got my text. Good. Come through here I'm just baking."

Beryl gesticulated that she didn't want anyone to hear their conversation; she led Evelyn into the kitchen and turned the mixer and the tumble drier on.

"Evelyn. We are all being taken for idiots. Partridge didn't get a degree for Archaeology; he got a degree for molecular science. Toby was his Government minder."

"Why would they cover that up?"

"Because he was also a psychopath; he was a genius in chemistry and electronics. And, yes, in his teens he did use his models as experiments; the thing is he was able to prove he could create autonomous molecular nanobots and that counted for so much more than a few dead bodies to the State. He was whisked away from Newcastle and spent every living moment in a lab. Then he vanished. Toby came up with the notion he would head for Newcastle and the whole business of the stone and the microbial parasites was thought up. Toby is no more infected than I am, these nanobots do as they are told. Toby tells me Copley's cure for him was they should shoot him."

"How do you know all this?"

"Toby rang me not long after Copley suggested they shoot him; he couldn't put up with it anymore. He's gone to ground, and I don't blame him. Whoever is behind this project is frankly insane, these nanobots are so small they can wander around inside you and get into the neural pathways. Copley was right but he was thinking it was a natural parasite, it isn't; somebody in power is telling it what to do."

"But what's it got to do with Copley?"

"Partridge wanted Copley to find his site in Newcastle, that's all Toby knew; he could get Copley down to Oxford regarding a piece of archaeology with reasonable ease; the story of the removal of the inscription stone is true, but the nanobots were planted by Partridge. He needed Copley to find the Crown Posada site. That's all I know"

"I can guess where Copley is."

"So can I."

"I've issued a code Re evacuation notice for Newcastle and forty-mile radius, that will keep a lot of people very busy. Are you suggesting the PM is responsible for this?"

"Somebody has spent twenty plus years funding research, hiding a psychopath and has developed a deadly weapon without anybody knowing about it. Whose powerful enough to cover their tracks?"

"So, she's played us all for mugs"

"Precisely. Good old Toby, I hope they never find him"

"What are we going to do?"

"Save Copley for starters."

"Jean's busy encasing the Crown Posada; I knew I had to have an excuse for the code Red and nobody is going to question it, not even the PM; if she was testing the weapon in the Witches Hole, she has succeeded; this is merely clean up."

"Why would Partridge want to make sure Copley found his work at the Crown Posada?"

"Because Toby, as Partridge's minder, will have spoken of Copley, no doubt about where he drank and also his abilities. A perfect match. All he had to do was get him into the cellar, but that was done for him by the PM."

"Fine, but we need to get to Copley."

"I have an idea; we will need a bulldozer and some men and some wet suites"

"Are you serious?"

"Absolutely! Get them down to the remains of Bessie Surtees; bring them in down the Close and along Sandhill, two large diggers, and two bulldozers as quick as you can. Get me there with them; twenty chaps will do. It's going to be messy and warn Jean, but I mustn't be hindered. Can you do this?"

"Give me an hour."

"Call it forty minutes. Copley is in real danger."

"They will be there in thirty."

Beryl turned the drier and mixer off and Evelyn left; issuing instructions to her secretary and phoning at the same time. Beryl called George in and having one last swipe at the security team, satisfied, he duly followed Beryl.

The cavalcade left. Sumerhill was quiet. Beryl found her gumboots and raincoat, popped George into his cage and stepped back out of her front door. A car was pulling into the road. Evelyn was on the case.

Copley's party had duly introduced themselves and there was suddenly an awkward silence; it had been quite fascinating to hear of people's hobbies and interests. The major problem being the lack of interaction. Copley had a brain wave. He stooped down and drew a smiley face on the floor, as he went to do so the floor moved back to reveal the real floor beneath the microbes. He drew a smiley face and next to it a sad one. The floor covered up the sad one, leaving the smiling one.

"Well that's good news; they've obviously seen enough trauma; they like happy."

Bob wasn't so impressed.

"Fair enough, but what are we going to do; these things are quite capable of killing us all."

"As we are physically walking through an atmosphere physically to the brim with them, they don't seem to have any inclination to injure us"

"They killed the engineers!"

"Only because somebody threw a brick at them."

"They've only experienced extreme violence, so that's what they use in return. They know that I didn't have their fellow microbes destroyed, they know they are safe. Otherwise we wouldn't be standing in here"

"Well at least we can communicate with them."

Bob started drawing with a stick, it was a long elaborate sketch which had both microbes and his team fascinated. Copley read it out loud.

"Man steps down into cellar, digs up stone, puts it on ship, it sails, then man drops stone into sea, time passes, big storm, wrecks city."

The microbes responded it with uncovering the gloomy face and covering the smiley one.

"Well that's something, at least they aren't happy about what they've done."

"They didn't do it. Look."

The microbes covered everything after man enters cellar and digs up stone.

"So, they are saying they know nothing about where the stone went; they wouldn't they're still here."

"Yes Bob, but because they've been inside me, they know what happened."

"Hang on, what's happening now. We've done something"

"We haven't; they seem to be fighting each other; it's to do with the memories of those microbes that were on me; the fact that they knew the second half of the story; most of these here didn't know. I think we should withdraw whilst we can. Run."

The party threw themselves into the passageway as the water began to change colour; the microbes were attacking each other.

They jumped into the boat, cut the lines and started the motor; the microbes were spilling out through the broken warehouse.

"This is not the place to be."

The boat headed for the tunnel; except the tunnel was gone.

"That's impossible."

"No Bob, they are blocking the route."

"What do we do Professor?"

"I don't know."

At that moment the boat began to sink beneath them, it was going down vertically.

The boat sank beneath them leaving all of them swimming in the water; they warehouses were translucent with microbes.

"Stay together."

The crew faced outwards and their head torches illuminated the battle going on around them; on the quay side figures emerged.

"My God, look they've created Partridge and that must be Gurndy; what the hell is going on?"

"They seem to have split into factions; but look at the Gurndy figure; it's an outline; they've recreated Partridge; as if he was whole."

"Look over there Professor. It's you"

"Least I'm whole. And here you come Bob. They are recreating the actual; they don't seem to know Gurndy, that's odd. Here's the rest of us."

The whole party was standing on the quayside facing down Gurndy; behind him there were wisps of figures.

"It's the refugees. Why can't they acknowledge them?"

"Look Professor"

Six young women stood next to Partridge.

"This is madness Professor, what's happening."

"It seems to be a battle between the actual versus the unknown; nothing to do with our morality; it's to do with what they have actually seen and experienced. This suggests they never saw Gurndy or the refugees; they didn't like the second part of your drawing because they hadn't experienced it themselves. Yet some were willing to side with the unknown; to accept as fact without observing. It's truly fascinating, absolutely fascinating"

"That doesn't help us much at the moment, if you don't mind me saying; how the fuck are we going to get out of this?"

Evelyn walked to the construction site around the Crown Posada, Jean was waiting to meet her.

"Hello Jean. I can see it's progressing well. Can I have a word in your office."

"Certainly."

"Actually, let's have a stroll, get some air; I'd like to see how the works are going along Sandhill and have a look at the Bessie Surtees site."

"I got the message. What exactly is Beryl going to do?"

"Leave it to Beryl. Just stay calm, take a deep breath and hold on tight. Have you warned your crew? Yes. Nobody will be near the Posada. Team brief."

"Good. Here we go. My God."

Evelyn and Jean rounded the corner to face Beryl standing behind the driver of a bulldozer with another alongside; two excavators and twenty hefty demolition workers. Evelyn could distinctly see George in the other bulldozer cab. Beryl saluted Evelyn and yelled

"Tallyho"

The bulldozers slowly moved forward and began pushing the remains of Bessie Surtees house aside; the timbers and walls gave way like paper; the excavators were piling up the remains right and left; the instruction was to dig through and down as quickly as possible.

The dust clouds rose; the splinters flew, masonry shot through the air; the noise was terrific; the building was sufficiently cleared in twenty minutes for the large excavators to start digging down.

Beryl dismounted from the bulldozer that was now busy shifting the bulk of Surtees house into a pile by the riverbank

"We have to go down over thirty feet, it's going to be touch and go but we should reach them. The archaeological record shows Roman foundations at about that depth; if I'm right we should reach the tunnel at this point"

"I hope your right; this vibration could be causing all sorts of problems"

Below, Copley and Bob were watching a light show, as they floated, treading water; the battle continued around them; there seemed to be at least four different sides, as if they were now even more undecided as to what they took as fact. The most alarming aspect was the stonework was beginning to shake and shake violently; the tunnel towards Corbridge was beginning to reappear.

"Their weakening; they can't keep up their ability to construct; they're putting all their energy into destroying each other. This place is going to come down if they carry on."

There was an ominous sound at the broken warehouse end of the quay; just beyond where they had gone ashore.

"I don't like the sound of that Professor"

"Well it's not being caused by the microbes, look at them, they are moving away."

More ominous stone snapping noises were followed by masonry falling into the water. The light show went out; all sides stopped fighting. The wall collapsed creating a bow waved that sunk all of them; they struggled to the surface.

Copley broke the surface and was staring up eight workmen and Beryl

"Ahh there you are Copley. Come along, better get you chaps dry"

"Thank you, Beryl, but we do have a bit of a problem with microbes down here, you better have this area cordoned off"

"Nonsense; they are not what you think they are."

"They're bloody dangerous Beryl."

"Copley, just get out of the water and let your chaps get dry."

"I'm telling you."

"Shut up Copley and get out before any of this falls in."

Copley dragged himself out along with Bob and the crew.

"Evelyn. What are you doing here? Look we are contaminated; you must take care."

"Copley. Thank you for your concern. Might I ask what you were doing in there when I specifically told you not to go?"

"My doing Lady Copley. I said he could go."

"Thanks Bob, but it was wholly my doing."

"Well let's get you chaps dry. Come along."

Beryl and Jean escorted the crew to transport whilst Copley, Bob and Evelyn looked at the hole where Bessie Surtees house had been.

"That was undoubtedly the most bizarre thing that has ever happened to me Professor"

"Unfortunately, it's not that unusual for Copley is it darling"

"It was quite unusual; I'm more worried about those fungus microbe things getting out."

"They're nanobots, invented by Fred Partridge; long story short. Partridge is a genius, but he has a problem, he's a psychopath, cutting up women to work on his molecular level experiments means nothing to him; Toby was his minder and Partridge's degree was not in Archaeology. Thing is somebody in government has been funding him and covering up his youthful experimental misdemeanors ever since she realised he had developed not only a useful servant to humankind but a very powerful weapon."

"Would that be somebody, who is your best friend by any chance"

"It would"

"Toby couldn't tell you, but he could get you to Oxford and he could get some nanobots on you. Partridge had gone walkabout probably the moment he realised his research was being exploited. Toby had told Partridge about you and your association with The Crown Posada; Partridge knew that he could point you to his research. He succeeded. What is clear, these are not ancient biological hazards; we've been hoodwinked. Partridges original research is under the Crown Posada. When the storm came it nearly destroyed everything; it's obvious nobody knew that his work was here. "

"But what about me and Gurndy; Arthur seeing Partridge in the seventeenth century? "

"I can explain that."

Beryl had reappeared with Jean.

"Partridge kept his nanobots in the cellar of the Crown Posada; nobody would notice them, and I suspect he gave himself an insurance policy by letting them find a niche of their own when he left in a hurry. The staff wouldn't even know they were there; all the time they were busy building more of themselves down in the ancient bowels of the place; these things really are microbial size. Then the regulars did the rest, I'm as guilty as any; talking about Partridge, Copley giving his lectures; so when Arthur steps outside on Christmas Eve and he has a nanobot wandering around his brain, no wonder he saw Partridge; amazing he didn't see anything else, but of course these things had Partridge's signature. We were doing exactly what Partridge envisaged, seeking out his babies. Except."

"Except, the nanobot on you was a recent one, not like the ones in the cellar."

"Which is why there was a problem in the cellar; we were in the midst of a civil war down there; they were taking sides.

"Partridge, obviously developed a version for his master, or should I say mistress."

"There was a shadowy seventeenth century dressed figure on one side, a more structured one of Partridge on the other, like standards for an army.

"That's a definite then; the nanobots on you would have related to the Gurndy story and the location."

"But they all left me."

"I think they left their mark; this is neuroscience territory; they were reading your mind."

"All well and good. What do we do with the fighting nanobots right now?"

"Why not ask them."

Everyone looked at Jean and then at Copley.

"We need to find a way of shutting them down."

Copley was not in a negotiating frame of mind. He was wet, annoyed and he felt violated. He didn't like anyone getting the better of him. He had empathy for the creatures, he couldn't have empathy for a thing. He had considered them sentient beings and they were just robots. Toys of a psychopath. A psychopath who was allowed to get away with it; he was looking forward to telling Arthur "Plod" the truth.

"We could ask them to shut down"

Everyone looked at Jean again.

"It's worth a try."

Evelyn scowled at Copley, putting down his likely response"

"Very well. Jean if you would like to have a word with them."

"No Professor. It has to be you, they respond to you well."

"They'll respond to you Just as well; they enjoyed listening to our stories"

"Alright I will talk to them. How should I ask them, do I give them instruction?"

"Tell them; Fred says sleep tight"

"Why that Beryl?"

Copley was puzzled.

"Because that's what Partridge said when he called last orders."

"Give it a try"

Bob approached the slope and eased his way down. He looked into the murky depths and shouted the instruction; it echoed around the warehouses; he stood up and shrugged his shoulders. Since Beryl had crashed through the wall the activity had stopped. Bob climbed back out of the hole. He reached the top and as he did a soldier rounded the corner and waved at the party; they all made their way to the Crown Posada; there they found the work crew standing looking at the screen, the camera operator provided a view of the ground floor of the site. The water was gone, a bare stone floor remained; the blocked stone arch remained.

Evelyn broke the silence.

"Where have they gone?

"No idea, the water just drained away"

The camera operator replied.

"Well, that worked then, except we don't know where they went."

Copley was less than impressed.

"I think for the moment they are not our biggest problem. They seem to do as their told; now we have a much more pressing issue"

"Your best friend."

"Exactly.

"Copley; I've got a Code Red evacuation underway, purely to give us a chance to do something; this distraction won't last long. I don't want to contact any other members of the cabinet directly: I simply don't know who to trust. Somebody must have known about Partridge and his work?"

"Your friend is responsible for murder and any member of the Cabinet that was involved with her."

"How do I prove it?"

"More to the point how do you stop it happening again? The nanobots here aren't the ones causing the problems at The Witches Hole."

Beryl intervened.

"You said that these critters were fighting amongst themselves. There's your answer. You set them against each other, but you make sure your critters win."

"Well it would help if we knew where ours have gone and then how do we persuade them they must get rid of the others."

"You tell ours that Partridge has been killed by the critters from the Witches Hole."

"we don't know that."

"Doesn't matter; these things will take the information we give them; I doubt if anybody is giving any further information to those in the Witches Hole"

"Fair enough, I can see the logic; I agree they will react. But we need them to understand and cooperate"

"Well you can do that; Copley, you can bore for England and they know you. Go and talk to them."

"Where are they then"

"In the Crown Posada, in front of us; just because we haven't any water in front of us, doesn't mean that the stones are really there.

Flat stone floor, regular pattern, whole floor. Impossible. They are still there; they just need a simple message. Off you go."

"There are times Beryl. I hate it when you are right. Well observed."

"Thank you, Copley,"

"Jean, can you get me down there?"

Ten minutes later Copley was lowered into the Crown Posada; he softly landed and the floor shimmered back. He sat down and talked to the floor.

"Now then; yes, it's me, you recognize me; I have to tell you Fred Partridge has been killed by the nanobots that were made elsewhere. Fred sleep tight."

A sad face appeared on the floor.

"Yes, it is very sad; you don't like sad things; I know you don't like death, do you. Would you help me to stop it happening again?

A big happy face appeared.

"If we can pick you up from here and take you on a journey and take to you where the other nanobots are, will you teach them to be good and not hurt people; not create anything that would kill people or change the weather again and when you have changed all the nanobots will you Fred says sleep tight."

The face was huge smile.

For a moment Copley felt an attachment to these nanobots; Partridge had invented something as close to life as he could, perhaps with those in the Witches Holes were sentient. But they had to be stopped, silenced forever. Something meant for good by a man that had no true idea of good or evil; perverted by a politician for her own aims; it was a novel scenario.

"Thank you. My crew will ask you to get into some containers and you will be taken by a boat and taken deep into the sea to meet the other nanobots. You are to make them Fred says sleep tight. Thank You."

The words 'Thank You' appeared on the floor.

Copley felt sick to his stomach. He tugged his rope and was lifted out of the cellar.

"They will co-operate; we will need the lads from the boat crew to move them, they knew them. Bob can you arrange that."

"No problem. Professor. You ok?"

"I admit I have become quite attached to them; they don't frighten me. I suppose if you've had them in your head you get used to them."

"They certainly calmed you down Copley"

"Thank you, Evelyn, I've done my part; it's now up to you to get these Tynesiders to the Witches Hole before your friend destroys us and that will take more than two hours. Plus, I anticipate this activity down here is going to get reported to Downing Street pretty sharpish. I think you need Bob. He knows how to get things done. I leave it to you"

Copley left Evelyn and Bob to manage the move. He had nodded to Beryl and Jean to join him.

"If we can take the strain off Evelyn and Bob by creating some sideshows; the regions under an evacuation order; it will be pretty difficult for the Prime Minister to act; except she has MI6 officers and can counter any of Evelyn's orders. We must take out our own communication hubs the moment Bob moves the Tynesiders; that means taking out the Civic Hall communication centre. Can I leave that to you Beryl?

"Leave it to me and George. I already know where to hit them, in fact everyone knows the weak point; the power supply is outside the building; pull that plug and heyho silence."

"Fine, just don't get caught."

"Jean take out the Keep, shut it down, black it out and can you shut down the airport anything and everything else you can. Have you anyone you can trust to assist you?"

"Yes. I'm certain we can shut down communications here, but the real problem is elsewhere, the secure network to the satellite feeds is what you need to remove."

"How do we do that; is it possible."

"Yes. But Evelyn will have to sign some security clearances, unless, you can do it. You can go anywhere."

"Very well. Leave it me; where do I have to go and what do I have to do?"

"It's basically the same as Beryl. You turn the power off. The difference is Beryl can do a little breaking and entering and you put the codes in with me helping you."

"What codes?"

"The codes on your pass, on the inside of the cover. You can access them with infrared light. Didn't they tell you?"

"They might have. I might have nodded off."

"I don't blame you, its onerous. The problem is when we do it, we need to be as far away from wherever we access the system; because believe me it will be a matter of minutes before they will be onto us."

"Fair enough. I have an idea, for that."

Evelyn and Bob joined them.

"We have a plan; we need to move the nanobots now; I've got to disappear; I've got to get the PM off your back for as long as possible. The Code Red hasn't been questioned, because it's obvious that there are serious problems here. I'm not going to communicate with any of you; it won't be safe; good luck everyone. Copley a word please"

Evelyn took Copley aside.

"Be careful darling, no heroics. I love you"

"I promise Evelyn."

"Beryl will keep an eye on you."

"Don't forget George."

"Well with him on the team we are going to be just fine."

"Take care Evelyn. It's hard when a friend turns out to be a megalomaniac"

"Love you."

With that Evelyn left Copley. He waved his fingers at her and mouthed Love You. He wondered where he could safely access the system to switch it off and then be none too close to his point of access. An idea occurred.

"Professor; the crew are ready."

"How are you going to move them?"

"Shipping container"

"Well that's nice and inconspicuous."

"Four identical Army shipping containers all going in different directions"

"Fine; wont the one going to Dundee be a bit obvious."

"It will, but they aren't in the containers, they are going in body bags by special train. The crew have started; the nanobots are cooperating; they've coloured up; bright blue so we can see them. Your talk seems to have encouraged them."

"Allowing for a clear run that's seven hours; aren't all mass burials supposed to go along the Waverley route. Why's this one going to Dundee?"

"Lost crew of Dundee based oil supply vessel."

"Fine; then you need a vessel to get you out to the Witch's Ground and penetrate the exclusion zone."

"We don't need to."

"Why not?

"We give the nanobots the coordinates and they make their way there; we give them the depth and a search area."

"Well I admit that has me beat; if we wanted to wait long enough, they could get there themselves, but I don't think we have that long. But you still have to get them 150Km out to drop them.; that's going to take some doing?"

"Helicopters."

"And how are you going to arrange that. No don't tell me. Just make sure the nanobots understand where they are going, they know what to do. Only the crew from our little adventure to go anywhere near them."

"Absolutely"

"Eight hours from when you finish loading."

"That's the moment we leave and that is about now"

"What?"

"Well there's no shortage of body bags in this town and the Body Special is being, held waiting for them. I'm re-routing it as we speak. Good luck Professor. Seven hours from now switch all the communications off and create chaos. You're good at that."

Bob walked over to Jean. Pulled her close, kissed her on the lips."

"Take care less. See you soon"

"Seven hours from now Professor."

Bob was gone, along with the body bags.

"Well, you heard him; we have seven hours. Beryl; just don't get caught or hurt; I know it's a waste of time saying be careful but be careful."

"We won't let you down; me and George, we have a trick or two up our sleeves. I must get going; things to do. Good luck both of you"

Beryl left Copley and Jean.

"I have no idea how we can switch the system off and be as far away from wherever we turned it off from as quickly as possible. I take it something very uncomfortable would happen if we stuck around?"

"I would suspect the PM would issue an elimination strike; anything she could point at you. Although it would probably give the game away, but it seems that she is playing for very high stakes and I think we should issue a message to her cabinet and all MP's the moment before the system goes down; along with the Chiefs of Staff. Put her on the spot. It has to be done; she's killed thousands of people. It might give us breathing space, because she has the power to basically do anything until they take her out"

"Over a hundred thousand, an atomic bomb wouldn't have killed as many. Yes; it's a good idea; write it on a piece of paper; we will type it in as we do the code thing; we don't want anyone knowing what we are doing. Which reminds me I must remove my underpants."

"Professor"

"No. Evelyn has a transponder sewn in, so she knows where I am; no phones, no underpants; I'm relatively invisible and that goes for you too. Not the underpants bit."

"Agreed. Where do we go?

"We stay right here. We appear to be continuing as normal, we have command access from here I take it?"

"Yes. But we will be a sitting target."

"I don't think so. Can you get a crew down into the tunnel via Bessie Surtees and get a ribbed craft that will fit down the tunnel and an outboard motor?"

"Yes. No problem."

"Well I will leave that to you. Meet me in the ware ruined warehouse by the Surtees entrance when your free; I need some lamps; I need to check something out."

"You will need a boat to get there; if you can wait, we can organize it; get a hot drink."

"Yes; I could do with a drink; a pint's out of the question, tea will do."

"Must get on Professor."

"Fine. Thank you, Jean."

Copley leaned against a wrecked beam of Bessie Surtees house; the scene around him was of chaotic destruction; yet he saw beyond it; as an archaeologist, he spent his life looking at destruction; rebuilding; patching up; destruction, decay; rebuilding; a cycle. Everything had its grand moment and then was gone. It was the way of things. He recorded rubbish, he theorized on decay; this was harsh; but it would be cleared away, some pieces would survive; rebuilding would take place; another page of history written. There was something puzzling him about Partridge; he understood he could have easily hidden his nanobots in the modern Crown posada cellar; nobody would have seen them. He could even have visited the pub and infected Arthur Nicholson; with the nanobots inside him he could have driven anywhere; they were driving him; he could track anybody because the nanobots were communicating with each other; that he could understand; along with the elaborate charade to get him into the ancient cellar. It was this that puzzled him. How had Partridge managed to get into the cellar. Gurndy's access route would have been blocked long ago; there was no access to the ancient cellar; if there had been there would have been plenty of beer in it if Nicholson had his way. So how did he get into it and exactly what did he do; there was no work bench, no equipment; just two skeletons.

"Tea Professor"

Jean held out a green mug; Copley took it, he realized he had a slight shake.

"Come on Professor let's get those underpants off"

"There was a time Jean when I wouldn't have said no to that."

"I'm sure that's the case; you've just been through quite an experience; you need dry clothes and a rest."

Copley enjoyed a hot shower and clothed in basics, he felt generally better; he also liked blending in; a portly soldier, but it was less obvious as his Harris tweed jacket. The skeletons still puzzled him.

"Well you look better; how do you feel?"

"Fine; the shower, the clothes and the tea; a proper prescription."

"You're frowning Professor, what's wrong?"

"The skeletons. I need to look at them."

"Would you mind if I come along."

"Are you sure?"

"Yes. I've got to end this; it's been with me long enough; at least I know they are not lost; there will be somewhere to go and grieve; their Mams are still alive."

"I do understand. Sometimes in my profession the dead become mere scientific objects; I've seen inappropriate burial; no burial at all; dumping. I treat the dead as if I'm a doctor with a patient; respect; understanding and just like a good doctor, observation is everything. We will learn as much as we can; then the Police can be informed, though I doubt nothing will happen considering what has happened."

"The boats ready; lamps ready and I've got a camera"

They made their way to the hole and with some assistance got into the small boat; they gently paddled across to the ruined warehouse quay; ashore, they made their way to the skeletons, side by side."

"We found you Maggie, Julie; we found you."

Jean bent down and with tears in her eyes kissed the skulls. Copley stood back; grief was personal; she had obviously recognized the rags of clothes; the shoes. Clothed, shoes still on; that was puzzling considering he was supposed to be into nude photography and liked cutting young women into bite size pieces. Why hadn't he and how had he got them here? Jean stood up; wiped her eyes.

"Sorry"

"Not at all, you honoured your friends; I don't need to ask if you know them; the clothes. I don't see any handbags."

"They were never found. But it's definitely them."

Copley knelt down and looked closely at the relation of the bones to the ground beneath it; he looked closely at the bones; no gnaw marks, no rats. In fact, he had seen not a single rat anywhere at any stage of the journey along the tunnel; the nanobots may have kept them away, it was odd. He gently lifted one of the skulls, it was lying on its left side; there was no doubt it was a young person, the wisdom teeth hadn't come through and then it came to him in a flash. He put the skull back exactly where it had lain. He stood up, looked at the remains; they were laid out, they were being presented to the viewer; they were straight; too straight, as if they had been in coffins; even the hands; there was no sign of ligatures on the wrists. Partridge had lain them out and he had done it after the floor had collapsed; he'd meticulously lain them out or got his nanobots to do it. The bones were clean; there was no cartilage, no gristle. He'd boiled them; he'd kept them; as if he was waiting for the moment; to revolt, to abuse Jean and the parents, to abuse him. Disgust didn't come close. Partridge's parting shot to the World and it was bloody petty; he knew exactly who his audience was; he'd found Copley, he'd found Jean and his nanobots had thrived. Had he known that his nanobots had caused the storm? Copley thought not; he was busy with his talents for killing young women. He wanted recognition, the recognition that he was being denied by the State who had covered up his crimes.

"Are you alright Professor?"

"Yes. I should be asking you that question"

"Yes. We've found them. That's all that matters."

"I've seen enough. When you're ready, there is nothing more for us here; I think it would be better if we leave them where they are now and make the necessary report. They may well be needed in evidence regarding the States involvement in this whole sorry saga."

Copley looked at his watch.

"We need to start getting that boat and equipment in here."

"It's all in hand."

"Before we go any further, how strong is the transmission signal; would they be able to pick up the signal if we were, say, underground?"

"You could be in a coalmine and they could track it; it's designed for nuclear war. The most important part is you have to put the codes in; the system has retina recognition and you will have been told a set of numbers to remember, just like a pin machine. You do remember them Professor?"

"Yes. Brilliant. No problem with the numbers; I wondered why they took so many pictures; I just went along with it. As they say bring it on."

Copley looked at his watch, Jean noticed.

"We are alright for time Professor; Beryl has to knock the Civic Centre bunker out at two, we have to start the procedure twenty minutes before; there's a time lag in the system; nothing we can do about that; for about five minutes what we are doing would slowly become apparent; but there's nothing they can do without authority and by the time they've got it the system will be down. I've had an idea regarding the message; we send it by email and social media; we go global."

"Good idea; whatever you think is best; this is a team effort."

Copley was getting the hang of cooperation and accepting that others may have solutions better than his own.

"We need a backup as well; so, we are sending a message on the night ferry to Rotterdam; to the Reuters office. It will be ready for your signature once we get out of here"

"Well done indeed."

Copley felt whatever happened, he was truly impressed with the efforts of others; he felt proud to be working with them all.

"I'm truly sorry about your friends."

"Did they suffer?"

"My initial examination would suggest they were not cut; there was no obvious indications; lack of any tissue doesn't help, and the bones have been placed in the warehouse as if on display; this is not where they died that's for sure. Psychopaths like recognition; that's why Partridge came back; that's why he found you and me. He wanted me regarding the Crown Posada; he wanted me to find his creations; he wanted you to see his work. The two things that mattered to him.

Beryl said he went to the archive quite a lot; she hasn't had any opportunity to find out why."

"That will be ships; all the Partridges were interested in sailing boats; they had all sorts of pictures of boats in their shops; mostly old sailing vessels, galleons; they had a trawler; used it for line fishing. People used to say they should have been fishmongers"

"So Partridge had an interest in old sailing vessels; I wonder if he wanted to know about the Commonwealth; I was spouting all this stuff about Gurndy and Captain Premm; it was the nanobots playing with my brain; Partridge really did his homework; he wanted us to know about the Witches hole, even though there officially was nothing to connect it to the storm, because the data was being frigged. I knew it was the Witches Hole; the nanobots confirmed it with the tale. He obviously wanted to make sure we investigated it."

"Why would he do that; he liked killing people."

"I don't think he was into mass extinction; I think he liked the one to one experience. Sorry that's very hard on you."

They gently paddled back to the hole and clambered out; they walked onto Side and the work to protect the Crown Posada continued; the threat had passed, but nobody was to know and protecting the structure was no bad thing as far as Copley was concerned; it was beginning to look like a Victorian glass domed specimen. A fragile intricate frame that shone amongst the rubble all around.

"Copley dressed in military basics was anonymous and he intended to stay away from the Castle but within close range of Jean, who was busy organising the boat and outboards; the hole would need widening; but it appeared there would be no delay, so Copley settled down in a quiet corner of the ruins for a nap. He dreamt of Evelyn; he knew not where, likewise, setting down her own false trail of activity; hopefully creating enough chaos to keep the suits busy; she was more than capable of that; of Bob on his train; with his precious cargo. He had to have an escape route for Jean; as for Copley he had his own plan. Two hours later Copley awoke. He was aware it was dark, the cold bit at him; the lights around the hole created strange unearthly shadows; one of them was coming towards him.

"Jean; you gave me quite a shock; is everything ready?"

"It is, all in place; just ready for you, as you wanted, they had some problems with the props and the depth, but they've solved it. I need your signature on this statement for Reuters."

Jean handed over the document; it outlined exactly what had happened and who was responsible; it named names; Toby would be safer in the open, they wouldn't dare kill him; nobody was going to come to the PM's rescue, it would be suicide. Copley signed. Jean handed it to a driver, and it was gone. She handed him another, identical letter. He signed with a flourish and it too was gone.

"That one is going to Dublin, just in case."

"Belt and braces. Right Jean. I need you to vanish as soon as we send the message; get yourself away; don't go to Birmingham, that would be obvious; don't use your phone but get yourself across to West Cumbria, a village called Nether Wasdale, the Strands Inn. Ask for Lesley; tell them I sent you. They will hide you away until things quieten down. Might get a bit tough but we will get through it."

"What about Bob?"

"Bob can look after himself, I'm sure of that. Remember radio silence, no contacting the boys. I know you can do this; you just have faith in Bob."

"Now let's do this."

A pile of cardboard and pallets provided George with an excellent vantage point; a very proactive look out, he could distract with a swift between the legs manoeuvre and roll on his tummy for a tickle, or jump all claws out straight onto anyone's face, it depended on how he viewed the situation. He was currently in distraction mode. The dilatory soldiers patrol seemed to have less routine as it got darker and as there were very few civilians in the City centre, patrol was more of a chore than a necessity. The bunker was equally quiet; no one noticed the tipper bin move in front of the wooden door to the plant room; the certainly didn't notice the legs behind it, moving it along.

George meowed and the bin stayed still, as the soldier gave George a stroke and George obliged with his tummy; suitably, assured that all was well with the World the soldier moved on. The tipper bin was now across the door. Beryl checked her watch, five minutes to go; bolt croppers at the ready, only to find the padlock was unlocked; merely through the hasp. Infuriated but relieved by the fact she had not to use the bolt croppers, which she was uncertain she could handle quietly, she removed the padlock and moved the upper bin forward to get clearance for the door to open. She was in and carefully closing the door she turned her torch on; a long corridor clearly stating power pointed her to the right, she followed it and then was confronted by a locked push lock door. Panic set in. No wonder the outer door was undone, the inner was locked; she swung her torch around and there scratched in the paintwork of the door surround was the code. She pressed the keys, the door opened. A staircase heading down which she leapt from step to step; aware that time was passing. Another corridor and there before here large shiny grey switch panels clearly identifying themselves as the master switches for the bunker. Out of her pocket she produced a rubber face mask, she put it on. Then rubber gloves. From her other pocket two plastic containers with phials inside them; she wired them onto the master switches; she then traced her way to where the cables went through a concrete wall, to descend into the depths, her third and final phial was attached. She checked her watch, wished everyone else good luck and smashed the phial closest to her with a toffee hammer; she ran back to the master switches and smashed the second and third and fled for the stairs; she kept on running, she had to stop to unclip the key door and then ran along the corridor, she was sweating inside the mask, she could hardly see, she knew she had to get out; she pushed the outdoor ajar and the tipper moved forward; just as the soldier was coming round the corner; before he could react George was on him. There was smoke rising from the plant room; the lights in the civic centre went out; the soldier was being ripped to shreds, his screams were going to attract attention; Beryl beckoned George and George obeyed and ran with Beryl across the road and into the ruined University building. The acid had done its work; there were now flames and acrid smoke rising; the bunker was out of action.

"Our job's done George; we've done our bit. Now it's time to disappear and sharpish.

Copley had tapped the numbers in; amazing how he could keep numbers if they reminded him of historic dates, or beers; he had passed all the sections, stage by stage and Jean had prompted him; every protocol was duly completed. All he had to do was push the button.

"Well here we go Jean. The moment I push this, we put the laptop on the boat over there, we open the throttle and let it go. It zooms up the tunnel and hopefully it just crashes at the other end of the tunnel; if the PM is more clued up than we think it gets blown up in the tunnel; are you ready?"

"Yes Professor."

"Here we go. Done. Now let's get this laptop into that tunnel."

Copley paddled across dropped the laptop onto the floor of the craft turned the ignition and the outboards started; he opened the throttles enough to get the boat underway; the water churned and he cut the line holding it back; it moved off into the tunnel."

"No point in opening the throttles too much it won't make any difference in that confined space, but it will keep moving forward, I've set her nose against the left-hand side of the tunnel wall to clear the caverns. righto. Let's get out of here and get you away. I don't want to know how you get yourself away, just do it"

"What about you Professor?"

"I have a suspicion the PM will try and get me; I think Evelyn can distance herself; I'm definitely going to be on the wanted list; if Bob fails to get those nanobots into the Witches Hole, the PM can sit quietly picking us off and then wait her moment to do it all over again. You get off to Cumbria now and you stay hidden."

"But what are you going to do?"

"Leave that to me. Now get us out of here."

They paddled back to the entrance. Jean kissed Copley on the cheek and was gone.

"Good luck"

Copley's words fell into the darkness. He stood alone, the lights making him feel naked to what was going to unfurl by the dawn. He didn't have a plan; he thought his nap would have supplied one, if not a myriad of possibilities, he had none. What was he to do? He had turned off part of the nation's defense systems it wasn't going to go unnoticed; he had a decision to make, he could go into hiding until, or flee. Evelyn had provided cover, by issuing the Code Red; people were moving out of the region, there was mass movement; it would be unlikely he'd be noticed, even by the best cctv. His head, still undecided, his feet started walking up from Side, towards the Castle and the Keep. There was another way.

Riverside Drive was quiet; the three vans pulled up next to the goods entrance to the airport. Dundee lay silent; the moon threw beams across the Tay, the bridge breaking their path into ever changing pools of light on the surface. The vans proceeded onto the airport runway where three helicopters stood; the body bags were duly loaded, and the helicopters departed; the vans drove back onto the Drive and vanished into the night.

Bob checked his watch; as long as Beryl and Copley had done their jobs, he had a chance; the three helicopters separated; the plan was a Southern, Western and Northern approach; reflecting commercial traffic heading to the platforms; there was commercial traffic out there in the dark. The helicopters split up; Bob was in the Western approach, the most likely to be challenged; he looked at the body bags.

"Tom. Talk to them, make sure they know what they have to do."

A thumbs up; Tom, unzipped the first bag; then the second and third. Over the noise Tom proceeded to check on the passengers; this involved a certain amount of mime acting, which created much merriment for the rest of the crew. The good news was they understood what they had to do. There was no sign of any aircraft or incoming missile and they flew on in silence; they crossed the exclusion zone; they saw the Northern team using the exclusion zone in an arc; ready to come down to the site; there was no sign of the Southern team. Bob looked to the pilot.

"Where are they?"

"I suspect they've gone in low as they can, conditions are really calm, thank goodness, but that means a problem; they passed over a British frigate."

"No communication; nothing; the Professor did his job. No sign of them sending their helicopter up either; that's odd. If I was in their position, I would send it up and ask who goes there?"

"No chance of that, no helicopter; they've not arrived yet. See the Minister of Defence for details"

"Men in suits. God bless 'em. Hang on, what the fuck is that?"

In front of them a huge silver green swirling mass of water was rising out of the sea.

"The mad bitch has started it up again. My God."

"We're on target; I was right, look over there."

Bob looked down to his right as the Southern team approached the column of water; it swung round and Bob could see in the helicopters lights that the bags were released into the sea.

"Now for the Northern team."

"They've gone!"

"What; there's no sign of them."

"Right. We are going in. Zips on the bags open"

"Zips open Sir."

"Here we go."

The helicopter approached the churning mass and swung hard right just before the blades were dragged into the column.

"Ok. Bags over the side."

The load was delivered; they swung away.

"Right gentlemen; we are off to Norway for a short holiday."

Bob turned to the pilot.

"Nothing on the Northern team?

"Nothing"

Bob grimaced. It was never easy loosing personnel. He just hoped it was not in vain.

Unbeknown to him the Northern team had decided on a wider path and zig zagged at low level, so low that they were creating waves on the sea.

The pilot had turned to confirm that the bags were unzipped; distracted the helicopter ploughed straight into the column of water. The blades cut into the upward flow and passed straight through, the body of the helicopter passed through and the crew found themselves on the inside of the column.

"Release the load"

The nanobots rained down into the sea, as they did, the crew who were now hovering in the circle of calm, were witness to a light show as the released nanobots started spreading their message. Patches of light started appearing in the wall of water.

"That's the Southern batch; we have to wait until Bob's passengers arrive before leaving the party. It's getting a bit lively in here."

"Over there to starboard, what the hell is that doing?"

A seventeenth century warship moved into view; then two smaller sailing ships that came alongside the larger craft.

"Well gentlemen we are in the Witches Hole and it is living up to its reputation. I hope Bob turns up soon; I'm not sure any of us will be sane if it last much longer."

"There they are; Eastern load deployed."

A green, red, blue sparkle flowed down the column. The water beneath them was purple and bubbling.

"We need to get out of here fast."

Before the pilot could react, the helicopter was forced upwards, as if in an express lift. After an age the helicopter was thrown out of the column; the pilot struggling to control the descent as the engine faltered; he struggled, managing to level out, but a ditching was inevitable.

"Prepare to ditch."

Ten minutes later the crew were sitting in the two life dinghies watching an incredible light show. The automatic emergency beacon was giving their position away.

"Let's hope it's worked; I can't make any sense of what's going on at all; if that column moves it could get interesting. But our main hope is a Norwegian recuse vessel, so start paddling East.

Copley walked up to the Keep, he was stopped by a sentry, but his pass was accepted and an apology for stopping him; he was still unsuspected, which was good. He climbed the steps and into the Keep. It felt like entering a prison; he needed to get some clean clothes and tidy himself up, he was exhausted. He walked up to the great hall; the monitors were blank, the room empty; curious, there was always a shift on duty; the Keep was quiet at night, but he felt a difference. He was expecting to be arrested; he was so tired he wouldn't have minded the experience, at least for a few minutes. A cup of tea and some clothes were his only priority and he could manage that, anything else was a blank. Tackling the PM was not an option. To his office and kettle on, tea bag in; boiling water and milk. Strip off and back into his style, if he had one; at least he was going to face the furies as him, not as somebody trying to hide and escape. Copley knew his responsibility, he hadn't started any of this; the person behind all this was the PM and her manipulating of people; taking a talented psychopath, covering up his deed; giving him a minder; letting him develop his nanobots and then testing them on a City. At least Partridge had looked his terrified victim in the face; one to one; not sitting behind a desk and giving an instruction. How many people knew about this weapon? How was the instruction to start the storm given; how was it done. What turned them on? Copley stripped, removed the tea bag and dressed; the tea was hot but sipping it he waited for the inevitable stomping steps of his captors. He waited. What was taking them so long; his watch suggested that by now the satellite would be back online and the PM would know who had turned it off; the Reuters message would have gone out; the emails. She would be fighting back, but the state would be questioning what she had done. She wouldn't give way, she never had. She would be trying to get at Evelyn, but Copley knew she wouldn't succeed. If he fell, Evelyn would finish her off, he waited and sipped. Nothing. Copley was thinking.

Fred Partridge is identified as a genius; how did the State find out about this genius of his.? When he was interviewed by a policeman? Unlikely. No. he must have done something so horrendous, so amazing that MI5 were involved; whilst they were slowly getting a handle on his operations, his ability; good, for them, and bad news for his victims; Fred was allowed his freedom and continued to work in the real World. When he was eventually so unpopular and Arthur "Plod" recognized him, he had to disappear. It seemed likely that the State was using him on a local basis and then decided his work, his ability was of worth, enough to promote him and send him to Oxford where Toby kept an eye on him. Fred had obviously been of use; perhaps the young females were a cover for his real targets and perhaps a bonus for him. In the end his usefulness ended in a ditch. Or had it? They had only been informed that Fred was dead, who had seen it?

Copley had concluded that Partridge had gone on the run from his minders; that Toby was not averse to his escape, had gone along with the ploy; Toby was fully aware of the test of the weapon; which was not his purpose for the nanobots. The best person to put a spanner in the works was Copley and Copley had definitely done that for him. Fred had made sure that Copley was on target, but the Alnmouth expedition had been unexpected and vulnerable to being captured, which he had. The PM had him. No wonder she wasn't worried about Copley, or the Cabinet, or public opinion, she had the trigger to the weapon, and she could wipe Copley off the planet. Except Partridge had provided the means of deactivating it. It was hard to smile, but Copley did, a psychopath had provided the evidence to capture a mass murderer. Now where was Fred Partridge, where could she be keeping him and how did she trigger the nanobots?

Copley finished his tea and noted the lights were coming up and some of the team were turning in.

"Good morning Professor; didn't expect to see you this morning. Well done"

"Well done?"

"The Prime Minister and the Cabinet has resigned; arrest warrants out on all of them; most claim to have known nothing. Lady Copley is in charge. Which is good news. She's on the TV if you want to see her."

"Not at the moment, thank you. Does anybody know where the ex-Prime Minister is? It's vital we find her. Also Fred Partridge is still alive, least I'm pretty sure he is, I suspect he's with the Prime

Minister, not necessarily of his own free will. Can I have two mobile phones please and a bacon sandwich."

Copley sat down; that was quick, he thought. She obviously knew the game was up the moment he had appeared on the scene; the storm must have hampered her trying to find Partridge. It was of course quite possible nobody had predicted the size of the weather bomb and she had been desperately trying to cover her tracks, it made no difference she was responsible; she'd groomed Partridge ever since she'd got junior ministerial office. She was going to get her just desserts. Where could she be?

"Has anybody got a report on the ex PM?"

Copley yelled from his office.

"Any news on my bacon sandwich?"

The bacon sandwich appeared, along with two mobiles.

"Were getting reports of a column of water rising from the Witches Hole, vertically; over a mile high."

"Oh my God, we were too late."

"Reports state it's not moving; it's multi coloured and sparkling with light."

"Well that's something. I've witnessed that firsthand, it means they are fighting amongst themselves; it seems to be a case of logics clashing; they eventually agree what to do. We can only hope and pray the Crown Posada nanobots persuade the ones in the Witches Hole to go Fred says sleep tight and go to sleep."

"Your boat arrived at Corbridge; it's a bit of a mess, there was no air strike; the media broadcast and the subsequent resignation, Lady

Copley taking control; the system wasn't in the PM's hands anymore."

"Ayton Castle. That's it. The other end of the tunnel. Tell Lady Copley. Top Priority; surround Ayton Castle, prepare to air strike it and block all radio signals around it. It's the stone; Gurndy and Premm wanted to quarry good stone; the easiest was on their doorstep, but they couldn't take anymore out, the whole of Side would collapse, so they ventured up the tunnel. There was a structure that they could strip, at least of it's outer walls, good masonry too, Ayton Castle; it was cut stone, they didn't have to quarry it, all they needed was to break out of the old tunnel entrance and the rest was easy."

"So why do you think the PM is there?"

"I think Fred Partridge is there and the PM has control of him. Eliminate Partridge and the PM is dead in the water, no control over the weapon. Nobody lives at the Castle, its English Heritage property, it has an impressive hall; after the Civil War it was an easy target for them, right in line with an easy means of transportation, a forgotten spot, of no great military value, Gurndy and Premm only got to strip the very top layers; they just shaved the outer defensive walls down, trip after trip; then the game was up and the Commonwealth sailed with the final cargo. The PM knows there's other nanobots, all she knows is Partridge worked at the Crown Posada and that there's a tunnel, she will be able to see the activity, between the two. My God there could be other nanobots, in the quarries."

"Why do you think he's there?

"He deliberately left us two skeletons, very carefully laid out, two. Firstly he wanted us to know he'd been there, the bones and clothing he'd kept for a very long time, he was giving up his trophies because he wanted to mark something, somewhere very special and he wanted me to know it; he brought both bodies, because Jean lost her friends, the skeletal remains. It was a conclusion, an ending for her; he was meticulous, he wanted us to know it was an end; so, you then go back to the start and that is the other end of the tunnel. He was bringing the nanobots to work, he was storing them there. But where was he living when he worked at the Crown Posada? Check if Browns Butchers had a branch in Corbridge."

"I don't need to. They did. I would go there with my Mum."

"I hope I'm, wrong. But if Partridge did his work at Corbridge then we have a major problem. Check with English Heritage if they had a volunteer at Aydon Castle by the name of Fred Partridge; get the Chairman out of bed if you have to; I need to know."

One of the telephones in front of Copley rang.

"Copley."

"Evelyn."

"Are you alright Copley?

"No. I'm positive Fred Partridge is alive and the Roman quarries along the tunnel are full of his nanobots and I'm pretty sure your ex best friend also knows; I'm sure Fred is in her clutches; she will be looking to use the trigger. How's the situation at the Witches Hole?"

"Well thank you for that nugget of news; I wondered why I was getting requests for air strikes. Can you confirm Partridge is there; I can't see your friend getting that far North, we haven't found her yet, but it's a long shot she's with him; she's obviously got supporters; were mopping up here. It's a mess Copley, but you have my authority to wipe the place off the map. Just give the word. Haven't you got the tunnel team just across from the Castle?

"Yes, we have"

"I'll give orders for them to make their way to the Castle and knock on the front door."

"If nothing else it will act as a diversion until you get anybody else there. If we can take Partridge alive. I stress he's obviously dangerous but he's definitely being manipulated, and he has certainly assisted us trying to stop what's happening. I stress, try and take him alive."

"Very well, but the most pressing priority is locating the ex PM, especially if she has the means of triggering God knows what; if we have a mile-high column of water in the North Sea, God knows what would happen if she triggered the nanobots in those tunnels."

"You look for her; I'll deal with the nanobots."

"Copley, please be careful. You are not going anywhere alone. That's an order."

"Yes, Lady Copley."

"Remember; call if you need Aydon taking out."

"Last resort."

"Understood. Take care."

"Love You"

"Love You Copley."

"Electric boats and six armed personnel to the hole at Bessie Surtees, twenty minutes"

Copley barked out to the white board staff in the great hall. He finished his bacon sandwich and put the phones in his pockets; he missed his old jacket; he suddenly had a brainwave; they still had some nanobots, in the lab, the result of Copley's dramatic self-purging of them.

He walked out of his office and politely asked the screen team if the lab could release to him the nanobots that were in the shower froth. This was duly agreed, and a vehicle was sent to pick them up; delivery was to be to Copley at Bessie Surtees.

Copley was pacing up and down, thirty minutes had passed, he was standing waiting for the nanobots, eventually a vehicle up with a white handled clear plastic container with a large biohazard sticker.

"Hello there, I see you are alright."

He said to the box.

"We are going for a trip in a boat to find some of your friends."

The boat crews looked somewhat surprised at Copley's behaviour, but they were soon in two crafts heading into the tunnel. Copley lifted the box up and proceeded to show it to the wall. It was noticeable that the nanobots were clustered to one end, observing the progress; the first cavern was reached, they came alongside the jetty and Copley spoke to the box again.

He sat on the stone floor.

"Some of your friends maybe here, we have five more places to visit, will you divide yourselves up into six groups; one group to find your friends and tell them that Fred says sleep tight."

The nanobots created a smiley circle, glowed blue to make it clear they would co-operate, and Copley opened the container. A minute blue thread disappeared into the dark cavern beyond.

Five hours later the crew were quite sad to see the last of their strange little passengers depart into the gloom. As the boats pulled away Copley just hoped that they were enough to stop Armageddon. By the time the boat reached the tunnel breach across from Aydon Castle there was an obvious fire fight taking place between forces loyal to the ex PM and those sent by Evelyn. The outer defenses had given way easily, the defenders were holed up in the inner courtyard and heavily defended hall. Copley assessed that the only option was to bomb it; Partridge would be dead either way, they only needed him alive to operate the trigger; he was about to use his phone when he noticed what looked like a thread of cotton work its way down his trouser leg onto his shoe, onto the grass and make its way across the shooting ground and into the Castle. He put the phone back in his pocket. Mortars had been brought up, and the inner gate was breached easily, another went straight through the door, leaving a gaping hole. Copley, attracted a soldier's attention and had him pass a message to his commander, to continue small arms fire, but to lay off the mortars as Copley's forces were at work.

This message was received with some consternation, but was duly followed, no more mortars were fired. After ten minutes, the guns in the Castle fell silent, a white flag appeared at the doorway; the man holding it was Fred Partridge. He walked down the steps.

"Where's Copley? Where's Professor Copley."

"I'm here Partridge."

"I see you got my message"

"I did."

"Clever of you to send my friends in"

"They went of their own accord; I like them."

"I thought you would. This destruction. This has nothing to do with me. That bitch kept me safe; I was a coward, I should have just walked into a police station and admitted to what I'd done."

"It wouldn't have worked; they would have had you back out and in a safe house in hours. Anyway, apart from you, these gentlemen want to know where the ex PM is and whether you wouldn't mind not triggering the nanobots in the tunnel?"

"You've already put them to sleep."

"Yes. My hitchhikers must have told you."

"They are really quite amenable creatures if you treat them right; you'll find a few drowned bodies in there."

"I take your hat off regarding the water business, no point me asking because you won't say."

"Correct"

"Can you turn off the problem in the Witches Hole?"

"Well you've managed that quite well; give it another couple of hours and they will all go sleep tight."

"Fred. Give them the ultimate command, then we can end this for you."

Partridge looked straight and deep into Copley's eyes. Copley was going to free him. He wanted that. He wanted that more than anything.

"The bitch is dead."

"She had you brought here."

"I wanted to be here; I told her where I needed to be, to trigger the nanobots. She had to go along; you see she couldn't talk to them like you or anybody else; she ordered them about. They don't take to being abused, they fear death, they are terrified."

"Because you taught them what terror was"

"Correct. I did; that's what the girls were for; terror. Real terror"

"Where is she?"

"The moment you cut the satellite she went off her head; thing is she's talking to me by video link and she tells me she's going to kill you, whatever it takes. I can't have that. So, I just give my friends in her office a friendly little message; nothing she would even realize was meant for them. You get this lot to go and pick the pieces up. It's alright they had their instruction their sleep tight now.

"Where is she?"

"Well, let me see; on the way to becoming a batch of Cornish pasties I expect. You going to finish this then?

"Only when you give the ultimate command."

"Deal. You know Copley, I know you detest me for what I did, I don't ever see a problem with it myself, but that's me; with you I know that when you say you will do something, you do. You never will be part of their system; you couldn't care a toss about them. Happy Returns. There you go. Happy Returns."

A dust began falling from Partridge. He smiled.

Copley turned to the officer standing at his side.

"Gun"

"But I have orders"

"Gun. I am the senior authorized person. Give me the fucking gun"

The officer handed over his pistol. Copley took the safety catch off.

Partridge was surrounded by tiny grey specks

"Thank you"

Copley pulled the trigger.

Partridge was blasted backwards; the bullet went straight through the temple and took half his skull away. He fell in a bloody pool of mush as the dead nanobots soaked up the blood.

"Thank you. Bad business that, but it was the only answer, nobody will have his ability, it was lethal. The nanobots, they're all dead. All of them. You better get word to every meat pie factory that they need to check for human remains."

"What are you going to do now Professor.?

"Help clear up this whole sorry mess, then I'm going to have a pint at the Crown Posada.

Chapter Eight

Copley stared out onto the quad.

His office smelt of new paint; the University smelt of paint. The City smelt of paint. A year of rebuilding, restoring the fabric; sweeping away and starting again. Another month and the students would be back.

Here he was, back in his World, the responsibilities of saving heritage safely back in other's hands.

"Copley"

"Yes Evelyn."

"Are you alright. Are the paint fumes upsetting you?"

"No. Not the paint fumes."

"We've had an invitation to Bob and Jeans wedding."

"I'm glad that worked out. I'd never have believed Bob would pack in soldiering to run a canal boat business in sunny Birmingham"

"Worcester and they needed to get away for the children."

"Good luck to them. New horizons and adventures. Ah well. Good luck indeed."

Copley's screen showed a newsflash of the funeral of the PM.

"It's taken a whole year to put her back into some resemblance of remains. Some poor sods chomped through the better part of her anyway Why did she do it?"

Evelyn stood next to Copley and stared out of the window.

"I haven't the faintest,"

"She was your friend. Best of pals from schooldays."

"One of my friends Copley. Let's get that straight. You keep on saying we were best of pals. You think you know somebody; I suppose power just got the better of her."

"No. There's more to it than a power crazed politician. Something or somebody was behind all this; she wasn't pulling all the strings. Nobody can."

"Copley. I really don't think there is anyone or anything. I do think she underestimated how destructive a weapon she was handling."

"She knew exactly what she was doing, and she didn't care."

"All I know is we can do what we are doing, putting things back together, making things better. You've done a marvelous job"

"I'd rather not have had to in the first place. What a bloody awful mess."

"Yes, it was; now it's time to move on, a new day; we pick ourselves up"

"You are beginning to sound like a politician"

"I suppose I am. But I'm here with you."

"Yes, you are, and I can't tell you how I feel about that. You could be in power yourself now and you came back to me."

"I'll never leave you Copley"

"I know that. I believe in us. I know I'm a selfish pompous old fart; I'm simply not complete without you."

"Same here and yes you are a selfish pompous old fart and I wouldn't have you any other way. Between you and me, you can be quite brilliant on occasions"

"Thank you, Lady Copley"

"Were going for a walk. Get out of this smell."

"The paint"

"No. Not the paint; the perfidious stench of the State at its very worse. We've been taken for mugs. Come on. We're going for a pint"

Copley and Evelyn strode down Westmorland Street; bright, shiny and bustling, the centre of the City was bright and clean; crossing to Greys Monument the scene continued to be one of renewed vigour, the buskers plied their trade, the smell of coffee filled the air and the Metro spewed another train load of passengers up from the bowels into the throng. Down Grey Street, onto Dean Street, the renewal continued; more scaffolding, building continuing in all its noise and dust. They stopped outside the Crown Posada on Side, paid their respects. The building was still covered in scaffolding; Copley had agreed the plans to retain the tunnel features, which meant the whole structure had to be anchored on a bridge; this allowed both the tunnel and the old Roman Quay feature to be displayed beneath the pub. It was just taking forever to complete. Copley would have to wait for his pint a little longer. Behind them the open expanse of water; the Quay area was gone and a decision as to what was to be done was dragging on. The Roman Quay edge was being bolstered with supports but was intact and sound enough to allow a water taxi service to use it. They boarded and headed down river to the Free Trade; a short climb up to the pub and they were soon attached to two pints. In Copley fashion they faced the bar and thus saw the reflection of the scene behind them through the crackled silver of the mirror.

"Your old school chum may have been a mad bitch, but even you must think it's odd that nobody was even suspicious as to what she was up to. She allowed a convicted killer to have access to scientific facilities, to roam free. Somebody had control of the budget for all that. Especially for the surveillance. Some Whitehall nobody must have seen what was going on. Nobody, no one in the Cabinet, nobody did a thing. I cannot believe she was able to pull so many strings all at once. Then to drag us into it as well. Perhaps that was the idea; she certainly had me followed; but of course, she knew me, my character."

"Because I told her. Yes. Can't disagree. Over the years your exploits came up in conversation. It isn't difficult to understand you Copley. You are a very public figure with a reputation. All of your own making."

"Fair enough. But what in the World makes her experiment with a weapon in the North Sea."

"She had to try it out somewhere"

"Which leads me to one conclusion"

"And that is?"

"We've been taken for fools. This whole business was meticulously planned. I doubt your friend could manage all of it alone; somebody did their homework; good thorough research. Toby admitted he'd known about the inscription and that the rest of academia were uninterested, but he wanted me to see it. Somebody knew me too well. They knew I'd jump at the chance. I fell for it. The whole thing. I can't understand why they went to such pains?"

"Deflection."

"Agreed, but why so elaborate and devastating; what was the purpose?"

"Partridge was a complex man capable of deception and with a deadly weapon, one that they, whoever they are, decided to test."

"By wiping out the North East"

"Precisely.

Copley finished his second pint. He stared straight ahead; the mirror looked back at him. Copley looked at himself.

"Hang on a minute. I'm an idiot. A fool. The whole business of the inscription; the reason no academic would consider it was it really was rubbish, a work of fantasy. Somebody knew I'd be drawn in by Toby. I wanted to believe in what I saw, because it fitted with my research, my theories. All of which is widely known. I'm not saying the stone isn't old; it was well established in the bell tower; it was a piece of ancient bunkum when it was set in the tunnel. That inscription provided a wealth of material, everything that I wanted to see. It drew me in. It was meant to. Getting me to travel to Oxford was part of the plan. A distraction. Toby was told when to contact me and I scuttled off to him as they wanted. I admit I got completely taken over by the idea. Getting you involved; well I really wanted that. No external influence. But I do believe I was being manipulated, played. Somebody wanted us to do what we did throughout this. Why us? "

"Because somebody wanted the past to survive the destruction."

"Somebody that came from the North East"

"Partridge"

"I believe Partridge decided he had to save something. Remember, he worked in the Crown Posada, he would have known of my work. I unwittingly became his candidate and how convenient Copley's wife is known to be a personal friend of the PM. Ideal candidates."

"So. If the PM wasn't working alone, whom knew of her intentions and why destroy so much; thousands of people dead. Why? From what I saw in Westminster and Whitehall it was a chaotic mess. I wasn't exactly sitting on my arse; whoever and whatever was behind this, it wasn't obvious from where I was standing"

"Hear me out Evelyn; this whole business seems to revolve around us. I know the house was built like a proverbial bunker, but it was completely unharmed, nothing wrong with it. How can that be? I tell you how. Partridge and his nanobots, that's how; he knew the Crown Posada; he knew where we lived, that wasn't difficult and through co-operating with your friend he kept us safe and busy."

"But Partridge was safely under the State's control for years; he couldn't have...."

"His nanobots could quite happily scuttle about right under the noses of his keepers; his cage was wide open; he just chose to sit in it. I don't believe Partridge wanted his nanobots to cause the devastation that ensued, but he couldn't stop it; he just made sure somebody he knew would do something to put things right."

"Partridge was a killer; those poor girls."

"Yes. He had no need to put the bones on display, so neatly arranged; other than as a signpost. Confirmation of his presence; his manipulation of all around him; his bragging rights. I don't deny it.

But if your friend thought she could control him, well look what happened. "

"I'm glad you shot him."

"Yes. So am I. He had to go; like the tunnel; it had to be stopped up. Buried and forgotten"

"Why was the tunnel blocked up in the first lace?"

"Fear. Pure and simple. Would you want to travel that distance with little or no light; penetrating darkness. A World full of water Gods and mystery; every trip would be a living hell. Plus; the local population knew of it, the Romans only improved an ancient navigation, the tunnel potentially could allow an enemy to appear anywhere behind the Roman defensive line. A superb bit of engineering that was infamous."

Copley supped at his third pint. He was on a roll; as ever the ale was playing its part.

"I think the tunnel was completed under Trajan and quietly blocked by Hadrian. Trajanic frontier control being fluid a tunnel which would allow relatively fast movement of personnel and supplies completely invisible to the enemy is a major bonus. Except the troops go mad from being in the pitch-black wet tunnel. Not quite as good as planned. The tunnel gains such a reputation that it's sealed up as part of the formalization of a physical barrier, the attribution is spurious, anything to do with the tunnel becomes folklore. Not a nice place to be; the stones themselves are bad luck. The whole thing is deliberately covered over with the new harbour."

"Plausible"

"I think so. I think Partridge played on every same factor; the history of the Crown Posada; the quarrying of cut stone but more importantly the fact that stone is taken to a specific location"

"The site where the storm starts."

"Exactly"

"Copley. Evelyn. Good to see you"

Michael the Free Trade's manager interrupted the couple's train of thought.

"I'm pleased to see you both. I have something for you Copley. A letter. Marked for your attention. In all the chaos it got itself into the cat's bed and it only came to light when we changed the blanket."

Copley looked across to the jukebox selector. The pub cat looked its usual menacing self. Somebody was risking life and limb thought Copley. No accident the letter was in the cat's basket.

The brown envelope was just marked for Copley's attention. Copley opened it. Inside was as single A4 piece of lined paper. Nothing else on either side.

"Odd. Very."

Michael was called away and Copley looked at Evelyn with a quizzical if perplexed stare. Copley held the paper up to the light. Nothing. He laid it down on the bar. Nothing. He took his mobile phone from his pocket and turned the light on, examining the paper thoroughly. Nothing.

"Who sends a blank piece of paper?"

"And puts it in the cats' basket. That was no accident. They didn't want it found immediately. That cat isn't human friendly"

"Copley. Look"

Evelyn pointed at the paper. The lines were moving, they were flowing down the paper towards Copley's phone. In front of their eyes the lines flowed into the power input socket. The phone flashed and the screen changed to the face of Partridge.

"Hello Copley. Somebody has braved the cats' basket. I believe you and Evelyn deserve an explanation. I don't have all the facts and I'm not going to plead my innocence. Whatever has happened to me, I deserve it. Not a nice person me. I led you a merry dance. But I never meant so many people to die, no I didn't. That wasn't me. You look elsewhere. I may have invented the means, but I didn't release it. They knew what it would do. Sorry Copley for playing with your brain, all that business of the old steps and the Castle. They went walkies inside you; I knew which buttons to push in your brain. I owe you plenty. So here it goes.Tell Evelyn to destroy her security pass; as soon as you've seen this message. Make sure she does. Destroy it. Then get yourself to the Witches Cauldron, get yourself as close as the skipper will dare to the whirlpool and throw this phone into it. Remember; destroy Evelyn's pass. It's essential. She, like so many others is just a pawn and I owe you one Copley. Time to bring the game to an end. Good Luck."

The phone's screen filled with a set of coordinates.

"I suspect that's going to match the Witches Cauldron. Give me your pass Evelyn; I know you are no longer in Government, but you still have clearance and passes. Hand it over."

Evelyn duly took her pass from her purse.

"Are we going to do what Partridge says"

Copley twisted the pass in two and duly tore it, breaking the plastic coating. He smiled to himself, then threw it into the bin behind the bar.

"We are going to do exactly what Partridge desires. Come on. We have packing to do"

Two days later, Copley and Evelyn were holding onto the rail of a fishing trawler heading to the precise coordinated on the phone. Copley raised his hand towards the wheelhouse as the phone confirmed they were exactly on the spot. The deck rose and fell alarmingly. Copley threw the phone into the maelstrom and indicated to the skipper to get out of the white water as quickly as possible.

"Copley. What was the point of that?"

"I have no idea. But I suspect it's not going to be good for some. Partridge knew we would survive; he knew we were singled out. Not one other member of the department stayed, all whisked away' the house intact with army protection; you in Government. Partridge was party to all of it. His masters were playing with his genius and laughing at us all, as we scurried around picking up the remnants. Partridge was a killer, those two girls are testament to that, I've no doubt he was sadistically warped, but nothing compared to those who exploited his genius."

Evelyn was distracted by the skipper waving from the wheelhouse, pointing towards the Witches Cauldron. Three conning towers appeared moving towards the trawler.

"They must be something to do with the release for the nanobots. So much for the nothing in the sector nonsense. Three nuclear submarines. Did you know they were here Evelyn?"

"No. I would have told you Copley"

"Partridge sent us fishing. Let's hope we are not the bait"

The submarines eased to a crawl, line abreast, the trawler was in the shadow of the nearest now fully above the waves. Copley looked up. There was movement; the hatches were opening along the deck; armed personnel were appearing. Copley began to wonder if Partridge was having the last laugh on him.

"Copley. What's going on."

"End game for someone, but I'm damned if it going to be us. Partridge used the phone as a beacon or the like, those subs obviously hide in that turbulent sea; the source of the great storm. But you don't need nuclear subs to launch nanobots"

"But you can hide on them; perhaps we get to see those really responsible. We will see, or not. I have a suspicion it's going to be rather sticky for them"

"Copley. What do you mean?"

Activity on all three submarines was intent. The skipper waved to Copley and Evelyn for them to join him in the wheelhouse. As they did it became obvious that the naval personnel were not carrying weapons, but fire extinguishers. All three submarines had fire parties on the deck; smoke began billowing from the hatches. More personnel emerged.

"They're on fire."

The skipper stated the obvious.

"Don't worry they are safe; just one or two of the passengers might have ignited,"

"Ignited?"

Evelyn and the Skipper looked at Copley.

"Remember Partridge told me to destroy your pass. The phone sent out a signal that I suspect the subs transmitted automatically to wherever the holders of the passes were; Partridge spiked the passes. Heyho. Grilled faceless despots. Clever. Very clever. But why most of our nuclear fleet was sitting in one place is a puzzle, other than Partridge didn't trust anyone to be out of his immediate control. Perhaps they were going to hold the country to ransom; Partridge being dead along with his weapon; they just might have been plotting their own coupe against him? I doubt they will say a word. They can't they're dead. It will all be quietly brushed under the carpet. Never happened."

"Things seem to be getting sorted Copley; time to leave"

The skipper eased the trawler gently away from the nearest submarine. There was no reaction from the submarine.

"They've no instruction to go after us; anybody onboard that had ill will towards us is just slightly charred. They have their hands full. I wonder how deep this conspiracy really went. I suppose we just follow the smell of burnt flesh"

"Copley."

"Evelyn. Now let me see, a "Thank you" for saving my life would be rather appropriate; but I will settle for a pint"

"Done"

"They certainly are"

FINIS

For Now

More Professor Copley Adventures

Available from Amazon